A Fashionable Affair

Jacqueline Parrish

First paperback edition: August 2020

Cover design by Bailey McGinn

ISBN: 978-1-7390491-2-6

To Mom, Dad and Megan
For your endless encouragement, love and support.

Contents

Chapter 1: Tinsley

"Name?"

"Tinsley Tomlinson, *Fashionista Magazine.*"

"Ah." The headset-wearing clipboard girl scanned the list, flipped past two pages and scrolled through the names.

"Tomlinson, here you are!" She smiled, uncapped the highlighter and crossed off Tinsley's name. "Love your magazine!" she gushed. "Will anyone else from *Fashionista* be joining us today?"

"Ah . . ." Tinsley hesitated. "I don't believe so."

"Perfect." The woman smiled warmly. "So happy that you could join us."

Tinsley smiled back and casually strode past the velvet rope. Her fake magazine persona had surpassed second nature and was currently vying for first—she almost believed that she was the fashion editor of a famous women's magazine herself.

Another headset-wearing woman in a short black dress greeted her just inside of the venue.

"This is Patricia." The woman gestured to the smiling, curly-haired lady to her right. "She's coordinating this afternoon's event."

"Hello, Tinsley." Patricia, also clad in black, thrust her hand forward. "So lovely to meet you! Can I get you anything to drink?"

"Oh! Yes, thank you," Tinsley replied, shaking Patricia's hand. "Lovely to meet you as well."

"We've created a line of custom cocktails for this afternoon's event." Patricia turned to the bar beside her where a framed list of drinks and their accompanying descriptions sat. "The orange creamsicle martini is one of my favourites. It tastes just like a popsicle."

"That sounds good." Tinsley smiled, watching as the bartender poured an orange liquid into a stainless-steel cocktail shaker.

Patricia disappeared while Tinsley waited for her drink—a neon-orange concoction that came rimmed with sugar and garnished with a slice of orange. She thanked the bartender before adjusting her suit jacket and taking in the room. It was a gathering of empowered women in art and fashion. Or at least that's what the invitation had promised. Looking around she saw a room of mostly familiar faces. It hadn't taken her long to realize that when it came to the art and fashion industries, social circles were very small indeed. She was on her second orange creamsicle martini, waiting for the presentations to begin, when she spotted Patricia walking towards her.

"You were right." Tinsley smiled and raised her glass. "These martinis are fantastic."

"Tinsley," Patricia began, looking uncomfortable. "I was curious how someone so young managed to snag such a prestigious job, so I went and checked your name on the *Fashionista* website."

Oh fuck. Tinsley's heart stopped. *She knows I'm not an editor.*

"Patricia!" Tinsley said, her stomach twisted in knots. "I can explain! I know what you're going to say and I'm so, so sorry!"

Patricia looked at her uncertainly.

"How could you do something like this?" she asked, sounding disgusted.

"I didn't mean for it to go this far," Tinsley pleaded. "It just . . . kind of happened."

"You're promoting designer diet drinks and trophy wife T-shirts?" Patricia interrupted. "I cannot believe that you've given that misogynistic company your endorsement! And to think that we invited you here today as one of our empowered women." She paused, shaking her head. "What the hell is wrong with you? Endorsements like that set back the women's movement."

Tinsley's heart started beating again. Diet drinks and trophy wife T-shirts? Patricia was right—what the hell was wrong with this Tinsley woman? She's a total weirdo.

Chapter 2:
Tori

Tori sat at the tiny desk in her fourteenth-floor cubicle sorting through the new marketing material that she would be using to question consumers with. Her firm, Staten, had a handful of big company clients but as an entry-level marketing assistant, Tori was on the bottom of the totem pole. She was the coffee runner and consumer call girl for the company's smallest client: Impotentia. The small red pill was marketed as "the world's first all-natural male stiffening solution". She had been mortified when she'd found out what she would be working on, and, as an entry-level associate, Tori had the embarrassing job of phoning up customers and asking them about their Impotentia experience. It was far from the glamorous job that Tori had envisioned for herself when she'd first set foot in the city, but it paid the bills. Writing was her first choice of career but when *Fashionist*, her fashion and lifestyle blog, had failed to make its mark, she had had to find something fast. Toronto was an expensive city and her savings would only cover two months' worth of rent. Marketing had sounded okay. Prestigious even.

She would still get to write—crafting promotional material for companies—and she would still get to be creative—pitching marketing ideas for new products.

Oh, how wrong she had turned out to be.

At the age of twenty-three Tori thought that she had landed her first adult job. Immediately after being hired she had gone out and dropped a month's worth of salary on smart suits and separates. At H&M and Joe Fresh, of course—a month's salary wouldn't go very far in Toronto's upscale Bloor Street shops. And with her closet full of corporate clothes and a smart new "adult" haircut, she'd shown up half an hour early on her first day of work, ready to prove her marketing skills to her new employer.

Instead, she'd spent the day fetching coffee for her colleagues and answering the telephone. Her Monday-to-Friday schedule hadn't deviated much since that day. She still spent a large portion of her time quenching her colleagues' coffee thirst and fielding phone calls, but her responsibilities had extended to managing the database of Impotentia consumers and talking to them about the product's effectiveness while addressing concerns, suggestions and questions.

Tori looked at the clock. It was 10:42 a.m. and she had already blown through her coffee run and phone call questionnaires for the morning. She clicked through her office emails, refreshing the page just as she'd done less than a minute ago.

Still nothing.

Heaving a sigh, she switched browsers and opened up a different email tab. TTomlinson@Fashionist.com, she typed, entering "muffin"—the pet name given to her by her high school boyfriend—into the password box. She'd started her blog while still in high school and it had received a lot of hits recently. Unfortunately, the hits were owing to the fast-rising popularity of a recently launched fashion and lifestyle website named *Fashionista*, and not owing to Tori's articles.

Her inbox loaded and twenty-seven email notifications popped up on screen. She'd stopped posting articles to her website over six months ago, demoralized by her less-than-fulfilling day job and inability to garner a single industry invite. But while the posts may have stopped, the spam mail just kept coming. She checked her *Fashionist* account every few weeks now just to keep from drowning in it. Looking at the bottom of her screen she scrolled up the list: Viagra (oh, the irony), Hot Russian Singles, Prince Abaeze Wants to Give You $10 Million (if only, she thought), Munger Carlson's Four Seasons Penthouse Party, Nasty Gal's 40% Off Sale.

Hold on.

Munger Carlson's Four Seasons Penthouse Party?

Odd, she thought. Then she looked at the from line: Black Widow PR. Black Widow PR, as in North America's hottest luxury brand public relations firm? No way. Tori dismissed the thought as she clicked open the email.

Dear Ms. Tinsley Tomlinson,

To celebrate the launch of the new Munger Carlson Vodka collection, which is distilled with the purest water from the Rocky Mountains and crafted with only the highest quality, hand-picked wheat, we would like to invite you to a private party at the Four Seasons penthouse residence to celebrate. You are invited to be among the first in North America to experience the crisp, cool taste of Munger Carlson with the city's most celebrated socialites, celebrities and tastemakers. Join us Thursday, May 4 for an evening of specially curated Munger Carlson cocktails with special guest performances and finger food. RSVP by Monday, May 1 and dress to impress.

Hope to see you there!

Claudia Everett

Black Widow PR

Holy. Fuck. Tori read through the email a second time before her eyes snapped back to the salutation. *Tinsley?* She was confused. *Who the hell is Tinsley?* They must have just gotten her first name wrong, she thought, shrugging it off. Then it hit her: Finally! All of her hard work had paid off! All of those years spent hanging around outside of industry events in order to get a first-hand scoop for her website and she was finally in the big leagues! Black Widow PR managed everyone from Tom Ford and Hugo Boss, to Birks and the Cosmopolitan Hotel. They were *the* PR company of choice when it came to luxury brands. And Toronto-born Munger Carlson was one of the world's biggest playboys. *They must have seen the article that I wrote about their Peter Pilato chocolate launch*, she thought brightly. Sure, the article had only garnered twenty hits and two comments (one of which was from a spammer), but it was well written, Tori told herself. Of course, she hadn't actually been inside of the party. She'd spent the better part of ninety minutes trying to talk her way inside before being firmly escorted to the sidewalk. There, she'd watched minor celebrities and socialites stroll past the velvet rope and into the event. Later, she'd managed to get her hands on a discarded chocolate wrapper that one of the attendees had carelessly tossed aside after leaving the venue. And with that, the celebrities that she had seen, the music that she'd heard every time the door was opened and snippets of conversation that she'd caught from exiting guests, Tori had crafted together a 600-word article that sounded like she had been inside.

Another wave of excitement overtook her as she looked at the date of the email. It had been sent two weeks ago. Today was Monday, May 1. She was lucky that things had been slow at the office today and that her colleagues had been sufficiently caffeinated. She might have missed the invitation otherwise.

Tori clicked the reply button and began to type.

"Dear Ms. Everett," she wrote. "Thank you for the invitation. I would like to inform you that I will be attending the Munger Carlson penthouse party on Thursday." She paused. "And I will be dressed to impress," she added, thinking that it sounded professional. "Regards, T.," she ended the email before hitting Send.

Tori sat back in her chair, an elated smile painted on her face. It didn't matter how many coffee runs or phone calls she'd have to field today, nothing could bring her down from her vodka launch, private-penthouse-party cloud.

"Tori?" came her boss's voice above her. "Tori? Hello, Earth to Tori!" he exclaimed, poking her on the shoulder.

"Hmm!?" Tori sat up straight, exited the browser and turned around. "Keith!" she exclaimed, the ecstatic smile still stuck on her face.

"Why do you have that funny grin on your face?" he questioned, eyebrows furrowing. "Are you on drugs?"

"No!" She immediately wiped the smile off of her face. "Not at all! It's just"—she paused and looked around the room desperately—"such a nice day today!" She gestured to the window, which revealed a veritable monsoon outside.

Keith looked at the window and then back at Tori, both brows raised in question.

"Right," he deadpanned. "Anyway, sheet rain aside, I need you to make sixteen copies of this presentation and then run it to the conference room on the tenth floor. Jensen's presenting our third-quarter results to the shareholders tomorrow morning." He handed her a folder filled with papers. "Think you can handle that?" he asked, eyebrows still raised to his hairline.

"Yes! Definitely! Looking forward to it!" she enthused.

Keith looked at her again, his expression unchanged. "Great," he said, backing away from her slowly before turning on his heel.

Tori's smile returned as she remembered the Black Widow invite. Nothing could burst her bubble, she thought. Not even cranky old Keith. She scooped up the file and headed to the copier. Plopping back down at her desk several hours later, Tori once again opened her *Fashionist* email. Her fifteen-minute task had turned into a nearly three-and-a-half-hour ordeal after being sidetracked by tenth floor coffee requests and a secretary who begged her to cover the phones while she stepped out to pick up her sick son from school.

Tori logged into her account. Sitting there at the top of her inbox was a reply: "Re: re: Munger Carlson's Four Seasons Penthouse Party."

Dear Ms. Tinsley Tomlinson,

RSVP received! So happy that you are able to join us!

Looking forward to seeing you there,

Claudia Everett

Tori's heart rate shot back up again. It was happening! She was going to be on the other side of the velvet rope for a change. She was going to the Munger Carlson launch party on Thursday!

*

The next few days passed pretty uneventfully, minus Tori blowing up the photocopier and spilling coffee all over herself in the Wednesday morning meeting. And finally, after three days that felt more like three years, it was the evening of the party. On Monday night she had torn apart her closet trying to find a dress that would impress and had finally settled on a plain black jersey frock. She'd pulled out her sewing machine, scissors and box of scrap fabric and set to sewing every day after work. The result? Tori looked at herself in the mirror. She'd hacked and sewed and bedazzled to within an inch of her life, taking the dress from simple to . . . if not quite sophisticated, definitely statement making. What that statement was was up for debate, but her outfit would do a drag queen proud. Slipping on black

10

off-the-rack heels Tori grabbed a handful of her business cards (a fashion illustration on one side, T. Tomlinson with her email address and phone number on the other) and stuffed them into her glittery purse.

At the office that day she'd barely been able to contain her excitement. When the workday ended, she'd hurried home as fast as she could to get started on her party prep. And finally, after a three-hour ordeal that included a lavender-scented bubble bath, half a can of hairspray and a liberal application of foundation and black eyeshadow, Tori was ready for her first industry party.

She stood back and surveyed herself in the mirror. Smoky-black eyes, feather-trim dress with a plunging neckline and rhinestone-studded skirt, black heels and slicked-back hair. She looked confident enough. How she felt was an entirely different matter. Tori frowned at her reflection. She didn't feel confident. She felt like an imposter.

Face scrunched up in derision, she put down her purse and headed for her side cabinet. Popping the top off of a bottle of Stoli, she hesitated for a second before putting the bottle to her lips and tipping it upside down.

Fake it till you make it, she thought as she gulped. *Or let vodka fake it for you.* Besides, she justified, she was going to the launch of a premier Rocky Mountain hand-picked wheat vodka tonight. It was necessary for her to imbibe beforehand. How else would she be able to appreciate the crisp, cool taste of Munger Carlson?

She wiped her hand across her mouth and put the bottle back. Picking up her purse, she shrugged on a faux-fur jacket and headed out the door. It took a few minutes for her to flag down a cab and then she was on her way to the Four Seasons.

Traffic wasn't too bad for a Thursday—it was a warm spring evening so there was more foot traffic than car. Tori sat in the back seat trying to keep herself calm but she was unable to contain her excitement. She hadn't told anyone about her invite. She still couldn't believe that she had been invited to this party and she didn't want to embarrass herself if it turned out to be a mistake. She pulled out her cell phone and scrolled through her contact list to the letter *M*.

"Maggie!" she typed. "You're never going to guess where I'm going tonight. So much to tell you!" She hit Send and popped her phone back into her purse. Maggie, her best friend since second grade, lived only a few blocks away from her. But despite the closeness of their living quarters, the pair managed to meet up only once or twice per week, both busy with work and extracurriculars. Well, Maggie was mostly busy with work. While Tori was a journalism graduate with an unrelated nine-to-five and poor advancement prospects, Maggie was a financial analyst for a hedge fund—a job that left her working crazy hours every week with limited time for a social life.

As the vehicle weaved through the city the Stoli came back to haunt her; Tori felt her face flush as the alcohol coursed through her bloodstream. Liquid courage indeed. She was already feeling more calm, cool and collected. The car pulled into the courtyard of the Four Seasons behind a lineup of black town cars and limousines. Leading to a roped-off area, a red carpet lay rolled out in front of the residence. Flashes of light punctuated the scene as photographers clicked away at people exiting the vehicles and making their way down the red-carpeted path. Through the doors Tori could see a large step-and-repeat backdrop. She'd never stood in front of one before, always being relegated to standing outside of the event.

Her taxi finally made it to the front of the queue, and she watched as a handsome tuxedo-sporting man opened the car door and offered her his hand. Tori stood still, momentarily stunned as flashbulbs went off around her.

"Are you okay, miss?" asked the handsome man, gently urging her immobile body towards the carpet.

Tori realized her mouth was gaping and shook herself off.

"Yes! I'm great!" she exclaimed as she willed her legs to start working.

"What's your name, love?" he asked.

"Tori," she replied, stumbling a little as she exited the car. "Tori Tomlinson."

"Well, you'll have a great night tonight, Ms. Tomlinson." He smiled, half dragging her down the carpet. "They flew in Beluga caviar from the Caspian Sea this morning, and Munger Carlson himself designed the drink menu." He deposited her in front of the clipboard-wielding party gatekeeper and bowed to her with a wink. "Enjoy your evening, Ms. Tomlinson," he said before turning away.

"Tomlinson?" asked the clipboard woman.

"Yes." Tori smiled nervously. This was it. This was the moment that they were going to tell her that she wasn't on the list and that there had been some sort of mix-up—that some intern had messed up the invites and that she shouldn't have received one.

"Here you are!" The headset woman smiled warmly. "Tinsley Tomlinson. *Fashionista Magazine!*"

Tinsley. *Fashionista*, not *Fashionist?* Tori was suddenly sober.

"I . . ." she began, and then paused as the headset woman looked at her inquiringly.

"Yes?" the woman asked, one eyebrow raised in question.

Tori was right. She had been mistakenly invited. She would do the right thing and fess up to being Tori Tomlinson from *Fashionist*, a blog with a pitifully small number of readers whose author had never seen the inside of an industry party, and not Tinsley Tomlinson from *Fashionista*, a world-renowned website with millions of monthly readers whose author was probably invited to every exclusive event.

"I . . . I . . . I'm so happy to be here this evening!" Tori gushed.

Okay. She would fess up to it next time. She would pretend to be Tinsley from *Fashionista* just this once. Just for one night. She'd finally experience the glitz and glam parties that she'd longed to be inside of and then she would send Black Widow PR an email telling them that they had her mixed up with the other T. Tomlinson.

The woman smiled and unclipped the red velvet rope.

"We're very happy to have you, Ms. Tomlinson." She motioned for her to walk inside. "Enjoy the evening!"

Tori stood there, her heart beating wildly, not sure if she should make a run for it down the step-and-repeat. Deciding that that was probably the quickest way to get caught and thrown out like the imposter that she was, she shuffled her way down the red carpet, trying to avoid the sea of photographers blinding her with their flashing lights. She quickly found herself at the end of the carpet amongst a small crowd of strikingly attired men and women waiting for an elevator. Helmed by two black-suited bodyguards, she watched the numbers decrease until they hit L and the doors slid open to reveal a spacious compartment with three mirrored walls. The crowd filtered into the elevator, chatting amongst themselves as Tori squished herself into the only available space—right in front of the elevator doors. As the doors slid shut, the man next to her fumbled on the pad, pressing PH, the only button on the lift besides Door Open, Door Close Ground, and Alarm.

Tori struggled not to breathe too deeply as the box began its ascent, her stomach twisting as the lift continued its climb. After what seemed like ages the elevator stopped with a sudden jolt. A faceless voice announced "Penthouse" as the doors opened onto what could only be described as semi-contained chaos.

She had never seen anything like it. Her first timid steps off of the lift bathed her in blue light. Dance music pulsed above the chatter of the bursting-to-capacity crowd and white and clear balloons littered the ceiling between aerial performers conducting sky-high acrobatics. Swan ice sculptures flanked a frosted sign advertising Munger Carlson Vodka and the room danced with bright white and blue lights, casting dark shadows onto the walls and the crowd. She spotted a bar to her right and walked over as a large crowd of people made off with their cocktails. She didn't know anyone at this party, but she wanted to.

Tori stepped up to the empty bar and looked at the drink menu.

"What can I get you?" the bartender, who was sporting a brush mustache and black-rimmed glasses, asked.

"Umm . . ." She hesitated. "What would you recommend?"

"The Mango Munger is pretty good," he said. "A splash of mango, lemon juice and syrup with two ounces of Munger Carlson and a pineapple garnish."

"Okay." Tori nodded. "I'll try one of those, please."

As the bartender poured, shook and stirred, Tori looked around. She should network, she thought. This was her chance to make industry connections. But how? The PR firm thought that she was someone else. She could hardly go around advertising the fact that she wasn't, in fact, Tinsley Tomlinson of *Fashionista*. It would be more embarrassing being escorted out of the party than it ever would have been not being allowed into it in the first place. She picked up the Mango Munger from the bar and took a sip.

Her face scrunched up at the sweet-and-sour combo in the glass before she shrugged her shoulders, threw it back and ordered another.

The bartender laughed.

"One of those nights, hey?"

"You have no idea." She smiled back at him.

Four Mango Mungers later and Tori was lacking neither confidence nor enthusiasm for the sweet-and-sour cocktails. With every downed Mango Munger she felt more self-assured, and after an hour of chatting with the bartender while he mixed up cocktails for the assorted guests, she finally felt confident enough to face the fashionable crowd.

Rick—she'd caught his name after he served her her second Mango Munger—supplied her with a fifth cocktail and bid her good night as she spotted a two-woman, one-man threesome that looked open to out-group conversation.

Tori steeled herself for any potential awkwardness and took a large sip of her drink.

Chapter 3:
The Morning After

She woke up to the head-splitting sound of her beeping alarm clock. Head and heart pounding from dehydration, Tori reached over and slammed her hand down on her nightstand, feeling around for the offending device.

Oh fuck, she thought to herself. Sitting straight up in bed she felt a knot in the pit of her stomach. What happened last night? She had been having a great time talking to the bartender and the last thing she remembered was walking over to a crowd and taking a sip from her fifth Mango Munger. She was hit with a wave of fear as she realized that she had no memory of last night. She'd been on autopilot. Fortunately, Autopilot Tori had had enough sense to set her alarm clock before she passed out, ensuring that she wouldn't miss work. She'd also been nice enough to leave a tall glass of water and a packet full of pain pills for herself. Head spinning, she reached for the hangover cure and downed both almost as fast as she'd downed the cocktails last night. Christ, she grimaced as her hair swept across her face, she smelled like a goddamned mango tree.

Setting the glass down on the nightstand she scanned her surroundings. Last night's outfit, purse and shoes included, lay strewn about the floor. At least she appeared to have made it home in one piece. Gingerly lowering herself to the ground she picked up her purse and rifled through it. Bank cards, ID, credit cards, grocery store card—all there and accounted for. The only thing missing was the enormous stack of business cards she'd brought along with her last night. Well, she thought, trying to find a silver lining, she had wanted to network.

Suddenly the floor began to vibrate. Confused, Tori looked around. Her brain cells connected moments later, and she realized it was her cell phone that was buzzing and not the floor. Tossing her crumpled dress out of the way she spotted and snatched up her phone. "6 missed calls," the screen read. She dismissed them all, then held her head in her hands and prayed to the vodka gods that she wouldn't find evidence of anything too embarrassing on her mobile.

There was a sharp intake of air as she opened up her messages folder. Name after unknown name appeared, starting at 8:40 p.m., with the final message received at 3:45 a.m. She clicked on one from "Big Wally". Big Wally? Who the hell was Big Wally? "Tinsley, you are totally crazy, girl!! Can't wait to see you on Saturday at Cartier's party! XOXO."

Message after message oozed admiration for Tinsley, all telling her how much fun they had had and how they couldn't wait to see her on Saturday. Tori suddenly felt nauseous.

Tinsley. These people thought that she was Tinsley. In her Mango Munger autopilot mode she'd passed out her T. Tomlinson *Fashionist* business cards and pretended to be Tinsley. She wanted to crawl into a hole and die. Throwing herself back onto her bed, she started scrolling through the photos that people had sent her: there were several pictures of her with different groups of people; one of her with the swan ice sculpture's beak in her mouth; one of her sitting on some dashing man's lap while he whispered into her ear; one of her clinging on to a very unhappy-looking waiter's back, holding his platter of hors d'oeuvres in her hand. She looked fairly sober, at least—minus a few photos with a gaping mouth and lazy eyes—no one would have been able to tell she was completely out of it. She let out a gasp as she stumbled onto a video that someone named Merrill had sent her. It featured her, Tori Tomlinson, on stage with Drake. Waving a shot glass back and forth she grabbed the microphone out of the rapper's hand and yelled "Cheers, bitches!" while the crowd enthusiastically woo-hooed her.

Oh God. She turned off her phone and threw it on her bed. She was never going out in public again. Not at night, anyway. From now on she was going to go straight home from work, and she was going to have her groceries delivered. Maybe she should dye her hair and invest in a large-brimmed hat and big sunglasses, too.

Work!

Tori jumped into high gear and ran into the bathroom to survey this morning's damage. Mascara and black eyeshadow smeared halfway down her face and her hair stuck out at all angles. Judging by the lion's mane that she was sporting, she must have face-planted into her pillow last night and stayed that way until morning. She marveled at the fact that she hadn't managed to smother herself in her sleep. She wouldn't have enough time to wash the mango scent out of her hair but that was nothing a tight bun wouldn't fix. It would also pull double duty by forcing her puffy and squinting eyes open. *Practical and functional,* she mused.

Stepping into the shower, she tried to scrub away the residual shame and the hangover. The effort was futile, but it did make her feel slightly more refreshed.

Miraculously, she made it into work with two minutes to spare. She held on to her thermos full of coffee, anchoring it to her desk to save herself from the spins.

"All right there, Tori?" asked Sierra, her short, grey-haired senior colleague. "You smell like a mango, is that a new perfume?"

Tori held back a dry heave, her stomach flipping at the mention of mangos.

"Uhh," she managed weakly, "no, it's shampoo."

"Smells amazing! You'll have to tell me the brand," Sierra said absentmindedly.

She managed to get through most of the morning without succumbing to her hangover and without too many people asking why she looked so pale. While she fielded phone calls in a much raspier voice than usual and moved much slower than normal, she didn't throw up on anyone or pass out at her desk, so she considered that a win. After running files to the twelfth floor and photocopying pamphlets for Keith, Tori slumped into her chair to check her email. There was one from a customer who, concerned that his Impotentia wasn't working properly, had tripled his dose, ended up with a five-hour erection and was wondering what he should do. On a normal day, Tori would have giggled and sent a sympathetic email instructing the man to head to the hospital. But she couldn't see the humor in it through her mango haze today. She fired off an email to the man, telling him to get to the emergency room as soon as possible, and then clicked open another message.

Work emails dealt with, an hour later she clicked open another browser and entered her *Fashionist* email. She closed her eyes as her inbox loaded and thirteen email notifications popped up on screen. Oh God, the first one was from Black Widow PR. Subject: "Re: Munger Carlson." *Here it comes*, she thought. It wouldn't even matter if they thought that she was Tinsley. She'd probably managed to get the poor, unsuspecting woman banned from all future Black Widow PR events.

She clicked open the email.

Dear Tinsley,

We would like to thank you for joining us last night in celebrating Munger Carlson Vodka. So happy you could make it!

Warmest regards,

Claudia Everett

Tori let out a breath of air that she hadn't even realized she'd been holding. She clicked Back and scrolled up the list. There were event invites, new friends laughing about inside jokes they'd apparently made last night, and at the very top was one from Munger Carlson, the vodka man himself—subject line: "?" Her cursor hovered over top of the email before she bit the bullet and clicked on it.

Tinsley,

You made quite an impression on me last night. I would love to continue our conversation this week in a more intimate setting.

Drinks this Sunday?

Munger

Oh fuck. She'd talked to Munger Carlson?! What would they even have to talk about? Munger was a handsome, Rolex-wearing playboy who dated Paris-Hilton-y types of women. She put her head down on her desk, intending to stay in that position for the remainder of the day until her cell phone started vibrating next to her ear. She looked at her phone—two missed calls from Maggie. "Call you back in 10," she typed, then stood up and asked who wanted coffee. A resounding "me" came from all corners of the office as she jotted down names and orders.

"Right. I'll be back," she murmured. And grabbing her purse and jacket, she swept out the door.

"Maggie! I'm a disaster," she wailed, clutching the phone to her ear.

"What the hell happened to you last night!" exclaimed

Maggie. "I get a text from you telling me I'll never guess where you're going and that you have a lot to tell me, and then the next thing I know I receive pictures of you deep-throating an ice sculpture and making out with Munger Carlson."

"It's terrible, Maggie. Absolutely terrible," Tori moaned. "Promise that you won't judge me!"

"Cross my heart and hope to die," Maggie said. "Now spill!"

Tori obliged, telling her everything that she remembered, right up until this morning when she realized what she'd done.

"Oh my God. This is hilarious. Black Widow PR thought that you were the T. Tomlinson from *Fashionista*, and now half of the industry thinks that you're the T. Tomlinson from *Fashionista*."

"I know!" said Tori, walking into the coffee shop. "It's horrible! I don't know what got into me! It was the Mango Mungers! I was only going to pretend for the one night!"

"What's a Mango Munger?" Maggie sounded interested.

"A horrible, evil, Satanist concoction."

Maggie snorted.

"I can't believe you drank so much that you have no memory of the only event you've ever made it inside of. The irony."

"It was a party celebrating vodka!" Tori said defensively. "How else do you celebrate a liquor launch!"

"Whatever helps you sleep at night, Tor," said Maggie. "Or should I say Tinsley?" she laughed.

"This is serious, Maggie!" Tori exclaimed. "Hold on." She walked up to the counter and rattled off her nine-drink order. "I just looked at my *Fashionist* email and I have all of these invites to events, and Munger Carlson—whatever the hell kind of name that is anyway—wants to take Tinsley on a date!" She handed over the company credit card and glared at the judgmental-looking barista.

"I'm being judged right now, Maggie." She stuffed the card into her pocket, moved to an empty back corner and continued her conversation. "What am I going to do?"

"Tori," said Maggie in an are-you-stupid tone of voice. "You've always wanted to be a fashion writer and now you have access to all of these events. What you're going to do is RSVP to everything you can get your hands on and you're going to write about it."

"But I'm Tori, not Tinsley!" she protested.

"So what? They don't have to know that. There's no harm in pretending to be Tinsley. No one knows what she looks like anyway. I just Googled her name and there are zero photos of her where she's not hidden behind dinner-plate-sized sunglasses. You both have long black hair and pale skin. You're as good as Tinsley!" said Maggie. "And besides, you're a great writer. Once you start dishing on all of these events, no one will care that you weren't the intended recipient of the invites. They'll care about your writing skills and their clients' coverage."

"I don't know," Tori hemmed, feeling herself wavering. "It feels wrong."

"It only feels wrong because you're suffering from a massive hangover and the shame of embarrassing photos floating around of you deep-throating a swan," Maggie said practically.

"Will you stop saying that!" Tori hissed. "I do not need to be reminded that there is a photo of me throat-deep in an ice sculpture, thanks!" The hairy, heavy-set man sitting close to Tori suddenly looked at her with interest.

"No dice, sir!" she said loudly. "I am not that kind of girl!"

She turned back to her conversation with Maggie when the barista called her name, indicating that her order was ready. "I have to go, Maggie. We're still on for sushi tomorrow?"

"Definitely," said Maggie. "Wouldn't miss it for the world. And in the meantime, respond to those invites!"

"I promise nothing," Tori said as the phone clicked off on the other line.

She made it through the rest of the workday, thankful that it was Friday. She was even more thankful that it was a slow Friday afternoon and that most of her colleagues had left the office early. Taking Maggie's advice, she'd RSVP'd to a total of six events including tomorrow night's Cartier party to celebrate their new "Timeless" collection at a car dealership. She'd also replied to the assorted emails from the friends that she'd apparently made last night, feigning remembrance and telling them that she couldn't wait to see them again either. Finally, twelve emails answered, three bathroom breaks taken, desk drawers cleaned out and work files finished, she clicked open the last email, the one that she'd been avoiding: Munger Carlson.

"Dear Munger," she typed, "I had a great time last night." She paused. She wasn't really lying. All photographic, text and email evidence indicated that she'd really enjoyed herself the previous evening. "Drinks on Sunday sounds great. My number is—" She typed in her digits, signed off with "T." and hit Send.

A quick after-work nap left Tori feeling more human, less walking dead, and thinking a little more clearly. If she was going to start attending all of these events and writing about them, she didn't want to start posting it to her *Fashionist* site. That would spell disaster if people clicked onto it expecting *Fashionista* instead. It wouldn't take a rocket scientist to put two and two together and figure out what was going on. To circumvent an untimely outing of her pretend persona, Tori spent her Friday evening setting up an anonymous WordPress website to document her industry experiences. Under the heading *On the List*, Tori posted a short "about the author" blurb that alluded to her being a society insider who wanted to dish on the industry. Given she had barely any memory of the party the night before, Tori figured she would throw up her first post after the Cartier party. If she didn't manage to get found out at the next few events, at least the site would allow her to put her writing skills to good use—something that had yet to occur at Staten Marketing. The clock read 9:42 p.m. when she finally snapped her computer shut, pulled on her fuzzy pajamas and crawled into bed.

Chapter 4:
Cartier & Cars

Tori awoke the next morning in great spirits instead of smelling like them. Sure, she might have made a bit of an ass—okay, a colossal ass—of herself at the vodka event the other night, but she was going to get to fulfill her dream of dishing on industry events! She wasn't getting paid—yet—but she felt certain that once senior editors read her writing, they would be fighting each other to get her on board with their publication.

She met up with Maggie at 2 p.m. for a late sushi lunch at a quaint little spot in their neighbourhood.

"This is the greatest thing I've ever heard," Maggie declared, stuffing an avocado roll into her mouth.

"I know what you mean. I wasn't crazy about the idea yesterday, but it's grown on me." Tori dunked a shiitake roll into soy sauce. "I'm excited to start writing about all of these events."

Maggie swallowed the last of her roll and reached for her water.

"Just try to keep your liquor consumption in check this

time."

Tori grimaced.

"I'm limiting myself to two cocktails tonight. Thursday night was different—I wasn't going for work, I was going for fun. I'll be strictly professional this evening."

"Well, either way keep me posted," Maggie implored. "I'll be at work all night keeping an eye out for any embarrassing photos."

"Just promise me that you won't tell anyone what I'm doing," Tori begged.

On the way home to her apartment Tori started putting outfits together in her head. With all of the events that she was slated to attend in the next two weeks, she'd need at least six different outfits. As the supposed fashion editor of a trendy online magazine she couldn't very well be seen in the same thing twice. But, as the entry-level marketing assistant at Staten, her budget wouldn't allow her to purchase a brand new off-the-rack outfit for every event. She was going to have to get creative.

After spending the rest of the afternoon designing her WordPress site, she climbed in the shower with three hours to spare.

Putting the finishing touches on her bright red lipstick, Tori pursed her lips, grabbed her purse and headed for the door. She'd chosen a curve-hugging black lace dress for the Cartier party, spicing it up with layers of her mother's costume jewellery. Like last time, Tori hesitated when she reached the clipboard woman who helmed the front of the line.

You're Tinsley, she told herself as the woman asked for her name.

"Tomlinson," Tori said nervously. "Tinsley Tomlinson with *Fashionista Magazine*."

And a few seconds later, the woman unclipped the rope and stepped to the side.

Tori could hardly believe it was so easy. All of those years that she'd longed to get inside of just one event and all it had taken was her pretending to be someone else. She walked down the steps and into the luxury car dealership. Cartier was celebrating their new collection by serving drinks and hors d'oeuvres to invitees as they mingled amongst the sexiest of European sports cars. Waifish models decked out in twenties-style outfits dripped in diamonds, emeralds, sapphires, rubies and pearls as they posed inside and on top of the vehicles and guests snapped their photos and inspected the new collection. Having forgone chugging directly from the Stoli bottle before departing for the party tonight, Tori's nerves were at an all-time high. She was definitely going to watch her liquor intake this time, but how was she going to talk to anyone? She took a deep breath and wandered over to the bar, ordering up a cranberry juice to hold in her hands because she didn't know what to do with them. Feeling self-conscious she moved to the back of the room and leaned up against a wall, twirling the cocktail straw in one hand while trying her best to look like she belonged there.

She had nearly finished her virgin drink when she spotted someone walking towards her. Some man, actually. One tall, blond-haired waif sporting a red fur jacket, sunglasses, impossibly tight skinny jeans, a large, slouchy man purse in one hand and a martini in the other.

"Tinsley! Darling!" He grinned devilishly, arms opened wide in a welcoming gesture.

"Hi!" she feigned recognition, covering up her ignorance of the man's identity with an enthusiastic smile. Without a hitch in his stride, the man wrapped his martini hand around her neck and enveloped her in a headlock type of hug, taking the opportunity to chug from the glass that was now in the vicinity of his mouth.

"How are you, darling?" he asked, air-kissing her once, twice and thrice.

Tori, ignorant of the air-kiss protocol, awkwardly bumped heads with the man who was now rubbing the side of his noggin with a grimace.

"Holy fuck, Tins!" the man exclaimed. "Are you shit-faced already? The party only started half an hour ago!" He started laughing and then, turning to his right, called out to a man and a woman who were being served at the bar.

"Alexei! February! Tinsley's here!"

The duo, drinks in hand, worked their way over to Tori and the fur-coated man.

"Tinsley!" The man, whom she was assuming was Alexei, opened his arms and went in for the requisite air kisses. This time Tori was prepared, and she managed to stumble her way through it without smacking any heads.

"Tins, doll," said the woman she assumed was February. A third round of air kisses ensued and then Tori stood back awkwardly smiling at the trio.

"What are you drinking tonight, Tins?" asked Alexei, his long black hair hanging down like curtains on either side of his head. "No Mango Mungers here!" he guffawed.

"Uhh," Tori started. "Just cranberry juice for right now."

"Smart girl," February chimed in. "Avoiding a hangover. Right, Marcus?" She glanced at the blond in the fur coat.

Marcus looked at her sideways.

"Suit yourself, Tins. My goal for this evening is to pass out on the hood of that Audi." He indicated the car to his left with an uptick of his chin.

Tori's eyes nearly popped out of her head. She could hardly believe these people. Here she thought that everyone attending these events was sophisticated and cultured. Sure, Marcus, Alexei and February looked the part, but "passing out on the hood of a car at a Parisian jewellery party" party goals? No wonder her vodka-fueled antics the other evening had proven so popular. She couldn't imagine keeping her current job if she'd shown up to an event as a representative of Staten and drank so much that she blacked out. But here, in the fashion industry, it looked like not only was that acceptable, but it had sealed the deal for her fake persona. Still, Tori did not want a repeat of Thursday night. Once was enough.

"What are you doing tomorrow night, Tins?" Marcus broke her train of thought.

"Umm, I have a date," she said vaguely.

Alexei eyed her with interest.

"Date with who?"

"Munger Carlson," she blurted out.

The fashionable trio's jaws dropped open and their eyebrows shot upwards.

Marcus was the first to regain his composure.

"Munger Carlson!? Well done, Tins! I mean, we all saw you with him the other night and assumed that he'd take you home for a good romp. But a date? Well done, indeed!"

Tori wasn't sure how to take this. She knew that she wasn't Gigi Hadid, but she thought that she held her own.

"The man is worth billions!" exclaimed Alexei. "Where's he taking you?"

"One billion, actually," Tori replied, having Wikipedia'd him the day before. "We're going to Lavelle for drinks."

Tori fielded a few more questions from the trio about her date before she excused herself to run to the washroom. She hadn't actually needed to use it, but she'd needed a moment to collect herself. Weaving through the crowd of fashionably attired people, Tori heard people calling out "Tinsley!" and she begged off as assorted men and women greeted her enthusiastically and tried to drag her into their conversations. After two minutes of navigating she finally found herself near the bathroom facilities. She pushed open the door to her right and came face to chest with a handsome, sandy-haired man wearing a slim-cut black suit and a surprised expression on his face.

Tori stepped back and put her hand to her face.

"Oh . . . oh . . . my God! I . . . I am so . . . so sorry!!" she stammered, her ability to speak rendered momentarily incapacitated by both her shock at finding the man in front of her and the man's devastating good looks.

He grinned down at her.

"No harm done," he said with a little chuckle. "Maybe just knock next time before swinging open the bathroom door."

Tori was mortified. She stood back as he exited the room, giving her a reassuring wink as he brushed by. Once he was out of sight, she closed the door behind her and leaned against it as her knees buckled. He was the most attractive man that she had ever seen, and she'd nearly left a makeup outline of her face on his suit jacket.

Splashing some cold water on her neck, Tori touched up her makeup before heading back to the party. She spotted Marcus, Alexei and February across the room. Martinis refreshed, they were chatting to a group of people—all of whom were completely ignoring the Cartier and car exhibit.

She headed in the opposite direction towards one of the bars stationed around the dealership. It was as she descended the last stair into the sunken area that she slipped on a spilled drink and pitched forward, grabbing on to the first thing in front of her, which happened to be a man's suit-jacket-clothed arm. Unable to maintain her balance, Tori toppled over, dragging the man down with her. She landed on top of the unfortunate individual with an "oomph" as the crowd around them parted and a glass rolled away.

"We meet again" came the voice of the man that Tori was lying on top of.

She raised her head off of his chest and glanced upwards. *Oh Christ.* It was the handsome bathroom man! And here she had embarrassed herself in front of him again. Twice in the span of ten minutes. She was really on a roll tonight.

"Already on the floor and it's only half past seven!" shouted a voice from somewhere above her. "That's the spirit, Tins!"

The man broke out into a boyish grin.

"Are you okay?" he asked.

"Yes! I'm so, so sorry!" Tori scrambled off of him, dusting herself off and grabbing for her purse.

The man pulled himself to his feet and turned to her. "Can I get you a drink, Ms. Spastic?" He smiled, raising one eyebrow in invitation. "Although given you almost walked in on me in the bathroom, then tackled me to the floor and spilled my drink, it should probably be you getting a drink for me."

Tori must have looked as mortified as she felt.

"I'm sorry," the man said, seeing the expression on her face. "I feel like an ass. I was only teasing, I swear," he said sincerely.

"I'm Alistair." He held out his hand. "Alistair Chase."

Tori hesitated before placing her hand in his, thankful that he hadn't gone in for a triple air kiss.

"Tinsley," she lied, while simultaneously wishing she didn't have to. "Tinsley Tomlinson."

"Right," said Alistair. "Well, Ms. Tomlinson, would you care to join me for a drink so that I can atone for my rudeness?" He gave her a friendly smile.

Tori melted. Good God, he was handsome.

"I would love to." She smiled back.

Not letting go of her hand, Alistair led her through the crowd that had flowed back in to fill the spaces that they'd vacated after the duo had fallen. At the bar, Alistair asked her what she'd like to drink.

Tori looked at the menu.

"Um"—she looked at the bartender—"what would you recommend?"

"The Pink Panther," the bored-looking bartender suggested, not even bothering to look at her as he inspected and polished a martini glass.

"Okay, I'll have one of those, please," she said.

"Make that two," Alistair interjected as the bartender grabbed a shaker and started mixing.

"You seem more like a scotch man," Tori mused. "I never would have taken you for a pink, frilly drink guy."

"Well, Ms. Clumsy," Alistair teased. "There's a lot that you don't know about me—yet," he added.

Tori's heart skipped a beat. *He's just being nice*, she thought practically, even though a part of her hoped with all of her currently fluttering heart that he was being *more* than just nice.

Two pink cocktails appeared on the bar and Alistair grabbed them both. "Better let me hold on to yours until we sit down," he teased. "We wouldn't want someone to end up drenched in your Pink Panther."

Tori laughed this time.

"Lead the way, Ms. Tomlinson." He gestured with a nod of his head towards a vacant couch beside the stairs.

Tori excused herself and apologized to several people in

quick succession as she attempted to squeeze her way through the crowd, dodging a bevy of assorted purses, oversized hats, clingy fabric and big hair. Emerging from the accessory-laden obstacle course, Alistair close behind, she deposited herself on a black velvet couch and took the proffered martini.

She cozied herself into the corner, pulling her legs onto the couch and Alistair sat beside her—one foot resting on his knee as he angled his body towards her.

"So," said Tori, taking a sip of the Pink Panther. "Are you in the industry?"

"Not really." He smiled. "I'm in finance. I do investing for Cartier so they sometimes invite me to their shindigs."

"Shindigs?" Tori raised her eyebrow at the ancient term, a teasing grin playing about her mouth.

Alistair laughed.

"Parties, then. Perk of the trade," he said, raising his martini glass. "And what about you?" he asked.

"I snuck in here," Tori said truthfully.

He laughed again and then took a sip of his martini.

She had just opened her mouth to elaborate when she was interrupted by Marcus.

"Tins, darling," he slurred drunkenly, his eyes still covered by giant sunglasses. "Who is this handsome man?"

Alistair smiled genuinely, extending his hand.

"Nice to meet you. I'm Alistair." He shook Marcus's hand. "Did you sneak in here, too?" Alistair asked lightly.

"Sneak in here? You snuck in here?" Marcus looked affronted.

"Not me," laughed Alistair. "Ms. Tomlinson here."

"I assume Tins here was just being drole, weren't you, darling." Marcus continued on without a pause. "Tinsley is the fashion editor of the hottest online women's magazine in the world," he said in a self-important manner. "She's an editor for *Fashionista.*"

Alistair looked impressed.

"Wow," he said. "I don't pay much attention to those sorts of things but even I've heard of *Fashionista.* So, you're beautiful, smart and successful." He grinned at Tori.

Tori plastered a smile on her face, wishing she'd had a chance to tell him the truth.

"I don't know about all that," she said uncomfortably.

"Humble, too!" Alistair enthused. "I should grab a ring and propose right now," he teased.

Tori smiled but inside she felt awful. She didn't want to lie to him and now there was no way that she could tell him the truth. Maybe she could pass Marcus off as an acquaintance who had had one too many martinis?

"So anyway," Marcus drunkenly interrupted. "We're going to get out of here, Tins. I couldn't possibly stomach another one of these watered-down drinks they pass off as cocktails." He grimaced at his empty glass. "We're heading for Kost. Are you guys coming?"

Tori looked at Alistair.

"If you don't mind me joining you, I'd hate to cut our conversation short." His eyebrows were raised in question.

He was giving her an out and there was no way that was she taking it. Of course she wanted him to come!

"I definitely don't mind!" she squeaked.

"Good," he said approvingly. "There is only so much bullshitting I can do about jewellery that I know nothing and care nothing about. If my sister could see me now." He shook his head in mock shame. "A pink, frilly drink, surrounded by people in weird outfits and talking about fashion. I'd never live it down."

Tori laughed and took a sip of her drink.

"Right," said Alistair. "Give me your coat-check ticket and I'll grab our jackets."

Tori obliged and Marcus slid into the vacant seat.

"You seductress, you," Marcus slurred. "First Munger Carlson and now this hottie! Bravo, Tins!"

They'd needed two cars to get to Kost. Marcus, Tori, Alistair and some man named James in one car, and February, Alexei, a short redhead named Stella and a blonde woman named Jess in the other. Tori sat in the middle of the car next to Alistair for the drive over. He'd squeezed her hand during one of Marcus's more colourful rants about the merits of top-shelf liquor over "lesser, pedestrian-type swill". She felt butterflies in her stomach as they shared a twinkle-eyed grin with one another.

After exiting the cars, they walked past the hotel's bouncer and into the waiting elevator. The blonde woman, Jess, pulled out a key card, popped it in the slot and pressed R for rooftop. When they stepped off of the elevators, the rooftop was vibrating. The air pulsed with Top 40 mixes and the well-dressed crowd milled about in groups talking, drinking and laughing. Marcus, the least in need of more liquor, led the way to the bar where he pushed his way in and rattled off a flurry of drink orders for everyone. After doling out the drinks, he sauntered away leaving the group with the bill. Tori was mortified as everyone else turned away until it was just her and Alistair standing there, the cheque sitting between them.

Alistair dropped his black Amex on the counter and the bartender promptly swiped it. She got a look at the bill: $186. *For eight drinks!? Cripes.*

"Thank you," said Tori gratefully. "And I'm so sorry. I can't believe that they stuck us with the bill."

"No worries, Tins." Alistair winked, teasingly imitating Marcus. "I'm the one tagging along on your night out. And given that I intend to keep you to myself for the rest of the night, I don't mind picking up the tab."

While the rest of the group they'd arrived with had dispersed into the crowd, Tori and Alistair wandered to the outside area where they found a secluded corner. They snuggled up companionably on the striped wicker loveseat and before they knew it, they were deep in conversation. Tori was telling him all about the small town that she'd grown up in and the summers that she'd spent with her family.

"It's so wild," said Alistair. "To think, you went from quading and camping and fishing, and wearing camouflage, and now you're at snobby fashion events and writing about it for a trendy magazine. I love that," he continued. "Landing a position like that would go to most people's heads but you're so grounded."

Tori shifted uncomfortably.

"Well, what about you?" she changed the subject.

"What about me?" He smiled.

"You're in finance," she said slowly. "The only thing I know about finance is that the guys in it all seem pretty slimy. Although to be honest, most of my knowledge comes from *Wolf of Wall Street*," she admitted.

"A lot of men in my industry are sleazy," Alistair agreed. "But hookers and drugs, and lying and cheating and stealing, and all of that other cliché stuff is not something that's ever appealed to me. My dad lied and cheated on my mom all throughout my childhood, then divorced her and left her penniless," he said thoughtfully. "I saw how it affected her and I never forgave him for it."

Tori felt her heart drop. In one stroke of mixed-up luck, she'd gotten her writing career and her dating life back on track. Except that she hadn't. She'd co-opted Tinsley's writing career and gotten Tinsley's dating life back on track. It killed her that Alistair thought that she was someone that she wasn't, especially after he'd shared such an intimate story about his upbringing, but what could she do now? She'd intended to tell him the truth. Right after she'd admitted to sneaking into the party. Marcus's untimely appearance, however, had put a stop to that. But everything that she had told Alistair so far, aside from her first name and her career, was true. Maybe she could just legally change her name to Tinsley?

They continued their conversation for several hours, only stopping when a waitress came by to refresh their drinks.

"Goodness!" Tori said, seeing the time on Alistair's watch. They'd spent three hours deep in conversation but to her it felt like it had hardly been three minutes. "I didn't realize it was so late! I'm so sorry but I should really get home." She thought about how she had intended to write about the Cartier event that evening.

"Already?" Alistair looked crestfallen.

"I'm sorry," she said regretfully. "I'm really enjoying

spending time with you, I just have a lot of things to do tomorrow."

"It's okay." He smiled. "Let's get you home before you turn into a pumpkin."

They took a taxi back to Tori's apartment and Alistair walked her to the door.

"I had a really amazing time with you tonight." Tori smiled at him when they reached the door to her building.

"I had an amazing time, too." He smiled back, brushing a stray strand of hair behind her ear. "I feel as if I've known you for ages," he said. "I really enjoyed our time together tonight. I'd love to take you out sometime. Can I do that?"

"Anytime! Absolutely!" she blurted out eagerly.

His smile widened and he cupped her face in his hands.

This is it! she thought. *He's going to kiss me!* She'd had a string of bad dates since she'd broken up with her high school sweetheart several months ago, and now she'd found an attractive, intelligent man with a great personality who genuinely seemed interested in getting to know her. Well, interested in getting to know Tinsley, at any rate. But even the knot that she felt at knowing that she had lied to him couldn't stop the feeling that shot through her when he bent his head, leaned in and pressed his lips to hers.

Alistair kissed her ever so softly, and Tori felt herself melt. He pulled back before kissing her again, a little harder this time, leaving Tori feeling jelly-legged and barely able to stand.

"Have a great rest of your evening, Ms. Tomlinson," he said, smiling as he swung the large glass door open for her. Tori staggered inside, hoping that she didn't look as dazed as she felt.

She floated into her apartment on a cloud of happiness. Evaluating her current mental state and the time, she figured she could put off writing her the Cartier piece for her website until tomorrow. After kicking off her shoes and dress, she flopped onto her bed and closed her eyes, still feeling the ghost of Alistair's kiss on her lips. It had been perfect. He was perfect. Tori, on the other hand, was anything but perfect. She was a grade A liar. She adored Alistair after spending just one evening with him, but what was she going to do about him thinking that she was Tinsley? Tori couldn't contemplate that at the moment. She would tackle that bit of business tomorrow, she thought as she fell into a deep, dream-filled sleep that featured soft kisses by a tall, blond-haired businessman.

Chapter 5:
A Fashion Faux Pas

The next morning, four hours and two cups of coffee later, a drained but invigorated Tori published her Cartier party article. She sat back to admire her handiwork. "Luxury Jewellery and Lust-Worthy Cars: Cartier's Latest Collection at Audi Inspired by Time," read the headline. What followed was a 654-word exposé on the previous evening's events. She'd received Cartier's press package full of photos that morning, which she'd embedded into the article. Probably owing to the cocktails that she'd consumed last night Tori had slept like the dead, finally waking up around 11 a.m. Normally an early riser, she didn't mind that she'd slept in this Sunday, savoring her memories from the night before.

Her first piece of writing accomplished, Tori focused on what else was in store for her today. Namely, her date with Munger Carlson. She'd been reluctant to go out with Munger given she didn't even remember meeting him (Lord knew what she had said to him). And now, after her evening with Alistair, she was even more reluctant. She didn't want word getting out that she was a serial dater. Ironic that she would even worry about that, she thought, given that last night and tonight were the first two dates (did last night count as a date? she wondered) that she'd gone on in months.

She'd woken up to a text from Alistair on her phone.

"Tinsley, I had a great time with you yesterday evening," it said. "Are you available this Thursday for dinner and drinks?"

Once again, Tori had butterflies in her stomach to contend with.

While she was reluctant to meet Munger, Tori still put effort into her appearance. She might not want to go but there was no sense in outwardly looking like it. She'd opted for a long and light spring dress and midi heels, accessorizing with the biggest purse she owned in an attempt to ward off any romantic advances on the part of Munger. He probably already thought that she was a floozie, she thought. Looking back at pictures of her from the vodka party, she looked like a floozie. But Tori figured that if he tried anything tonight, she could fend him off with her giant Fendi (fake, of course, who has $7,000 to spend on a bag?).

Wary of letting men know where she lived as a form of stalker prevention, she met Munger at the trendy King West rooftop bar Lavelle. The elevator doors led her into an open-air lobby and a warm breeze blew through her hair as she walked towards the hostess.

"How can I help you?" the girl in the short black dress asked.

"I'm meeting a friend for a drink," Tori replied. "Munger Carlson."

The girl's eyebrows shot up.

"Right this way, miss." She turned and walked out onto the dimly lit patio, past three small swimming pools and bottle service cabanas until she came to a large palm-leaf-covered cabana where Munger Carlson sat chatting on his cell phone.

"Danny," he said matter-of-factly, "I don't care what you have to do to get it done, just figure it out." He glanced up at Tori. "You have until 10 p.m. And if it isn't a done deal by then, you're fired." He clicked off his phone, smiled and stood up to greet her.

Oh no, thought Tori as he feinted to one side. *Here come the air kisses again.* How did they always know which side to start on? She'd never been good at dance, constantly mixing up her steps, so it was no surprise that she wasn't very good at the fake-kiss "nice to see you" waltz either. After stumbling through the air-kiss greeting, the ensuing date could be summed up in one word: *disastrous*.

While Munger had taken a liking to Tori, Tori hadn't taken a liking to him. She found him to be rude, crude and completely full of himself. As the hostess turned to go back to her station, he'd immediately grabbed Tori by the waist and tried to pull her onto his lap. She was having none of that. Tori decided that she would stay for one drink out of the sake of politeness, but that was it. After all, she could kind of understand him being touchy-feely with her seeing as she'd apparently given him the green light the other night. But the more time she spent with Munger, the less she liked him. And the colder that she was towards him, the hotter Munger seemed to be for her. She got the impression that no one had ever turned the billionaire playboy down before. He had just finished running through his list of expensive toys (two Porsches, a Lamborghini, a forty-foot yacht, vacation houses in Spain and Bali), which Tori had only half been paying attention to. She should be more excited about this, she thought. Millions of women would kill to be in her position right now, but Tori just couldn't do it. The man was an insufferable narcissist. Draining the last dregs of the vodka-cran that Munger had poured for her, Tori announced that she had a headache and was going to head home. Munger looked distinctly put out by that. After she thanked him for the drink, he promised to call her later that week. Tori cringed, silently hoping that he wouldn't.

*

It felt weird being back in the office on Monday morning. Tori had lived a different kind of life the past few days—going to private parties with the city's most fashionable and going on dates with a handsome businessman and a billionaire. There, she was Tinsley, celebrated fashion writer and party-girl extraordinaire. Here, she was Tori, entry-level marketing assistant and coffee girl. Despite feeling bad about her dishonesty, she allowed herself a small smile. It was kind of exciting living a double life. Like James Bond or something. Albeit without the fighting, guns and killing. Okay, maybe not like James Bond. But it was still exciting.

Her phone buzzed and a message from Maggie popped up on her screen. She'd completely forgotten to update her friend about what had happened at the party on Saturday night.

"Tor! Call me! I need to hear about the party and your date with Munger!" Tori read.

She quickly texted her back: "Call you at lunch, Megs."

Tori had brought her lunch to work with her that day (like she did every day), but instead of spending her lunch hour eating at her desk, she stepped outside and found an empty corner to sit in. Dropping her bag on the bench next to her she leaned against the wall and dialed Maggie's number.

"Spill!" Maggie answered without even saying hello. "And hurry. I have a meeting in ten minutes."

"I don't even know where to start," said Tori. "I think I'm in love," she said helplessly.

"What? In love!? With Munger Carlson!?"

"No, no, no, no, no!"

"Then who?" Maggie queried.

"Alistair," she said with a dreamy sigh. "Alistair Chase."

"Who is Alistair Chase and what happened to Munger Carlson?"

Tori filled her in on her impromptu Saturday night date with Alistair ("Oh my God, he sounds perfect, you lucky bitch!"), and her less-than-stellar Sunday night date with Munger ("What a cad!").

Maggie laughed.

"What a crazy weekend. If someone would have told me a week ago that you'd be hobnobbing with the fashion crowd and going on dates with billionaires, I would have called the hospital's psychiatric ward to see if they had room for another patient."

"I know!" Tori exclaimed. "It's still so surreal!"

"What events do you have going on for this week?" Maggie asked.

"A fashion show on Wednesday, Luminato launch on Thursday, and Fashion Cares pre-launch party on Friday."

"And what about Alistair?" she asked.

"He texted me yesterday to see if I wanted to go out for dinner and drinks on Thursday."

"What about Luminato?" asked Maggie.

"Luminato doesn't start until later," Tori replied. "I figured that we could do dinner and drinks and then go there together."

"This is hilarious," Maggie laughed. "Three days ago you were nervous about pretending to be Tinsley to get into parties, and now you're bringing people along as your guest."

Tori laughed herself.

"I know. It's totally crazy but I'm having an unbelievable time. I've always felt like just average Tori, but when I'm Tinsley, I feel so much more confident. I feel like I'm doing what I've always wanted to do."

"Well, enjoy it while it lasts," Maggie advised. "Someone will figure it out eventually, but until that happens, get as much mileage out of it for your career as you can. And if you happen to meet a handsome Mr. Right along the way, then that's a bonus," she added.

"I know," Tori sighed. "I really, really like this guy. And he really, really seems to like me. But everything that he thinks he knows about me is a lie."

"Everything?" Maggie asked, aghast. "What did you do? Make up stories about globe-trotting, fashion shows and premiere parties?"

"God no!" Tori exclaimed. "Actually, everything that I told him about myself is the truth, minus my first name. Marcus is the one who told him that I'm an editor at *Fashionista*. I haven't even mentioned anything else about it to him."

"Who's Marcus?" Maggie asked.

Tori sighed.

"A tall, blond-haired gay man who wears fur jackets, carries a man purse and sucks back martinis like most people suck back water."

"Sounds like you've made some interesting friends," Maggie observed.

"They only like me because I drank my face off at the Munger Carlson party and because they think I work for *Fashionista*."

"Ah," Maggie sympathized. "Fair-weather friends."

"Majorly," said Tori. "Anyway, I should get back to the office. Impotence calls."

Maggie laughed as a passerby in a business suit shot Tori a weirded-out look.

"Text me and let me know if you're free for lunch this Saturday," said Maggie. "My boss has me working late every night this week."

Tori promised to keep Maggie in the loop before she clicked off the phone and headed back to her desk.

She spent the remainder of the afternoon sifting through mail and reviewing the new questionnaires that she would be using to query consumers and non-consumers about. The silver lining to her embarrassing job was that no one ever saw her face to face. If she'd had to ask people these questions without the anonymity of a phone she would have died of embarrassment.

On her way home from work Tori made a mental tally of her wardrobe. She needed three outfits this week and she wanted Thursday's to be extra special for her date with Alistair. She would never admit it to anyone, but she was already designing her wedding dress in her head.

At the last minute she decided to make a pit stop at a vintage shop a few blocks away from her apartment. Vintage shopping was fun; if she slogged through enough racks she was often able to find a hidden gem. The only downside was the weird smell that usually came with the clothes. It didn't matter if the outfit was from two or twenty years ago, it always seemed to carry the same stale, moldy odour. She flicked through the racks at top speed, pausing to examine a promising-looking piece every now and then. She was just about to give up when she spotted a navy-blue dress with a Tom Ford label. She could barely believe it. Tom Ford dresses normally retailed for thousands! She pulled the dress out and examined it further. Cap-sleeved with structured shoulder pads and a navel-plunging neckline. As she admired the contoured seaming at the waist and the below-the-knee hemline, Tori knew she had found her dress. She immediately took it to the changing room and tried it on. Her H&M top and pants lay crumpled at her feet as she stepped back and looked at herself in the mirror. She didn't think she had ever looked so elegant. The tight navy fabric hugged her curves in all of the right places while the plunging neckline and demure hemline walked the line between sexy and sophisticated. The stretchy fabric definitely called for Spanx, she thought, turning sideways, but the dress fit her like a second skin. She beamed at her reflection before reluctantly slipping out of the garment and checking the price tag. Tori's heart sank; it was $500. The dress was an absolute steal in terms of what it would cost to purchase straight from Tom Ford, but for Tori, the dress would eat up nearly a third of her paycheque. She thought for a minute before making up her mind—it was too gorgeous for her to let go. She would just resign herself to a diet of ramen noodles for the next few weeks.

In short order, a once-again clothed Tori walked up to the counter and plunked the dress down.

"Beautiful dress, isn't it?" The retail clerk glanced at it admiringly.

Tori nodded vigorously. "Very."

"We just got it in yesterday. I figured it would be snapped up pretty fast."

"It fits like a dream," said Tori. "I didn't want to take it off."

After she'd handed over her credit card, the clerk placed the tissue-wrapped dress in a long-handled bag and passed it to Tori.

She tried it on again as soon as she arrived home, pairing it with her sky-high black stilettos and sparkling cubic zirconia studs. Perfect, she thought to herself. She couldn't wait to see

Alistair's reaction on Thursday.

*

Tori woke up with a smile on Wednesday morning, buoyed by the knowledge that after tonight she would have more material for her site and that she had a date with Alistair and another event to attend tomorrow night. She reached over to her nightstand, grabbed her phone and entered the passcode. An exasperated sigh slipped from her lips when she saw the message on her screen. She'd had to deal with late-night dirty texts from Munger the last two days and it appeared that this morning was no exception. Monday's message (sent at 2:42 a.m.) had just read "Hi sexxxy". Tuesday's message (sent at 1:35 a.m.) had read "can I cum see u?" And this morning's message (sent at 3:12 a.m.) read "Have u ever had a threesome?" Tori scrunched up her face. If Munger's personality hadn't been such a turnoff, his 2 a.m. sexts and substitution of *you* with the letter *U* would have turned her off anyway. Unfortunately for her it appeared that her lack of interest in the billionaire hadn't turned him off, it had merely emboldened him. As she'd done the last two mornings, she ignored his text and was about to put down her phone when a message popped up from Alistair: "Good morning, gorgeous. Can't wait to see you tomorrow night X." A smile spread across her face as she texted him back "Good morning, handsome :). I can't wait to see you either."

At the office, despite the drudgery of her task that day, she could hardly contain her excitement. Keith had given her a list containing thousands of names and phone numbers to slog through in an effort to compile more market research. Given the number of times she was hung up on or cursed at after her introductory spiel, it was understandable that the list was so large. From the seven thousand or so odd names, she would be surprised if she received 250 useable responses. As a rule, people weren't overly fond of telemarketers, and the ones that were were usually lonely individuals who welcomed any excuse for a conversation. She felt sorry for those ones, which often left her talking to them for longer than she should due to her empathetic nature. She did feel bad engaging in lengthy conversations during company time—especially given that their loneliness indicated that they would definitely not be using Impotentia any time soon—but when she heard the delight in their voices that they had someone to talk to, it eased some of her guilt.

One hundred and fifty calls later and she was done work for the day. While the majority of the consumers had hung up on her either before or after subjecting her to an unhealthy round of verbal abuse ("Fuck off, bitch", "Take me off your fucking list"), she'd managed to talk to three kind and cooperative people. One man had just broken up with his girlfriend and welcomed any kind of distraction (although the intimacy-related questions had caused him to start crying). And of the other two, one sounded higher than a kite, and the other was a polite, well-spoken retiree whom she promised to send a sample.

After packing up her things, Tori hurried home. She had just enough time to make a quick dinner (round three of ramen noodles) before getting ready for the fashion show that night. She'd chosen a striking, mid-length navy lace dress with see-through sleeves and peek-a-boo bust and waist detailing. It was another one of her vintage store finds. The designer wasn't anyone well known, but the dress looked like something straight from the runway. With a smear of hot pink lipstick and a tousled chignon at her nape, Tori inhaled the bowl of bland noodles and headed for the event.

Tonight's fashion show was by one of Toronto's hottest design duos. Greta Constantine was a label that she had been following for a long time. They were known for their masterful draping skills and their liberal use of jersey, and she had spent several seasons outside of their fashion shows, hoping to get a word or two from the designers themselves. In a bid to keep out the uninvited, the label's highly coveted invitations never disclosed the show's venue. An email containing the location was sent out two hours prior to the show, the details of which inevitably wound up online in a short amount time. Before the advent of the Tori-Tinsley, *Fashionist-Fashionista* mix-up, Tori would have spent all afternoon trolling Twitter in order to figure out where to stake out for the night. This time, she was the recipient of the secret info herself. With the show slated to start at 7 p.m., an email arrived in her inbox exactly two hours beforehand. Greta Constantine would be showcasing their latest designs at the one-hundred-year-old Burroughes Building. She'd arranged to meet Marcus, Alexei and February at the entrance to the building at 6:15 p.m. sharp. Marcus had wanted to get there early to allow for maximum martini intake.

Tottering on her high heels, she flagged down a cab and booked it to the building twelve blocks away. She spotted the trio as her taxi pulled up to the sidewalk and her jaw dropped open as she emerged from the car. Marcus had really outdone himself tonight. Sunglasses planted firmly on his face, his hair swept up high and an oversized Louis Vuitton hanging from his arm, it appeared as though Marcus had forgone the fur coat tonight and had opted instead for python. An enormous, shiny, very much alive and currently undulating python.

The three of them stood around chatting as Tori approached. Alexei, she noticed, looked very uncomfortable standing beside the snake.

"Hi, guys!" Tori waved cheerily.

"Tins, darling!" February enthused as she went in for air kisses.

"Hello, gorgeous." Marcus waggled his fingers at her as the heavy snake curled around his arm.

Alexei was too intent on keeping an eye on the serpent to spare Tori a glance.

"Marcus, what the hell do you have around your neck?" Tori questioned.

"A python, darling," he said matter-of-factly. "Goes by the name of Roger."

"I can see that," she said. "But why?"

Alexei looked as if he, too, would like an answer to this question.

"Because, Tins," Marcus snorted. "I want to be featured in the party pages tomorrow. Rupert and I broke up last night and I want him to see me when he reads it. I'll be on everyone's newsfeed."

February shot him a quick look.

"I thought that you broke up with him?"

"I did," Marcus said indignantly. "But I just want to make sure that he knows what he's missing."

February furrowed her brow as she tried to process this logic.

"Anyway, let's get inside," Marcus commanded. "Martinis are calling my name."

Marcus and his giant python led the way as they walked into the creaky old building and piled into the antique brass elevator. As the doors slid shut Tori realized just how small the space was. Alexei had pushed himself into one of the corners, putting as much distance between him and the snake as possible. Tori wasn't too fond of the slithery creature herself, but she managed to keep her composure during the ten-second ride to the fourth floor.

The elevator stopped with a jolt and an old-timey *ping* announced their arrival. Stepping off the lift Tori found herself in a spacious, tall-ceilinged room that was filled with a smattering of people. Two women wearing headsets took their names (it turned out that Marcus had a blog with a cult following, February was from *Elle Canada* and Alexei apparently just had money to burn). This time, Tori felt no trepidation when she said her name was Tinsley.

"Who's that?" Tori discreetly gestured to a man a few feet away whose face was obscured by a cloud of pink bunched-up tulle. "He looks like that cartoon character, Mr. Messy."

February squinted at the ball of tulle.

"Well," she said thoughtfully, "given his height, the fact that I haven't spotted him this evening, the fact that he's standing with James and Kennedy *and* the fact that he's a shameless, try-anything attention whore, I'm guessing that's Myles."

"Well-spotted, Sherlock." Marcus struggled to keep his martini from spilling while keeping the serpent from slithering off his shoulders. "I really should have thought this Roger thing through," he admitted—his regret lasting only as long as it took for a few photographers to come over and take his picture.

The room slowly began to fill up as the invitees found their way to the building. In addition to the minuscule portions of finger food being offered up by a bevy of black-suited waiters, Greta Constantine—sponsored for several years by Stoli Vodka—had servers passing around shots of the Soviet liquor. When they reached Tori's group, Marcus insisted that they all have one. Tori's face flushed as the vodka settled into her stomach.

The show didn't start on time—an expected occurrence Tori was given to understand. At twenty after seven, the PR women ushered the now jam-packed room full of guests into an adjoining space.

Fake birch trees filled with silver tulle and white twinkle lights lined the back rows of the room, while white fold-up chairs stood in three parallel rows that created a U-shaped runway. Guests clamored for their seats, each searching for the placard bearing their name that indicated their assigned chair and, consequently, their value to the label. The most important publications and people garnered front-row seats. These were the magazines, website and blogs with the biggest readerships, television hosts, the city's most wealthy and well-known socialites (often outfitted in clothes from the designers), and the less wealthy and oftentimes cash-strapped trendsetters. Tori looked around nervously as she tried to find her seat.

"Over here, Tins," Marcus called from the other side of the room. He was currently in the process of ripping Talia Fitz's name off of the seat next to "Tinsley Tomlinson, Fashionista Magazine", and replacing it with his own.

"Are you sure you can do that?" Tori was apprehensive. She may have gotten used to the Tinsley ruse, but the last thing she wanted to do was draw unnecessary attention to herself.

"It's fine," Marcus said, waving away her concerns as he slid into the seat next to hers and adjusted the python.

Tori took her seat, thankful that she was on the tail end of Roger. She felt sorry for whoever was seated next to his head. As the rest of the guests sauntered around chatting to friends and looking for their seats, the black-suited waiters reappeared with fresh trays of vodka, offering up shots to those seated in the front row.

"Cheers!" Marcus clinked his shot glass against Tori's before downing it in one gulp. "Greta Constantine knows what they're doing," he declared. "Get the people toasted before showing them your goods." Leaning back in his chair he added: "Also a dating strategy of mine."

Ten minutes later, the lights dimmed down and loud music began to blast through the speakers. Spotlights flicked on as a wafer-thin model appeared and stomped down the runway. Heads and phones followed her movements as she rounded the U, with necks snapping back in unison to the start of the runway when another model appeared. Fluid jersey dresses interspersed with stiffly constructed separates in deep reds, golds, blues and silvers took over the runway. It was a collection fit for royalty. Tori was in awe—it was her first live fashion show, but it had taken only one to get her hooked.

A brunette model had just appeared at the top of the runway in a royal-blue silk dress when shrill screams of panic exploded to her right. Tearing her eyes away from the model and looking in the direction of the screams, Tori saw three women in the front row leap out of their chairs and push each other out of the way. The cause of their panic was not readily apparent but their hysteria had managed to rub off on those around them, working others into a similar frenzy.

"Oh fuck," said Marcus under his breath.

Tori looked at him sharply.

"What's going on?"

"Roger." Marcus grimaced as Tori realized that the giant snake was no longer around his neck. "I was so focused on the show that I didn't even feel him slither off of me."

"Oh my God, Marcus!" she exclaimed. "You have to do something!"

By this time, the model, unsure of what to do, had paused on the runway, and someone flipped on the overhead lights, basking the room in a bright white glow. The black-clad PR associates were running around trying to calm the guests and figure out the cause of the commotion.

Marcus slid down in his seat.

"Marcus! You have to get Roger!" she said exasperatedly.

"I don't want to!" he hissed. "I'll never be invited to another Leaf PR event ever again!"

"Marcus!" she said firmly. "They already know it was you who brought the snake! Aside from several photographers taking pictures of you with it, everyone saw you!"

Marcus had now sunk so far into his seat that most of his body was on the floor. He stuck his lower lip out before standing up, letting out a loud, dramatic sigh and soldiering headfirst into the chaos.

*

Tori couldn't stop laughing as she finished typing up the details of the show (and sideshow, thanks to Marcus) on her laptop. It had been a crazy night. Marcus had finally managed to round up Roger while the PR representatives had worked to calm the crowd—a difficult endeavour given the amount of time that people had spent pumping themselves full of pre-show liquor. The president of Leaf PR had pulled Marcus aside for a little "chat" about what was and was not appropriate to accessorize with in the future (no live animals), and one of the designers had had a total meltdown. Leaf PR finally managed to calm down and corral the guests into the other room and finished the show by having the models stand in a row at the front of the room, giving attendees a chance to see the collection up close. Marcus, with Roger once more secured around his shoulders, sulked in the corner and fended off dirty looks from people who fingered him as the cause of all the chaos.

"Well . . ." February had stifled a laugh as Marcus scowled. "On the bright side, Rupert will definitely see you in the party pages tomorrow."

After a quick read-through Tori hit Publish. And with that, her second post for *On the List* went live. "Clothing and Chaos: Sexy Dresses and Uninvited Snakes Create an Unforgettable Evening at Greta Constantine's Show," the headline read. She'd included photos that she had taken herself of the runway show and of the snake-induced mayhem. She was pleased that her first blog post about Cartier had amassed five followers. Her Twitter account of the same name was definitely helping to drive traffic. She may have only five followers at the moment, but her article had been viewed 302 times since she'd posted it. She hoped that the amusing details of tonight's event would drive even more people to her page as she sent out carefully crafted 280-word tweets, hashtags optimized to capitalize on the Twitter searches that would inevitably follow once word and the party pages came out tomorrow.

Wiping the rest of her makeup off of her face, Tori pulled on her fuzzy flannel pajamas and curled up in bed. She'd managed to stave off after-show drinks with February and Alexei by citing a fictitious deadline. And, fortunately for her, Marcus wasn't around to goad her into it given he had to return Roger to his owner by 9 p.m. In bed, despite being tired, she tossed and turned for an hour—excited anticipation for tomorrow night preventing her from falling asleep.

Chapter 6:
Im-Potentia-L
Problems

Another day, another eight hours of telemarketing phone abuse. Tori was exhausted by the time she slogged home on Thursday evening but there were several silver linings. Between phone calls she'd checked the optics of her website. She was overjoyed to see that she had received several comments and over 300 page views in addition to gaining eleven new followers. She was confident that the Luminato launch this evening would also boost her numbers. But to Tori, the biggest silver lining of the day was that in just a few short hours she would be seeing Alistair again. She was also looking forward to having a real meal tonight as she was currently on day four of her ramen noodle diet. She'd forgone the finger food at the fashion show last night, knowing that her clumsy nature made it likely that most of it would end up on her dress instead of in her mouth.

She soaked herself in a lavender-scented bubble bath when

she arrived home before putting on a cucumber face mask and shaving her legs. Fifteen minutes were spent moisturizing her skin before putting on a fresh coat of black nail polish and meticulously applying her makeup. And ten minutes before Alistair was slated to arrive, Tori slipped on the Tom Ford, stepped into her high heels and grabbed her favourite clutch. Tossing face powder, lip gloss, an assortment of cards and some spare cash into the purse, which still held the remnants of previous parties (coat-check tickets and Impotentia samples from a party the company had thrown a few weeks ago, gum and some stray Starburst candies), Tori sat down to wait when her phone started to ring.

"Hello," she purred, knowing from the caller ID that it was her date.

"Hello, gorgeous," Alistair greeted her back, the smile evident in his voice. "I'm downstairs if you're ready. If not, take your time."

"No, I'm ready! I'll be right down!" She clicked off her phone and headed for the door.

Alistair was waiting for her in the lobby—she watched his jaw drop open and his eyebrows shoot up to his hairline when he saw her step out of the elevator.

"You look incredible!" he said appreciatively, having picked his jaw back up from the floor. "You look absolutely stunning in that dress."

Tori felt a rush of pleasure at the compliments as Alistair took her head in his hands and pressed his lips against hers. Seconds later she went weak at the knees. Again. Jesus, she thought to herself. She was going to have to do something about that. She couldn't very well lose all control of her motor functions every time Alistair planted one on her.

"That's a nice way of saying hello." Tori smiled at him after he pulled away.

"There's more where that came from." He winked at her.

Taking her by the hand, he led her out to the black town car waiting curbside. The driver of the vehicle stood patiently beside the back-passenger door, opening it up as they approached and helping Tori inside. Alistair got into the other side, grabbing her hand and interlacing his fingers with hers as soon as he settled into the back seat. Tori liked how comfortable and completely natural it felt—like the two of them were going out on their five-hundredth date instead of their first. After closing the door behind Tori, the driver slid into the front seat and put the car in drive.

"Where are we going?" she asked excitedly.

"Ah," Alistair said, grinning at her cheekily, "that's the first of many surprises tonight."

"I love surprises!" she enthused. "As long as none of them involve roofies," she added dryly.

Alistair laughed as he squeezed her hand.

"No roofies," he promised. "So, you're sure that it's okay for you to take me to the Luminato party tonight?"

"Definitely," she said more confidently than she felt. "I'll tell them that you're my photographer or something if they ask."

Alistair's one eyebrow rose as if to say *Really?*

Tori laughed.

"Okay, maybe not. But I doubt that they'll bother me about it. They want the coverage, after all."

They chatted about their week during the drive with Tori telling Alistair about the Greta Constantine disaster the previous evening. He shook with laughter as she described the look on Marcus's face when he realized that Roger the snake had escaped and was the cause of all of the commotion.

"Sounds like you had quite the night," he chuckled. "That Marcus guy is quite the character."

"Majorly," she agreed.

Just then the car came to a halt. Tori, who hadn't been paying attention to where they were going, saw a Hazelton Avenue sign and realized that they were in Yorkville. Outside of the Hazelton Hotel in Yorkville, to be exact. She rarely ventured up that way given the bank-busting prices of the boutiques, bars and restaurants in that area. She stuck to places in her neighbourhood that were a little friendlier to her pocketbook. But even without spending much time in Yorkville, she knew immediately where he was taking her. One was an established eatery with high net worth clientele. She'd always imagined that it was full of old rich men and their twenty-five-year-old trophy wives, and her first step inside didn't disappoint. The low lighting of the lounge created a smoldering atmosphere; couples (the kind that she had imagined) sat in shadowy corners sipping on cocktails and conversing. She tried not to stare as she and Alistair made their way into the restaurant.

"Chase," Alistair said to the hostess when she asked if they had a reservation.

"Right this way," she replied, turning on her heel.

"You made several women want to stab your eyes out just now," Alistair whispered to her as they followed the hostess to their private table in the corner.

Tori looked at him in alarm.

"What did I do?!"

Alistair laughed.

"You turned the head of every man in the room."

She blushed, feeling embarrassed, and, if she was honest with herself, a little flattered, too. Not that it mattered. She didn't care if she turned Prince Harry's head tonight. The only man that she wanted was Alistair.

The waiter held out the chair for Tori—something that she wasn't accustomed to. It made her feel a bit like a small child being seated at the table by her parents. She was even more bewildered when, after finally settling into her seat, the waiter placed her napkin on her lap. Alistair chuckled when he caught sight of her expression.

"Sorry," she said a little shyly. "I'm not used to places this nice."

"No apologies." He smiled at her. "That's one of the things I like about you. You're not pretentious, rude or demanding. It's a nice change."

Tori thought about that for a second, mulling over what that said about the company that Alistair kept, when the waiter reappeared with the wine list in hand.

"They have a really great selection here." Alistair gestured to the wine menu. "What do you like?" he asked.

Tori hesitated. She liked red wine, but she was ignorant about what constituted a good bottle. Usually she just opted for whatever was on sale at the LCBO.

"I prefer red," she said. "Why don't you pick something out for us?"

"Done." Alistair picked up the list and examined it for a second before deciding on a French Bordeaux.

The waiter disappeared before returning with the wine and Tori turned the conversation back to Alistair and his friends.

"So," she started, one eyebrow raised, "about the pretentious, rude and demanding company that you keep . . ." She trailed off.

Alistair smiled.

"I don't hang out with pretentious and demanding people. I have, however, wound up on several dates with attractive women who act like spoiled princesses. They're rude to wait staff, insist on top-shelf liquor and their ambitions only stretch as far as bagging someone with a seven-figure bank account."

Tori thought about this as she swirled her wine around and took a sip. It was delicious.

"Why do you go out with them, then?" she asked curiously.

"Well," Alistair said thoughtfully, "their real personality doesn't usually come out within the first few minutes of meeting them. But twenty minutes into a first date it gets a lot more clear. That's why I've stopped doing dinner dates," he said. "I only do drinks. That way, I can politely excuse myself after one drink if it turns out that she's not a nice person."

"But you asked me out to dinner," Tori pointed out.

He grinned at her. "That's because I've already spent enough time with you to determine that you are the very antithesis of rude, snobby and demanding."

At that moment a waiter approached their table and handed Alistair a small, expensive-looking red gift bag. He thanked the waiter. Tori was puzzled. Maybe they gave people gifts at fancy restaurants?

"I got you something," Alistair said, smiling as he passed the bag to her.

Tori's mouth hung open as she took the red bag.

"Alistair . . . thank you." She was flustered. "You didn't have to get me anything."

He shushed her as she reached into the bag and pulled out a red leather box. "Cartier" was embossed in gold on the top of the box and it was tied with a red ribbon that ended in a neat little bow.

Still in disbelief she paused and looked at him and he gestured for her to open it. Tori turned her attention back to the present, slowly undid the ribbon and placed it on the table before opening up the jewellery box.

Her eyes widened and she let out a gasp when she saw what was inside.

"These are the earrings from the other night!" she exclaimed, staring at an elegant pair of long, dangly diamond earrings. "Are you serious?" Tori was stunned. Not only had Alistair remembered the comments that she'd made on the way out of the Cartier party about the stunning sparklers, but he'd actually gone through the trouble and expense of getting them for her?

"Alistair, these are gorgeous," she said sincerely. "But I couldn't possibly accept them. I love them, really, but they must have cost a fortune."

Alistair smiled at her, taking obvious delight in the excitement that his gift had aroused in Tori, and in her modest refusal to accept it.

"Tinsley," he began. Tori tried not to wince as he called her by her pseudonym. "Don't worry about the cost. I called in a few favours to get them for you. Right now, you're the only one in the world with a pair of those earrings. They aren't available in stores until the fall."

Tori was shocked all over again.

"You went through all of that trouble for me?"

He laughed.

"I wouldn't call it trouble, per se. I saw how much you liked them the other night and I couldn't stop thinking about how they would look dangling from your ears." He took the box from her hand, removed the earrings and, leaning across the table, replaced the cheap cubic zirconia she was wearing with the Cartier diamonds. He sat back and smiled as Tori touched her ears, feeling the heavy weight of them on her lobes.

"How do they look?" she asked, grinning from ear to ear.

"They look gorgeous. Just like the woman who's wearing them," he complimented her with a grin.

"I absolutely love them, Alistair," she began. "Thank you so much." He held up his hand before Tori could continue.

"No thank-yous necessary." He smiled. "Just promise me that when you wear them, you'll think of me."

Tori couldn't stop beaming.

"Done," she agreed.

Holding up his glass of red wine, Alistair toasted Tori.

"To you, Tinsley." His eyes stared into hers with obvious affection. "Diamonds for my diamond." He clinked his glass against hers and they took a drink of their wine, their eyes locked together the entire time.

Tori was about to tell him how much she was looking forward to spending the evening together when she was interrupted by a tall, skinny blonde woman.

"Allistaairrrrrr," the blonde drew his name out in a singsong way. "What are you doing here? Client dinner?" She eyed Tori unkindly.

Alistair looked unhappy at the woman's sudden appearance.

"Tinsley, Corinne. Corinne, Tinsley," he introduced the two women. Tori had only just been introduced to the blonde woman, but she already didn't like her. And she really didn't like the look that Corinne was giving her. She looked like an apex predator—sizing up Tori for any sign of weakness.

"Ah, yes." Corinne looked down her nose at Tori. "I saw you at the Munger Carlson Vodka launch last week. Nice to see you sober."

Tori was floored. This woman didn't even know her! Why was she being so nasty?

"Corinne," Alistair warned.

An evil smirk crossed the woman's face.

"Poor Alistair." She put on a fake pout. "How far you've fallen down the dating ladder. You've really scraped the bottom of the barrel with this one." She eyed Tori up and down in a disapproving manner.

"At least I have a great personality," Tori said, smiling brightly. "That's one thing makeup can't cover up."

Alistair choked back a laugh as the blonde, who was actually wearing a rather thick layer of foundation, looked at her furiously. She opened her mouth for what would surely have been an icy retort when Alistair cut her off before she could even begin.

"Corinne"—he looked at her levelly—"I'm enjoying my date with Tinsley right now. You've insulted her and I don't appreciate it, so please leave us alone and don't bother us again."

Corinne's mouth dropped in indignation as Alistair turned back to Tori.

"Now, Tinsley," he said, pointedly ignoring Corinne. "Finish telling me about the Greta Constantine show last night."

Tori smiled at him gratefully as Corinne, whose face was set in a scowl, slunk away, shooting dirty looks at the duo as she went.

"Remember the pretentious, rude and demanding women we were talking about?" Alistair asked.

Tori nodded emphatically.

"Corinne is Exhibit A."

"You actually dated her?" Tori said in disbelief. It made her feel uncomfortable that Alistair would go out with someone who was so mean.

"Two dates, to be exact," he admitted. "She was pleasant enough to me the first time that we went out. But the way that she treated the restaurant staff, bartenders and drivers was appalling."

"So why did you go out with her again?" Tori was still processing the fact that he had gone out with such a bitch.

Alistair looked as though he was wondering that himself.

"I guess because she's attractive . . . and I thought maybe it was a one-off thing." He paused to take a sip of his wine.

"About ten minutes into our second date I realized that it wasn't a one-off thing, it was a Corinne thing."

"Well, that explains why she was so nasty to me," Tori said resignedly.

"I'm sorry about that," he said, shaking his head. "On the positive side, her behaviour just makes me appreciate you that much more."

They spent the remainder of their dinner in pleasant and teasing conversation. Tori ordered the mushroom risotto (which she was pretty sure would have tasted just as heavenly even if she hadn't been subsisting on a diet of ramen), and Alistair ordered the sea bass. They were nearly three-quarters of the way through the bottle of wine when the dessert menu arrived. Alistair insisted that Tori try the chocolate fudge cake and Tori stuffed a spoonful of the decadent dessert into his mouth after she'd finished her first bite.

"I could stay here talking to you for hours," Alistair said, propping up his chin with one of his hands. "You're a lovely person."

Tori smiled at him.

"We practically *have* stayed here for hours." She looked around at the sparsely populated restaurant that had been bustling with activity when they had first arrived.

When the bill came Alistair didn't even allow Tori a chance to protest, discreetly sliding his credit card into the cheque holder and handing it to the waiter.

"Thank you," Tori said gratefully as they stood up to leave. "For everything. I mean it. I really enjoyed myself tonight."

He grabbed her hand and pulled her in for a kiss.

"Likewise." He smiled after a lengthy lip lock.

Clutch and Cartier bag in one hand, Alistair's hand in the other, they exited the restaurant and stepped into an Uber.

She cozied up to Alistair for the entire ten-minute ride, feeling incredibly happy and content. Still, the ever-present pit in her stomach reminded her that Alistair thought that she was Tinsley, which was a massive lie.

The car pulled up to the venue and Tori reluctantly left

Alistair's side. He got out first and offered her his hand as she climbed out of the back seat. The launch party had started an hour and a half ago yet there was still a long line. The temperature had dropped several degrees during their dinner and Tori shivered as they waited for their turn to go inside. Tori rubbed her arms as Alistair removed his navy suit jacket and wrapped it around her shoulders.

In short order they were at the front of the line facing Tori's former nemesis—the list.

"Name?" the redhead with the clipboard asked.

Tori answered as Tinsley while the woman unhooked the rope and stood back to let them in. Despite the fact that she'd only RSVP'd for herself, the lady didn't bat an eyelash when she'd said that Alistair was her plus one. "Tinsley Tomlinson with *Fashionista Magazine*" seemed to be the private party equivalent of "Open sesame".

The launch was held in an outdoor area on the twentieth floor of the building. A large rectangular space with giant eight-foot-wide steps ascended to the sky. Heat lamps and table fires dotted the landscape, with string lights hoisted overhead and around the perimeter of the party. A DJ booth was set up in the corner and a crowd of people danced around a large pool while tuxedo-wearing waiters wandered around with plates of strange-looking finger foods. She saw several people who she recognized from the previous fashion parties. There was Kennedy and James following behind who Tori could only assume was Myles given the two-foot-tall popped collar and furry pants he was wearing. Alistair shook his head at that.

They were standing next to a tall table on one of the raised steps when Alistair gave Tori a nudge. "Isn't that your friend?" He gestured towards a blond sunglasses-wearing man who, drink in hand, was just leaving the bar.

"Oh Lord," said Tori. "It's Marcus!"

"At least it looks like he's left the python at home tonight," Alistair observed.

"Either that or he's just left it at the coat check," she said dryly.

Alistair laughed. "How can he even see anything in those sunglasses?"

"I have no idea," she replied. Tori was just as mystified as him by Marcus's refusal to remove the tinted shades after the sun set.

"Tinsley!" someone near her called out, causing several heads, including Marcus's, to turn in her direction.

"Tinsley!" Marcus exclaimed, forcing his way through the crowd with his oversized Louis and expansive personality. "How are you, darling?" He grabbed her around the neck before turning to Alistair and enveloping him in air kisses. "You should grab a drink," he suggested. "These bartenders mix one mean martini." He pulled out the olive garnish in his glass and popped it into his mouth.

"That sounds like a great idea." Alistair gave Tori's hand a squeeze. "I'll be right back." He leaned in and planted a quick kiss on her cheek.

"Tins." Marcus was watching Tori as she watched Alistair's departure with a love-sick grin on her face. "You look at Alistair like a teenage boy-band groupie." She turned her attention back to Marcus. "But there is a veritable smorgasbord of hotties here tonight, so just give me the signal if you want me to distract your date so you can prowl." He took a sip of his martini.

"Thanks, Marcus," she said dryly. "But that really won't be necessary."

"Never say never." He waggled his finger at her. "If things head south or you change your mind, just give me the signal!"

Tori didn't bother asking Marcus what, exactly, "the signal" was. She turned the topic of conversation towards Marcus's ill-fated snake stunt yesterday. Several people had emailed her (to her *Fashionist* account, of course) the party pages featuring pictures from the Greta Constantine show. The editors had decided to run a "Fashion Faux Pas" photo spread featuring a picture of a sunglasses-clad Marcus posing with Roger the snake around his shoulders before the fashion show began. This was followed by a series of photos depicting the ensuing chaos that Roger caused when he slithered through the crowd. There was one particularly unflattering photo of Marcus crawling on the floor between the legs of people who were hurrying away in his quest to retrieve the python.

"So," Tori began, wondering how best to broach the subject before deciding to just hit it head-on. "Did Rupert see you in the party pages?"

Marcus's head dropped back and he let out a sound that reminded Tori of a strangled cat.

"He did." Marcus's head snapped forwards again. "And then he texted me a long string of laughter followed by 'Thank you for breaking up with me. I hope you're not barred from future Greta Constantine events.' I have been, by the way," he added shamefully.

Tori tried not to laugh.

"I suppose that will teach me," he said morosely, the martini in his hand momentarily forgotten in his shame.

Tori, not knowing what to do, patted his arm awkwardly.

"I'm sure it will be okay. Who knows, someone could do something crazy tonight and by tomorrow your snake fiasco would be completely forgotten about."

Marcus perked up at that.

"You're right, Tins. Maybe I should push someone into the pool or something?" He started sizing up the crowd.

"No," Tori said firmly. "That is the last thing that you should do."

Just then a short-haired woman named Alice wandered over to talk to them. Tori had met her last night (and, as the woman had reminded her, she had also met her at the Munger Carlson Vodka party one week ago). Alistair returned shortly and Marcus wandered away to the washroom.

She and Alistair were soon flanked by a small crowd of people, all amicably chatting about what was lined up for the week-long Luminato Festival. The organizers this year had put together a jam-packed schedule that included shows by the London Symphony Orchestra, traditional First Nations dancers, opera singers, several plays and an assortment of other dance and music performances. Tori had attended the festival a few times in the past, bussing in from her small town for an afternoon, but she had never attended the launch party. She had never been invited.

While talking with a group of industry people, Marcus surreptitiously appeared at her elbow, taking her attention away from the conversation at hand.

"Tins!" he hissed into her ear. "Do you have any gum?"

"Sure," she whispered back, absentmindedly passing him her purse. "Check in there." She turned her attention back to the group, eager not to miss a moment of the conversation, which was currently centred on a juicy piece of gossip concerning the director of the festival.

She'd forgotten that Marcus even had her purse when she felt her clutch being pushed back into the crook of her arm. An enthusiastically whispered "Thanks, Tins!" came from somewhere behind her and she turned and gave Marcus a quick smile as he made off through the crowd once again.

Minutes later there was a break in the conversation as people branched off to talk to other people or take a quick trip to the bar. Alistair headed off to refresh his and Tori's drinks after planting a smoldering smooch on her lips. Just then, she heard Marcus's voice behind her.

"Tins, I've met my next boyfriend," he announced, then paused and took a large swig of his drink. "He's hung like a horse and he's a big old bottom." Marcus fanned himself with one hand.

Tori was stunned.

"You were only gone five minutes! How in hell do you meet someone, find out what he has in his pants and how he uses it in five minutes?"

Marcus winked at her.

"I have my ways, gorgeous." He chugged his drink and placed the empty glass on the cocktail table beside him. "Now make way—Thomas needs me," he said and sauntered off through the crowd.

Alistair appeared moments later with drinks in hand.

"Where's Marcus off to?" he asked, handing her a fruity-looking cocktail. "I passed him on my way back from the bar. He said he was off to give someone named Thomas a good pounding."

Tori's mouth dropped open.

"Did he get into a fight or something?" Alistair took a sip of his drink, completely oblivious to the fact that Marcus intended to bed, not beat someone. Tori wasn't about to enlighten him.

She took a sip of the pineapple-and-strawberry-flavoured drink then set it down on the table. Opening up her purse, she rifled around for her Chapstick. After a few seconds of feeling around, she paused. Something was missing. She opened her purse up wider to confirm her suspicions. It was just as she'd thought—the Impotentia packet was gone.

Oh my God, she thought. Marcus must have taken it when she'd given him her purse to grab a piece of gum. She knew that he was into alcohol and party favours but would he seriously pop random pills that he found in her purse? She hoped not, but knowing Marcus she'd be more surprised if he hadn't swallowed them.

"What's wrong?" Alistair had picked up on her panicked expression and he looked concerned.

"Marcus . . ." she began. "He took a packet of pills from my purse."

"He what? What kind of pills?" he asked.

"They're . . ." She couldn't finish her sentence.

Alistair's eyebrows rose in question.

"They're . . . erectile dysfunction pills," she confessed.

Alistair looked like he'd just walked into a wall.

"Erectile dysfunction pills?" He was incredulous. "Why are you carrying around erectile dysfunction pills in your purse?" he questioned.

"I was at an event a few weeks ago and they were handing out samples," Tori said truthfully. "And I didn't clean out this purse before using it tonight."

His expression softened at that.

"You have a weird job," he said with a half smirk.

They spent the remainder of the night snuggled up together

on one of the many wicker couches. Tori was tired but she didn't want to leave. Leaving meant saying good night to Alistair. And while she didn't want to do that, she knew that she needed to get home and write about the night for her website. She had completely fallen for Alistair (which was scary to admit after a total of only two dates), but her career (legitimate or not) was very important to her. If she wanted to build her brand and leverage it into a career that didn't involve being people's coffee bitch, she had to stay focused on why she was going to these events in the first place.

"The crowd's beginning to thin out," Tori observed late into the evening.

Alistair looked around.

"So it is. Does that mean you're ready to call it a night?" he asked.

"If I had my way, this night would never end." She smiled. "But as much as I would love to stay here and keep snuggling with you, I don't think my boss would be too appreciative if he found me face down on my desk tomorrow morning."

"All right then, sleepy head." Alistair stood up and held out his hand. "It's time to get you home."

Tori took his hand and hoisted herself up off of the couch as Alistair pulled her in for a kiss. Standing there under the night sky and a string of party lights, she felt another rush of pleasure.

They spent the majority of the cab ride to Tori's place making out like teenagers and, just as he had on the night that they first met, Alistair once again held the cab and walked her to the front door of her building. Their good-night kiss lasted much longer this time and was more passionate than the one they'd first shared one week ago—something that Tori wouldn't have thought was even possible.

"You know," she admitted to him, less inhibited after several drinks, "every time you kiss me, I go weak at the knees."

He laughed at her for a moment before kissing her again.

"Text me when you make it inside," he said after they finally broke apart. "I want to make sure that you don't end up as a quivering mass of jelly on the elevator floor."

She smiled at him and swatted him playfully on the arm. "Done." Tori opened the door and walked inside. She kept her promise, texting him as soon as she'd opened the door to her apartment.

"Good night, gorgeous," he messaged her back. "You looked breathtaking tonight. I had a really great time together. I look forward to doing it again soon. Saturday? X."

A perma-smile plastered on her face, she pulled off her shoes and dress, settling into her fuzzy pajamas before brewing a cup of coffee and setting up shop at her desk. An hour and a half later and she had crafted article number three for *On the List*. "Luminato Launch: Festival Kicks Off at TIFF Building and Promises a Fun-Filled Week," read the headline. Not the best one she'd ever written, but the best that her sleep-deprived mind could come up with at that moment. In the article she included tidbits of insider information that she'd picked up from various conversations, including that the director of Luminato, Terry Malven, had been fighting with the shareholders of the festival over the direction of the event, and touching on the diva-like behaviour by one of the artists (whom remained nameless). She'd snapped a few photos from the night—peripheral crowd shots, mostly—that she included along with the piece. Luminato had not sent out a post-party press packet yet but she wanted to be the first article about it up on the net. Giving the article one last read over, Tori clicked Publish, closed her laptop and climbed into bed. Exhausted from her hectic twenty-four hours, she was asleep almost before her head hit the pillow.

Her state of deep sleep didn't last long, however, as she was rudely awakened by a phone call from an unknown number less than an hour later.

"Hello?" she mumbled, still half asleep.

"Tins!" the man on the other end of the phone pleaded. "I took something from your purse and now it won't go down!"

"Wha?" she said, confused. "Won't go down? What are you talking about? Who is this?" Her brain kicked into overdrive as she tried to make sense of the call.

"It's Marcus!" he said indignantly. "I took a packet of pills from your purse! I just wanted to try it! I thought it might help me impress Thomas!" he insisted. "I didn't know I would end up with a four-hour hard-on!"

Her brain catching up to the situation, Tori tried to stifle her giggles.

"Marcus, you need to get yourself to a hospital," she told him between laughter. "I cannot believe that you took those pills from my purse."

"Okay," he said, sounding less stressed. "I'm getting an Uber. But why the hell do you have the equivalent of Viagra in your purse anyway?" Marcus demanded.

That made Tori sit up straight in bed.

"Umm . . ." She cast around helplessly. "I was holding them for a friend."

"Alistair's not that old," Marcus observed. "Unless! Are you secretly romancing a senior!?"

"No!" Tori was aghast. "I . . . I . . . they're for my dad!" she blurted out.

Marcus sounded stunned. "Your dad?"

"Yes!" She paused. "He was too embarrassed to buy it so I told him I would pick some up for him. It's not sold in stores where he lives and he wanted something natural instead of chemical-laden Viagra. I was going to send it to him, but I just haven't gotten around to it yet." Good God, she thought to herself, the lies just kept coming. It was like a snowball effect. The more she lied, the more lies she piled on top of it to cover up for the big lie, and the more she lied, the easier it became. She was pretty sure she met the diagnostic criteria for "pathological liar" at this point.

"You're a better child than I, Tins," Marcus announced. "Lord, if my father ever asked me to pick him up a stiffening solution . . ." He trailed off.

Chapter 7:
The Snowball Effect

She had finally gotten off of the phone with Marcus after he had arrived at the hospital and ascertained that he was going to be okay. Incredulously, he still placed part of the blame on her. This despite the fact that he was the one who had swiped the pills from her purse in the first place. She stood in front of the coffee maker like a zombie, eyes fixated on the steady stream of caffeine pouring into her cup. She really needed to invest in one of those coffee makers that had a timer. Maybe she'd think about that after she ate her way through two more weeks of noodle rations.

Setting the empty cup in the dishwasher she dragged herself to the washroom and pulled off her pajamas. Good Lord, she thought as she caught sight of herself in the mirror. Her late nights were starting to catch up to her—and to her face. She was off to a rough and late start this morning. Black marks under her eyes indicated that she was seriously sleep deprived. Her eyes, such as they were, looked like two little slits below her eyebrows. A long, defeated sigh escaped her lips as she pulled her frazzled hair up into a ponytail before stepping into the shower. Standing under the hot spray of the nozzle did serve to improve her mood but didn't serve to improve her looks. The hot water also couldn't atone for her foggy head—her brain's retribution for refusing to allow it to get anywhere near a full eight hours of sleep lately. Still, Tori thought to herself, if a puffy face and foggy head were the only prices to pay for spending time with Alistair and kickstarting her career, she'd find a way to deal with it.

She ran into the office fifteen minutes late, huffing and puffing from her medal-worthy sprint from the subway station. Carelessly tossing her things down on her desk, she shook off her trench coat and slid into her seat. Fortunately, no one seemed to notice her late entrance. Her boss, Keith, was a stickler for being on time. Tori was rarely late, but she didn't want her alter ego putting her daytime job—the one that actually paid her bills—in jeopardy.

She was still floating on cloud nine, daydreaming of Alistair, when she caught her reflection in her computer screen. The Cartier earrings caught the light, sending rainbow sparkles all around the room. They were a little over-the-top for everyday office wear, but Tori didn't care. She didn't even think that they went with her outfit today (black and white suit jacket with black pants and ballet flats) but she never wanted to take them off. Emails promptly dealt with, she grabbed her cell phone and sent a quick text to Maggie before setting back to work on the phone list.

"Drinks on Saturday?" she texted. She'd forgotten to keep her best friend updated throughout the week.

"Great earrings, Tori!" Sierra stopped by her desk, file folders in her hand. "Where did you get them?"

"Thanks!" Tori said brightly. "They were a present from my boyfriend." She thought that calling Alistair her boyfriend was probably stretching the truth, but she really liked the thought of having him as her boyfriend. And, if she was honest with herself, calling Alistair her boyfriend was the least of her lies.

Sierra perked up at that.

"I didn't know that you had a boyfriend." She leaned against her cubicle. "How long have you two been dating?"

"Um, a little while." Tori pretended to arrange a stack of papers on her desk to avoid meeting her colleague's eyes. Technically, it wasn't a lie. They had been dating for a little while. One week to be exact.

"Well, hold on to that one," Sierra said emphatically. "He has great taste in jewellery."

Tori beamed at that.

"Thanks! I really like him."

She checked her phone as Sierra walked back to her desk. A response from Maggie read "Yes, please!" and Tori quickly texted her back. "I'll confirm tomorrow. 1 p.m. at Hunter's Landing." She put her mobile down, picked up the phone list and dialed the next number—E. Adams. It was going to be a long four weeks to slog through this, she thought to herself. But on the upside, she wouldn't have to worry about showing up to work with a foggy brain.

"Keith wants to see you in his office, Tori," Ryan, the senior marketing manager, said as he walked past her desk. She had been just about to place another phone call but put the receiver back in its cradle. Her heart started beating eighty miles per minute. *Fuck*, she thought to herself. Keith *had* noticed her coming in fifteen minutes late this morning. *Damn it! And damn Marcus!*

Taking a few deep breaths in and out she tried to calm herself. What had that meditation book she'd read recommended? Clear your mind and find your happy place. She sat back in her chair and closed her eyes, thinking hard. She thought of the beach, her parents on the beach, margaritas on the beach, Alistair on the beach—in a speedo . . . with a ring in his hand. Her heart started beating even faster.

"Enjoying your nap, Tori?" Keith's voice came from somewhere above her.

Her eyes snapped open and she jumped up, startled.

"Keith!" she said, scrambling to regain her composure. "I wasn't sleeping! Ryan told me that you wanted to see me in your office, so I was just composing myself!"

Keith looked at her sideways.

"Whatever." He rolled his eyes. "I'll be waiting in my office whenever you've finished composing yourself."

She stood up immediately and followed behind him. Opening the glass door to his office, Keith crossed the room and settled into his seat behind the desk, motioning for her to sit across from him. Tori looked around. His office was almost as devoid of personality as he was. Stark white walls presented a single photo: a picture of Keith and his wife in their glory days, both sporting long hair, sunglasses, and outfits that were straight from the eighties.

"Now, Tori," Keith started.

Her attention snapped back to her boss.

"I know! I'm so sorry I was late this morning! But it was only fifteen minutes and I have a good reason! I was up late last night dealing with an Impotentia emergency!"

Keith's eyebrows shot up into his hairline.

"Tori, I don't need to know about your personal problems. And I'm not here to judge, but as an entry-level marketing assistant for Impotentia you should advise your bed mates of the proper dosage."

Tori was aghast.

"What!? No!" she exclaimed. "Not me! Not my boyfriend!"

Keith looked confused. He put his hands up.

"I don't want to know." That was pretty much his catchphrase where Tori was concerned. "Now," he changed track, "while I don't condone you showing up late for work, emergencies happen." He leaned forward and rested his elbows on his desk. "But don't let it become a habit."

Tori nodded her head vigorously.

Keith cleared his throat and sat back in his chair.

"I called you in here, Tori, because I've been noticing how hard you've been working lately, and I think it's time to reward that hard work with more responsibilities. You and I both know that you're capable of handling more than the office coffee orders and calling customers."

Tori felt her stomach drop. Two weeks ago, she would have leapt at the opportunity to prove herself more valuable to the company and to use her brain. But now that she was working towards her dream career and dating her dream man, more responsibility at her day job was the last thing she wanted. She couldn't do anything but sit there, stunned, while slapping on a fake smile that didn't quite reach her eyes.

Keith nodded in approval at Tori's upturned mouth, not noticing the lack of crinkled eye corners that denoted genuine glee.

"So," he continued. "I've decided that you're going to assist Sierra with putting together our city-wide marketing campaign for Impotentia's new women's line of products that we will be launching in six weeks. It's going to require hard work and a lot of overtime."

Tori felt the corners of her fake smile falter.

"If you do well, we'll see about getting you a raise. Are you up for the challenge?" He eyed her expectantly.

Tori could tell that he was waiting for her to jump up for joy and shower him with gratitude, but a small "I think so" was all that she was able to manage.

Keith's brow furrowed.

"You think so or you know so?"

"Um," Tori stalled. She was completely overwhelmed. She was exhausted from only two days of regular work and fake magazine work—how was she going to handle working overtime at her day job in addition to her fake job while still spending time with Alistair?

"Tori," Keith said firmly. "If you don't want this position and the responsibility that comes with it, I can find someone who does."

"No!" she protested. "I want to do it!" she added another lie to her growing list.

That seemed to placate him at least.

"Good." Keith relaxed his demeanor. "Now, you and Sierra will be meeting today at four to begin brainstorming. She will fill you in on the details. It's a tight timeline so you're going to be very busy in the next six weeks. Don't let this get in the way of your regular work," he warned. "I still expect the same level of dedication and effort in your daily tasks."

Because fetching coffee takes so much effort and dedication, Tori thought to herself.

"Right, well, thanks, Keith." She tried to muster up enthusiasm, but her sentence fell flat.

"Just don't disappoint me, Tori." Keith turned to his computer, which she took as a dismissal. She stood up and quietly tiptoed out of the office, sinking back into her chair when she reached her desk. What was she going to do? She still depended on Staten to pay her bills, and she definitely didn't want to disappoint Keith. She may not particularly enjoy her job most days, but she always put forth her best effort. But she was also excited about the possibilities her mistaken persona was presenting to her. And she didn't want to have to cut back on her time with Alistair. She may be getting ahead of herself given that they'd only gone on two dates, but she already wanted to spend every evening with him. A smile crossed her lips as she thought back to the text he had sent her this morning ("Good morning, beautiful. Missed snuggling with you all night. Hope your day is amazing X"). She shook her head. Now was not the time to get lost in Alistair-filled daydreams.

She took a deep breath before picking up the phone again—this time she was interrupted by several shouts of "Congrats, Tori!" from supportive colleagues to which she waved and answered back with a half-hearted "Thanks!"

At 4 p.m., while everyone else was packing up their things, Tori headed to the conference room. Sierra had emailed her that afternoon with an outline of their budget and timeline.

It was a small conference room with a table just large enough for eight people. The larger conference rooms were on the twelfth floor where most of the major company meetings took place.

"Hi." Tori plopped into the chair opposite Sierra, trying to stifle a yawn.

Sierra raised one of her eyebrows and a half smirk appeared

on her face.

"Late night, huh?" she asked. "Keith told me that you and your boyfriend had a little problem." Sierra paused. "Well, he didn't actually say little . . ." She trailed off, staring at Tori expectantly.

Tori flushed.

"No," she said. "Not my boyfriend." She sat up straighter. "My gay friend, Marcus."

Sierra's mouth dropped open.

"Not like that!" Tori squeaked.

Sierra blinked.

"Whatever you say, Tori." She looked down and shuffled a few papers on the table. "Anyway, let's get down to business," she started. "We have a tight budget and a tight timeline."

Sierra pulled a large tote bag from under the table, reached in and pulled out a long pink bottle that had sparkly blue graphics on the side. Setting it on the table she reached back into the bag and pulled out what looked like a pink highlighter, also with sparkly blue graphics on the side. Tori braced herself. Impotentia was, after all, a company aimed at helping couples improve their sex life. Was there a vibrator in the pink bottle? Was the highlighter a mini vibrator? Was she going to be coming up with a marketing campaign for sex toys? Her poor parents.

Sierra pushed the products across the table to Tori, who examined them closely.

"Wet & Wild" read the label on the pink bottle. "Sparkly, edible personal lubricant."

She put the bottle down and picked up the pink highlighter. "Sex & Candy" it read. "Sparkly, cotton-candy-flavoured edible body paint."

Tori put it down, relieved. Compared to the products that she could have potentially been marketing, edible lube and body paint seemed pretty tame.

From there, she and Sierra spent the better part of two hours brainstorming the best way to introduce the product to the public within the confines of a slim budget.

By the time Tori arrived home, all she wanted to do was

sleep. She had been counting on an after-work nap to boost her energy before tonight's Fashion Cares pre-launch party. She looked at the clock. It was already 6:25 p.m. She'd nearly fallen asleep in her meeting with Sierra and had gone for a quick double espresso when they'd taken a ten-minute break. She'd thrown it back like a shot of tequila and was rewarded with a serious boost of energy and a serious case of the caffeine shakes.

She startled herself when she caught sight of her reflection in the mirror, her purse dropping out of her hands in surprise. Tori stood back, aghast at her appearance. It was difficult to believe that a mere twenty-four hours ago she'd looked like she'd walked off the pages of *Vanity Fair*. Right now, she looked like the before picture on one of those frazzled-mom daytime television makeover shows.

Picking up the scattered contents of her purse, she popped a bag of ramen into a bowl of water and turned on the microwave. The thought of having to sort through her closet for a suitable outfit would have been daunting tonight so it was fortunate that she'd had the forethought to plan out all of this week's party clothes. Even if her forethought was owing more to excitement than to organizational compulsion.

She sliced a couple of cucumbers for her puffy eyes and lay down for a breather. One minute later the cucumbers went flying as she was jolted awake by the beeping of the microwave signaling that her dinner was done.

Thank God that tomorrow was Saturday, she thought. Her lunch date with Maggie was at 1 p.m., and she wasn't getting out of bed until quarter 'til then.

Dinner, as bland as it was, perked her up a bit and was immediately followed by a hurried makeup application. She lined the inside of her lid with a white pencil to make it pop and applied several coats of mascara to create some sort of definition. She quickly combed her hair out and put it in a tousled ponytail, leaving Alistair's earrings dangling from her lobes. Slipping into a black and white sheath dress with beading detail at the hem, Tori turned sideways and looked herself up and down. It was a definite improvement from this morning.

And at the very least she didn't scare herself when she looked in the mirror.

A little after 7 p.m. she had staggered downstairs and hailed a cab. She watched as the numbers on the taxi's meter climbed as they drove at a snail's pace through typical Friday night Toronto traffic. Traipsing around the city to parties was getting expensive. Tonight's event was at another Yorkville hot spot— STK. Wincing slightly as she handed the driver her credit card, she took the proffered machine and punched in her PIN.

A long line of well-dressed people stood on a long blue carpet flanked by a red velvet rope. Tori, too tired to feel nervous, walked straight up to the front of the line and was ushered through the door within seconds.

Two sets of black lacquered stairs opened onto a room with a white vaulted ceiling and a large crowd. House music pumped through the speakers as dim lighting cast the crowd in a shadowy light. A large banner at the back of the venue read "Fashion Cares" in bold red letters. Red and silver balloons towered above the crowd, and oversized white floral arrangements stood tall on bars and tables. Waiters walked through the crowd serving up champagne, wine and an assortment of cocktails. An oyster bar was set up in one corner while another boasted a three-foot spread of meat, cheese, bread and an assortment of finger food.

Tori said hi to a few people as she made her way through the crowd—she had spotted Alexei, February and Marcus at one of the bouquet-flanked bars and worked her way towards them. She could hear Marcus regaling them with the story of his 2 a.m. trip to the hospital. Alexei and February were shaking with laughter as she sidled up beside them.

"You!" Marcus said accusatorily as she placed her purse on the bar.

Tori looked around at him innocently. "Me?"

"Yes, you!" He fanned himself with one hand. "Remind me to never go rooting around in your purse for pills again."

"You shouldn't be taking random pills from people's purses to begin with," Alexei pointed out.

Marcus flourished his hand in dismissal and tilted his martini into his mouth.

"So, Tins," he changed the subject. "How quickly did Alistair get you out of your dress last night?"

Tori could feel her skin turn scarlet as all three eyed her expectantly.

"Uh . . ." She paused. "He didn't."

"What!" Marcus was aghast. "You had that sexy specimen all over you the entire night and you didn't take him home and ravish him?" He looked at her contemplatively. "I knew it," he continued. "You're not into him! You should have given me the signal!"

"Of course she's into him!" February chimed in. "He's soooo incredibly good looking."

Alexei nodded in agreement. "And nice," he added as an afterthought.

"He's more than that," Tori protested. "I *like* like him. I don't want to take him to bed on our first date."

Marcus looked confused, failing to understand how someone could possibly resist dragging the object of their affection straight to bed as soon as the opportunity presented itself.

"Right," he said. "Well, what about Munger?"

Tori had almost forgotten about Munger. She'd been on the phone fielding Marcus's emergency room call when Munger's requisite dirty morning text came in. "I want to sex u til u scream," it said. Tori had nearly gagged when she read it, but her sleep-deprived brain had blocked all memory of it out until now.

"He's not my type," she said firmly.

Marcus nearly spat out his drink.

"A billionaire is everyone's type!" he declared.

February flipped her hair back and leaned forward conspiratorially.

"Is he really as lecherous as the tabloids say?" she asked.

"Worse," Tori emphasized. "And he won't stop sending me dirty texts."

Marcus looked interested.

"Well, feel free to forward any and all dirty texts to me," he implored, causing February and Alexei burst into laughter.

Tori turned towards the bar and was nearly finished ordering a vodka martini when she was interrupted by the sudden feeling of a hand on her lower back.

"Speak of the devil," February whispered in Tori's ear.

Her stomach dropped as she turned and realized who "the devil" was.

"Hi, gorgeous." Munger grinned at her, motioning to the bartender. "Make that two vodka martinis. Munger Carlson Vodka. Extra dirty."

Oh. My. God. Did he really just order a drink with his own brand of vodka? Could this man get any more repulsive? Tori grimaced as Munger slid his arm around her waist and pulled her into him. He smelled like liquor. She struggled to extricate herself from his grasp, bending over and pretending to straighten out her shoe.

Unfortunately, this put her back end right in Munger's line of vision and resulted in a short squeeze to her left cheek. She straightened up, her jaw dropping open in outrage.

"What the he—" She was cut off by Marcus.

"Tinsley!" he interjected. "I don't believe you've introduced us." He extended his hand.

Mercifully, Munger pulled his hand away from her rear to shake Marcus's hand.

Marcus went in for air kisses after exchanging names and Munger reciprocated. Shake, kiss, repeat went around the circle until all three had introduced themselves. Tori reached for one of the martinis that was sitting on top of the bar and poured it down her throat. The combination of sleep deprivation and Munger left her longing to leave but she knew that she had to stay if she wanted another article for her site. The invitation had said that remarks wouldn't be made until 9 p.m.

The foursome stood chatting for several minutes with Munger dominating the conversation, which mostly consisted of him bragging about his lifestyle. It was all that she could do to keep herself from rolling her eyes but the other three were hanging on his every word. She couldn't believe that she'd made out with this man a little over a week ago. Fitting that it was the mango drinks bearing Munger's name that had caused her to black out. Blacked out was the only way in which she could ever see herself willingly spending time with him.

She tried to slide away from the group at that point, seeing her savior in a woman named Marty whom she had chatted with on Wednesday night. Munger unfortunately noticed her departure and begged off the conversation with her friends, following close behind her.

She felt his hand on her elbow and he gently turned her to face him.

"You haven't been answering my texts, Tins." He leaned in close.

"Um," she began. The last thing she wanted to do was end up in a confrontation with an obviously inebriated and aggressive billionaire. "Sorry, Munger. You're just really not my type," she said as kindly as she could while bracing herself for an onslaught of verbal abuse. Instead, Munger burst into laughter.

"I always get what I want," he said, mirth still evident in his eyes. "And right now, I want you."

Tori let out a squeak of indignation and yanked her arm away from his grasp.

"That's nice, but it's not going to happen." She turned and forced her way through the crowd, leaving Munger alone although she was sure it wouldn't be for long. Women seemed to throw themselves at him with wild abandon. She couldn't understand it. He was so obnoxious. Was the lure of money really that strong for these women?

*

She had vowed not to wake up before quarter to 1 p.m., but her internal alarm clock had her opening her eyes at an earlier hour. Still, it was late enough that Tori felt recharged and refreshed. She had spent the majority of last night fending off advances from Munger, who wouldn't take no for an answer.

Christ, she thought to herself. The man was as aggressive as his namesake vodka.

She'd also seen Corinne, and the woman had stared daggers at her. She really seemed to hate Tori, but Tori couldn't figure out why. The only reason she could think of was Alistair. Even Marcus had commented on it when he saw Corinne glaring at her from the other side of the room.

"Meeeow." He'd flourished his hand in imitation of a cat's claw. "What's up Corinne's ass?"

Tori had sighed.

"I don't know. I met her the other night when Alistair and I were out for dinner. Apparently she and Alistair went on a couple of dates."

"Ah." Marcus nodded. "That explains it." He took a long sip from his martini. "I'd watch your back with that one. She's rich enough and crazy enough to make your life a living hell."

Tori was taken aback and looked at Marcus in alarm.

"What do you mean?"

"Well." His lips curled away from his teeth in a dramatic grimace. "Let's just say that Rachel Morrow, the last girl that Corinne took a disliking to, is now an industry pariah."

Warning bells were going off in Tori's head.

"What do you mean?" she asked again.

"Rachel accidentally drenched Corinne and Corinne's white dress in red wine at Pepsi's party last spring. Prior to that fiasco she had a popular fashion blog and was the toast of the industry. *InStyle* had courted her for a possible contributing editor's position, companies were paying her to advertise their clothes and Saks Fifth Avenue had proposed a fashion collaboration with her."

"And?!?" Tori's heart felt like it was going to beat out of her chest.

Marcus looked at her sympathetically.

"*And* after Corinne was done with her, every sponsor, advertiser and contract that she had was terminated and she was persona non grata at every industry event. Poor girl moved back to the 'burbs to live with her parents. And last I heard, she was working retail"—he paused dramatically—"at Forever 21!"

Tori's jaw dropped open. Marcus patted her arm awkwardly and offered her his martini.

"Have a sip," he insisted. "It'll help with the shock."

She'd needed no prodding to take the proffered drink this time. She'd grasped the glass stem gratefully and thrown back the entire drink. Marcus's eyebrows shot up into his hairline.

"Maybe we should get you another beverage . . ." He'd trailed off and then made a beeline for the bar.

Tori had calmed down by the time Marcus reappeared by her side, fortified with two martinis. She took one but refrained from guzzling it down.

"Do you think Corinne would really do something like that to me?" she asked. "Over a man?"

"Well . . ." Marcus looked thoughtful. "Maybe not. I'm sure she's calmed down since then. I mean, sure, she has a history of doing awful, awful, totally terrible shit to people that she takes a disliking to—and I mean truly horrendous shit—but leopards change their spots!"

"Marcus." She stared at him incredulously. "The saying is 'leopards DON'T change their spots'."

His face had scrunched up then and, for lack of anything reassuring to say, he'd offered her a Xanax.

As she lay in bed, anxiety welled up in her at the memory of the incident. Regret for not taking Marcus's Xanax set in. If she was on Corinne's hit list, she would have to be extra cautious. Especially given that she was pretending to be someone she wasn't. Maybe she could have a cordial conversation with her about it, woman to woman? Corinne didn't seem like the type for cordial conversation, she thought doubtfully, but she was determined to give it a try. After all, if Corinne was that vicious towards those that she didn't like and she found out that Tori was pretending to be Tinsley, it would be all over for her. She vowed to approach Corinne the next time that she saw her to try to smooth things over.

She rolled over in bed on Saturday morning, her mouth stretched in a yawn as she reached for her phone on the nightstand. The blinking light made her heart skip a beat. She and Alistair were on daily texting terms that had extended from good morning messages to good night, sweet dreams and emoji kisses. "Sweet dreams gorgeous X," Alistair's last message to her read.

She had managed to sneak out of last night's party after all of the remarks had been made. She'd left via a back door, afraid that Munger would try to corral her into his car if he saw her heading for the exit. At home she'd stayed up for just as long as it took her to type out an article about the night's event. Too bleary eyed to properly edit it, she'd saved the draft and crawled into bed, forgetting entirely to text Alistair good night.

Ensconced in a sea of fluffy pillows, she smiled as she messaged him back. "Sorry! I crashed as soon as I came home," she wrote.

"Hope you had a good night X. Looking forward to seeing you this evening" was followed by an emoji smile and an emoji heart.

Suddenly she was struck with the realization that she had turned into one of "those" people! The sickening, lovey-dovey, multi-heart emoji people who had ridiculous pet names for their partner. But she didn't care. She figured she had only found "those" people so nauseating because she was bitter about not being one of them. Besides, she wasn't calling Alistair Schmoopsy or Babycakes. Yet, at least.

Sunlight flooded her tiny living room as the smell of freshly brewed coffee filled the air. Still swathed in her flannel pajamas and well-worn bunny slippers, Tori opened up her laptop and went over everything that she'd written last night. It wasn't half bad. But it wasn't half good either. Exhaustion really didn't lend itself to her best writing. Fortunately, with the bare bones laid out, it took her only the better part of an hour to turn it into a piece that was worthy of public consumption. The PR company in charge of Fashion Cares had sent out photos from the event early this morning, which made for a perfect accompaniment. "Fashion Cares: Behind the Scenes at the Pre-Launch for Toronto's Hottest Party," she wrote in the title bar before pressing Publish.

After draining the last dregs of her coffee, she spent a few minutes picking up around her place. She was going to deep clean the apartment after her lunch date with Maggie. She had a date with Alistair tonight and at the end of it she wanted him in her home, and in her bed.

Hunter's Landing was her neighbourhood's local watering hole. With a sixty-person patio, classic rock music, cheap beer and meals, it was one of Tori's favourite late-night, post-bar snack stops.

"Cheers!" Tori and Maggie said in unison, their glasses clinking together.

"So!" Maggie said, putting down her pint and leaning forwards in the booth. "Tell me all about it! The parties, the man, the site."

Maggie was a good friend, Tori thought. She was nearly as excited for Tori as Tori was for herself.

"It's unbelievable, Maggie!" she gushed. "I love it so much! It's funny, I've only been pretending to be someone else for a week, but I already feel comfortable in Tinsley's skin." She paused and took a drink of her beer. "I wasn't even nervous approaching the clipboard girl last night, and I've made so many contacts. It feels like I've been doing this for years, not just a week."

Maggie was an enthusiastic listener.

"And Alistair?" she encouraged.

Tori let her head drop back as a huge smile blossomed across her face.

"Maggie, I am so crazy about him!"

Maggie grinned widely.

"So, when do I get to meet Mr. Fabulous?"

A grimace etched itself on Tori's features—how could she let Maggie meet Alistair?

"I don't know if I'm ready for that," she said seriously. "If you slipped up and called me Tori it might ruin the whole thing. I want to wait until we've established a solid relationship before I tell him the truth."

Maggie squinted at Tori, took a sip of her beer and then set the glass down.

"You know, Tor," she began, "he's going to find out sooner or later. I really think that you should just be honest with him. The longer you drag it out, the more painful it's going to be for him and the more deceitful you're going to look."

Tori was confused.

"But you were the one who encouraged me to pretend to be Tinsley in the first place."

"Yes, for your career. But I think you should tell Alistair the whole story. You can't start a healthy relationship off with a lie."

Maggie was always so logical.

"And from everything that you've told me about him, he'll appreciate you being honest with him."

"But what if he tells everyone and then I'm blackballed from industry events?"

"Well . . ." Maggie thought about it for a minute. "I really don't think he would do that," she concluded lamely.

That wasn't enough of a reassurance for Tori.

"If we're still together in a few months, I'll do it then," Tori decided. "Because who knows! If he told everyone that I'm not Tinsley it would put a stop to my career before it even has a chance to get started."

Maggie said nothing and took another drink of her beer.

"Besides," Tori added, "maybe things won't work out. Maybe we'll be horribly incompatible in bed." She hoped that that wasn't the case. But it was always a possibility. Look at smart and sexy Jacob. He checked all of the boxes—tall, handsome, great personality, fun, fit. Unfortunately, another "box" was where it all went wrong—specifically, his inability to get it in due to an endowment that would put a packhorse to shame.

"True," said Maggie, trying to be supportive. "And I suppose it doesn't matter what I tell you either way. You'll do what you want anyway."

Maggie moved the conversation forward. "What are you and Alistair doing tonight?"

"We're going for dinner and then we're going to take a romantic walk along the waterfront . . . and then I'm going to bring him back to my place," Tori added confidently.

Maggie laughed.

"Well, at least one of us is getting laid," she lamented. Maggie had broken up with her most recent boyfriend a few months ago and she had yet to get back into the dating game.

"And hey!" Maggie exclaimed suddenly. "Don't forget that next Thursday you're supposed to be helping me finalize the plans for the SPCA fundraiser!"

Yikes. Tori had all but forgotten that she'd promised Maggie that she would help her plan and put on the event geared towards raising money for homeless, sick and injured animals. Maggie may work in a cutthroat industry but outside of finance she was the most sensitive softie. In her spare time (not that she had much of it) she volunteered at the SPCA as a dog walker and a cat cuddler, and she was often surrounded by a plethora of foster pets.

"Of course! I wouldn't forget it for the world!" Tori said with a lot more enthusiasm than the situation warranted.

Maggie eyed her suspiciously.

"You'd already forgotten, hadn't you?"

Tori cast her eyes sideways. "Momentarily!" She met a disapproving Maggie's eyes. "I'm so sorry, Maggie," Tori said. "I've just had so much going on with *On the List*, and with everything that's going on at work . . ." She trailed off.

"What's going on at work?" Maggie asked, her eyebrows raised in question. "Surely coffee runs and phone calls aren't keeping you at the office after hours?"

Ouch, Tori thought indignantly.

"Actually, Keith is letting me be in charge of brainstorming and putting together a marketing event for Impotentia's newest products. So that's keeping me at the office after hours. Not everyone has some super important finance job, but I have a lot of responsibility now, thanks."

They sat there staring at one another. Tori was waiting for another verbal smack from her best friend. They rarely fought, but when they did, it could turn nasty.

"Look," Maggie said, breaking the tension first. "I'm sorry I said that about the coffee runs and phone calls. That was rude and uncalled for."

Tori opened her mouth to apologize, too, but Maggie stopped her.

"I just get a little defensive over the animals," she continued. "I'm really excited to put together this event."

"I know," Tori said emphatically. "And don't worry, I'll make sure I'm there on Thursday. I'm putting another reminder in my phone right now." She typed out "SPCA fundraiser, Maggie this Thursday" in bold letters at the very top of her to-do list. The two of them ordered another beer and spent another hour catching up on everything. Maggie had gotten a new (and incredibly attractive) boss at work and he had been paying her special attention. One of the dogs that she was fostering (an overweight dachshund named Minnie) had a potential forever home but now Maggie didn't want to give her up. They chatted about their families—Tori's parents were slated to come down for an overnight visit at the beginning of next month, while Maggie's mom and dad were currently on a month-long Caribbean cruise, and her sister was off on a backpacking trip through Asia.

They parted ways a little while later, the brief moment of tension all but forgotten.

That afternoon Tori cranked up some classic rock, threw on some sweats and swept, dusted, scrubbed and polished her apartment to a veritable sheen. She placed a cinnamon-scented candle in the middle of her coffee table, folded a fluffy blanket over the arm of the couch and switched on the fireplace television channel. By the time she was finished, she didn't have a chance to kick back and relax as Alistair would be there in an hour. She knew she would never be able to top Thursday's outfit, so she didn't even attempt to. Still, she didn't want to look like she'd spent all afternoon elbow deep in apartment grime. A mound of clothes lay strewn across her floor by the time she'd finally settled on an outfit: a short, tight, off-the-shoulder dress paired with striped pumps. She ran a flat iron over her hair to smooth down the fly-aways and applied a black smoky eye with a nude lip. Punctual as always—at ten to 7 p.m. Tori's phone started ringing and Alistair's contact card came up.

His face lit up in a mirror smile of Tori's when she stepped off the elevator and into his arms. Their plan was to have a low-key evening tonight. They were trading in the glitz, glam and pretentiousness of Yorkville and Tori's industry events for an out-of-the-way diner. Alistair had told her that it was one of his favourite places. The drive there took ten minutes, which seemed like a normal commute time if you were travelling within a seven-block radius of her condo, but it was far away from the bustling downtown core. She smiled when she stepped out of the car and took in the eclectic hole in the wall where they would be dining tonight. It was definitely more her style. There wasn't a fake, face-full-of-makeup, look-down-your-nose fashionista in sight. The few clientele who dotted the landscape all looked like normal, down-to-earth individuals who had nothing more on their mind than enjoying their dinner. The long space was dimly lit—paper lanterns of assorted colours strung up across the ceiling; an old piano sat in one corner and a long wooden bar ran half the length of the room. The rest of the space was filled with diner-style booths and tables. Alistair led the way through the restaurant and slid into a cozy corner booth in the back. Tori eased in after him and he immediately snuggled up next to her. It was hard to believe that they had only met one week ago. She felt so comfortable with him and their conversation flowed so easily that it felt like they had known each other for years.

Classic jazz streamed through the speakers as a large, casually attired woman in her late fifties approached their table. There was no impossibly fake smile or ass-kissing air about her like there had been from the wait staff at One the other night. Pulling a well-worn notepad from the front of her apron, she introduced herself in a monotone voice before asking them what they would like to drink. Tori felt more comfortable with choosing wine this time—there were only three options and she could pronounce every item listed. Alistair's hand found hers as they pored over the menu, their fingers intertwining.

"I'll have the merlot," Tori said to the waitress.

"Make that two," Alistair chimed in.

The waitress disappeared back to the bar while Alistair pulled Tori close and whispered in her ear.

"So," he said conspiratorially. "Our waitress? I've been coming here for the past five years on a biweekly basis. She's served me nearly every time, but whenever I come in, she acts like she's never seen me before."

"Five years and she pretends she doesn't know you!" Tori giggled. "You can't be serious."

"Swear on my life." Alistair grinned. "Entirely serious."

Tori laughed some more.

"That's hilarious. Maybe she has some form of short-term memory loss?"

Alistair's grin widened.

"You know, I can't decide what's worse: over-the-top ass kissing or being completely ignored."

She thought about it for a second.

"Over-the-top ass kissing, hands down. Because you're always afraid that right when you put a forkful of food into your mouth that the waiter or hostess or bread man or busboy will pop up out of nowhere and ask you how it is, or ask if there is anything else that they can get you, or pour you more wine while you're in the middle of a conversation. It all feels so forced. It makes it difficult to fully enjoy the experience because you're constantly aware of their presence. And there are so many rules to follow!"

"Agreed." Alistair smiled before leaning in to kiss her. "That's one of the things that I adore about you, Tinsley. I can't imagine bringing someone like Corinne to this place."

Tori felt a weird mixture of pleasure and discontent at that. On the one hand, Alistair had just given her a massive compliment. On the other hand, this was the second time that Corinne's name had popped up during one of their dates. She couldn't get away from the woman.

Two glasses of wine suddenly appeared on their table and in

short order they were munching away companionably on their meals (quinoa salad and French fries for Tori, burger and French fries for Alistair).

"Dessert?" Alistair asked when she'd pushed her empty plate away.

She could do with some dessert. The two glasses of wine that she'd drank had not been tempered by her dinner.

"Sure." She smiled, reaching for her glass of water.

"Perfect." Alistair squeezed her hand and smiled back. "This is my favourite. I order it all of the time. You're going to love it."

The waitress reappeared to clear off their table.

"Dessert menus?" she asked.

"I'll have the usual," Alistair said.

Their waitress didn't even stop to ask what "the usual" was before she walked off to the kitchen.

Alistair and Tori broke out in a fit of laughter.

Following dinner, they took a leisurely stroll along the harbourfront close to Tori's home. They walked hand in hand along the warmly lit pathway, pausing every now and then to kiss. The park was quiet tonight and they passed only a handful of people despite the nice weather. A slight breeze ruffled the sails of the docked yachts and caused faint ripples in the water. Stars scattered the inky sky and the bright glow of the full moon cast a shining light onto darkened surfaces. They came to a stop under a large maple tree where Alistair pulled her off to the side and led her to a wooden bench. Tori snuggled up closely, her legs draped on top of Alistair's lap and his arm wrapped around her, holding her tight. They shared laughs together and Tori told him all about her family and growing up in Sudbury, and how she had always dreamed of being a magazine editor. Alistair regaled her with stories of his mom, stepfather and sister, and shared how he'd always dreamed of being a banker.

"I should get you home." He gave Tori a squeeze two hours later. There was a crispness to the air that had crept in without her even noticing. Alistair took her hand, they walked companionably back through the park, their hands tightly clasped together.

At the front doors of her building, Alistair cupped his hands around her face, leaned down and kissed her.

After several breathless minutes they pulled apart.

"I want you to come upstairs." Tori smiled, trying to catch her breath.

A slow smile grew across Alistair's face as he gazed into her eyes.

"Are you sure?" he asked, drawing her in closer. Butterflies welled up in the bottom of her stomach as he kissed her again.

"I'm sure," she whispered when they broke off.

Alistair's hand moved from her face and his fingers intertwined with hers. She fumbled in her purse for her keys, her hand shaking as she finally pulled them out with a triumphant jingle.

Hands clasped together, they walked into her lobby and stood waiting for the elevators, the up button emitting a red glow against the black tiles. Tori felt her nerves ramp up as the numbers of the lift decreased from 14 to G. With a mechanical whir, the shiny metal doors parted and Tori stepped inside with Alistair following close behind. The mirrored walls of the compartment allowed Tori to see the look of absolute elation on her face. She was mortified at her ecstatic expression and a bright pink blush crept into her cheeks as she pressed the button for her floor. She was going to have to play it a little cooler, she thought. Although Tori's embarrassment lasted only as long as it took for the doors to close, whereupon she found herself pinned up against the back mirror with Alistair's lips pressed against hers. His kisses were deeper now. His tongue urgently prodded the recesses of her mouth as Tori eagerly answered back. A tingling sensation spread through her torso as she pushed her hips against his body.

They barely made it out of the elevator when the doors opened onto her floor as the two of them continued to kiss each other with a single-minded abandon. Tori fumbled with her keys when they arrived at her door, blindly trying to stuff them in the keyhole with one hand wrapped around Alistair's neck and her eyes firmly closed as their tongues intertwined.

Several hours later they lay snuggled together. Tori, nestled in the crook of Alistair's arm, traced her fingers over his chest while he rubbed her hips affectionately.

It had been everything that Tori had hoped for and more. The two of them weren't just compatible in bed, they were dynamite.

They spent most of the next morning lying together in bed, only getting up around midday to go for brunch. Tori insisted that they go somewhere outside of her neighbourhood (the last thing she needed was for one of her neighbours to call her by her real name) and they wound up at an upscale French bistro several blocks away. Enjoying the afternoon sun on the restaurant's front patio they sat side by side, kissing between bites and teasing each other the entire time. In terms of the company and cuisine, it was the best brunch that she had ever had.

"Oh my God," she moaned through a mouth full of crepe. "This is almost as good as last night."

"Is that so?" Alistair grinned, giving her a playful shove. "Well then perhaps you'll give me a chance to redeem myself with round two later."

Tori giggled.

"Round two? More like round twenty-two," she shot back, thinking about the nearly fourteen hours that they had spent together in bed.

"Twenty-two, then," he conceded. "Although if we've gone twenty-two rounds and I'm still beaten out by a crepe, I don't know if I'll ever come out on top."

"That's okay." Tori smirked, a devilish glint creeping into her eyes. "I can be on top."

"Is that so?" Alistair's eyes answered her in kind.

She nodded her head as the mischievous grin spread further across her face. Alistair pulled her close and kissed her on the lips.

"What do you say we get out of here?" he said. "I have just enough stamina left for round twenty-two and twenty-three."

Chapter 8: Life on Repeat

Walking into work the next morning, Tori was on cloud nineteen. Alistair had spent the night at her place for the second night in a row and after their steamy post-brunch sex session, Tori had declared him the uncontested winner of Alistair Chase versus the Crepe. They spent the rest of the evening lounging around watching reality TV and talking until pink and orange streaks of sunset flooded the sky. After picking up a few items at the grocery store, Tori pulled out a bottle of wine and set to work making dinner. Alistair sat at the table sipping from his glass and reading the market futures. The past twenty-four hours had been so perfect that Tori could barely stand it. She happily bounced around her tiny kitchen, chopping up vegetables and pulling things out of the cupboards. They finished dinner (rice-stuffed mushrooms, French bread and a beet and goat cheese salad) and polished off the bottle of wine for dessert. The whole evening felt so relaxed and comfortable to Tori—it seemed like they had been dating for ten years instead of only ten minutes.

"Ooooh, somebody is glowing!" Sierra remarked as she walked past Tori's desk. A deep flush spread across Tori's face. "Did you and your boyfriend conduct scientific testing of the new Impotentia products this weekend?" she teased.

Her flush deepened, which caused Sierra to laugh.

"That's great, Tori," she said, still smirking. "Good way to compile market research. You can give me your review of the products at our meeting this week," Sierra laughed as she walked away.

She and Alistair hadn't actually gotten around to trying out Impotentia's newest line of women's products but now that Sierra had mentioned it, it was definitely on her to-do list. When she would get around to it, though, was anybody's guess. Currently her to-do list was two pages long. She had several industry events to go to this week in addition to several meetings regarding her project with Sierra. And a meeting with Maggie! She couldn't forget about that. And Alistair, of course. He had asked her to go for dinner Tuesday and Thursday, and to spend Friday, Saturday and Sunday together.

He had left her apartment early that morning. Usually in the office by 7:30 a.m., he had needed to go home and change his clothes. She hadn't been able to fall back asleep after he left, and consequently found herself stifling yawns throughout the morning. She couldn't wait to see him again. Mentally, she had already cleared out a space for him in her tiny closet.

*

Drained from the day's work and last night's lack of sleep, Tori crashed as soon as she arrived home from work that evening. Intending to lie down for a quick twenty-minute nap, she woke up on her couch three hours later in a puddle of drool and confusion. Disgusted, she wiped at her mouth, rubbing her bleary eyes into focus with her other hand.

Fuck—she looked at the clock. It was 8:30 p.m. and she still had to prep for her Wednesday morning meeting and pick out all of her outfits for this week's events.

Splashing cold water on her face she reached for a towel as the scent of freshly brewed coffee filled the air. Dropping the towel on the floor she braced herself for the onslaught of work she was about to face. Her dining room table was littered with papers strewn about in an unorganized fashion. Sighing at the mess, she sat down, took a deep breath and set to work. She and Sierra had settled on Thursday, June 22 as the date that they would host their event, which meant that she had about a month to get everything together. Fortunately, she had now been to enough product launches and parties to know what kinds of things she needed to plan for. Sierra was giving Tori a lot of room for input in creating this marketing campaign and Tori didn't want to let her down.

It had been decided that they would throw a launch party for the products, which was usually the easiest way to garner publicity. But in order to work within the confines of a small budget, they were going to have to get creative. Tori was confident that she would be able to find a liquor and catering sponsor for the evening. She figured that the hardest part would be finding a suitable, budget-friendly space.

Notepad at the ready she started making notes. "Potential alcohol sponsors?" she wrote at the top of the page. She had received a business card from the marketing manager at Steam Whistle Brewing at last week's Luminato launch. And the sales representative at Carnivore wine had given her her number and told her to call if she ever needed anything. And then there was Munger. She dismissed the thought as soon as it entered her mind. Nothing, not even the threat of losing her job, would prompt her contact him for a favour. Tori paused then. How would she manage to get all of these sponsors on board without them finding out that she wasn't Tinsley? She racked her brain. Maybe she could do everything via email and introduce them to "Tori" that way?

She sat back for a moment. Had she gone completely off the deep end? It was bad enough that she was faking her way through the fashion industry. She would be a total idiot to get that mixed up with her real daytime job. Tori sighed and shelved her idea of using Tinsley's liquor and catering contacts for now. That meant that she would really have to get to work. Scratching out the names of potential sponsors that she had already written down, she took to the Internet and conducted several searches.

Two hours later, her table still covered in papers, she made for her closet to pull together her outfits. Tomorrow she was having dinner with Alistair and then they were going to head to the Conair party. The beauty company was celebrating the launch of their latest line of hair-styling products and the invite promised drinks and finger food (an industry standard, as Tori had learned by now) and hair stylists on hand to give her mane a makeover.

She pulled out a floor-length black wool dress with a navel-plunging neckline and placed it at the front of her rack. Paired with her red pumps and a swipe of red lipstick, it would make for a very simple but very sexy outfit.

The Roots clothing party was on the following day, but that outfit fortunately didn't require much planning. Hosting their event at Chill Ice House meant that pants and a sweater would suffice given the invite indicated that mittens and knee-length down-filled parkas would be provided. She pulled a chunky knit sweater and a pair of black slacks out from the rack and placed them behind the wool dress.

While last week her outfit planning had been born out of overwhelming excitement, this week it was born out of necessity.

She continued on through her closet until she had an outfit for every day until Sunday. Only two of her outfits needed some kind of modification to counteract their blandness. She had set a style precedent with her previous looks and she wanted to keep it well above that baseline. Pulling out her sewing machine she looked over at the clock with a groan. It was 11:08 p.m. At this rate she would be lucky if she didn't sew over her hand in a fit of fatigue.

Shortening the hem and adding trim to the collar of one dark green dress and adding sequin sleeves to another, she finally fell into bed in the early hours of the morning. Alarm clock set for 6 a.m., she texted Alistair a good-night message and passed out cold.

*

The next day, she found herself once again trying to hold back a series of yawns. While she had slept like the dead for several hours after work yesterday, it didn't appear to have impacted her energy levels any. She worked her way through the morning calls and made sure to order espresso for herself when she went for the daily office coffees. She was sitting at a table waiting for her order to be completed when she felt her phone buzzing. Looking down she saw Alistair's contact card on her caller ID.

"Hello," she answered, beaming happily into the phone.

"Hello, beautiful," he replied. "What's my lovely lady doing? Product launch for Prada? Writing an article about the advantages of patent leather over suede? Martinis with Marcus, perhaps?"

Tori giggled.

"All of the above," she teased. "It's been a busy day."

"Ah, thought so," he laughed back.

"No," she replied with a smile. "Nothing as exciting as all of that, I'm afraid. I'm actually sitting in a Starbucks, waiting for my coffee order."

"Starbucks!" he exclaimed. "Well, I just called to tell you that I miss you and that I can't wait to see you tonight."

Tori melted.

"I miss you, too," she said sincerely. "I'm really looking forward to it."

"Good," he responded. "Because I need my Tinsley time. I've seen entirely too little of you in the past twenty-four hours."

Tori giggled again.

"You spent nearly thirty-six hours with me this weekend!"

"Yes," he replied. "And that's the absolute minimum amount of time that I need to spend with you in a two-day period."

"You're going to get sick of me," she teased.

"Never!" he said firmly. "I'll be at your place for 6:30 tonight. I figured that you could pick the restaurant this time."

"That sounds perfect," she said. "Although I don't know if

you want me picking where we eat . . ." She trailed off. "I'm horrible at choosing where to dine."

"Nonsense," he assured her. "You could take me to a flea-infested hovel best known for serving up food poisoning and I would just be happy to be spending time with you. And," he added, "I would happily hold your hair back while you were puking into the toilet later."

"Is that the definition of love?" Tori wondered aloud.

Alistair laughed.

"Holding back your partner's hair while they're vomiting into the toilet and still feeling content because you're spending time with them?" he teased. "I think it might be."

"Tori!" came the voice of the Starbucks barista. She rushed over to the counter and picked up her order.

"Sorry, Alistair! My order is ready and I have a full tray of drinks to bring back to the office."

He laughed.

"You're doing the coffee run? That's another thing I like about you, Tinsley. Most people would just pass that off to their interns."

Tori grimaced.

"Yes, well. I'm definitely not above grabbing drinks for my colleagues!" Wasn't that an understatement, she thought. Not only was she not above it, it was basically written into her job description.

"Okay, well, enjoy your afternoon and I look forward to seeing you tonight, Coffee Girl."

"You, too." Tori smiled. "I'm really looking forward to it."

The remainder of her workday consisted of her continuing to cold-call consumers. She also talked to Maggie, who had slipped out of the office for five minutes to talk to Tori. Her best friend was devastated—the family who had been looking to adopt Minnie, her foster dachshund, had been approved and they would be picking up the little four-legged sausage that evening.

"Oh, Maggie, it's okay," Tori tried to comfort her friend. "It's good that Minnie will be going to a loving family. And now you can take in another foster dog, which will free up more space for other pets to be saved."

"I know." Maggie sniffled, her voice sounding thick. "It's just so hard every time one of my foster pets gets adopted. I get so attached to them. And now my new boss probably thinks I'm bonkers."

Tori was perplexed.

"Your handsome new boss that you told me about? Why?"

"He was walking by my cubicle just now and saw that my eyes were all red and puffy." She sniffed again. "So he asked me what was wrong, and I told him, and he handed me some tissues and told me to take some time out to go and grab a tea and phone a friend or family."

"And you think he thinks you're crazy because of that?" Tori was aghast. "He sounds like a great boss—like he really cares about you. God, I can't image what Keith would say if he saw me crying at my desk. He'd probably just roll his eyes and tell me to get back to work."

Maggie shifted the phone and sniffled.

"You think so? I just don't want to disappoint him. Or lose my job. I work with all of these cutthroat, void-of-feelings types of men, and sometimes it feels like I can't show any kind of emotion because I'll be seen as weak."

"I know so," Tori said reassuringly. "Besides, you're extremely good at what you do. You're hard-working, smart, personable, and with one phone call you could land a job at one of your company's competitors in less than twenty-four hours."

Maggie's sniffs were getting more spaced out now.

"Thanks, Tori," she said gratefully. "You're a good friend."

"Anytime, Maggie." Tori smiled into the phone. "Now go and grab a tea like your boss suggested, and go and sit in the dog park across from your building for a few minutes."

"Will do," she said, her voice no longer sounding shaky. "Thanks, Tor. Love you," she signed off.

"Love you, too, Mags. And text me later! Let me know how the wiener-dog hand-off goes tonight."

At home, Tori pulled her long wool dress out of the closet.

It was pretty risqué looking, but she had discovered that at industry events, almost anything went. Hair pinned back in a loose bun, she splashed on some red lipstick and slipped on her shoes. She hadn't quite figured out where they should go for dinner and was still trying to come up with a plan when Alistair texted her to let her know that he was downstairs.

After whisking her into the black town car he sat back expectantly.

"So," he said, looking at her, "where are we going for dinner?"

Tori faltered.

"Um . . ." She thought for a minute. "How about Fresh?"

"Fresh it is." He smiled.

A low-key hipster hangout with vegan cuisine and tables that were way too close together, Fresh was easy on the wallet and ethically sound. They dined on a meal of tofu steaks and noodle bowls in a cramped corner of the restaurant and Alistair enjoyed his meal so much that he vowed that they would be back sometime for more.

Outside of the Conair party the clipboard girl recognized Tori and let her and Alistair walk right past the rope. The venue Parlour, a gothic-chic late-night lounge, was brimming with red-velvet furniture and wrought-iron accents. Up against a back wall several hair styling stations were set up, each seat occupied with men and women having their hair worked on. In usual fashion, Marcus was already there at the bar, accompanied by February and a few other acquaintances that Tori knew from various events.

Ordering up beers, Tori and Alistair spent the next two hours mingling and talking to others, but mainly talking to each other. Tori didn't bother having her hair done, not wanting to appear in any of Conair's event photos for obvious reasons, and by the time they decided to head home, she had made several more contacts and her purse was brimming with business cards. One of the PR girls had stopped them on their way out and given them large gift bags containing each of Conair's new styling products. A smaller bag held a USB stick containing Conair-approved product photos and an assortment of headbands and hair ties. Alistair gave Tori his gift bag, claiming that his sister wouldn't be interested, and she held it back with Maggie in mind.

It was late by the time their car pulled up to her place and Tori wanted nothing more than to spend the night with her handsome man. Disappointingly he declined, citing early morning work commitments, but Tori tried to look on the bright side. Maybe tonight she could get in more than five hours of sleep. He walked her to her door as usual, and they engaged in a lengthy kiss. Intending to get down to article writing as soon as she stepped foot in her door, Tori hadn't even made it inside of her unit when her phone started buzzing. Glancing at the screen, she saw a text message from Alistair: "I had such a great time with you tonight, Tinsley. As always. Get some sleep and I can't wait to see your beautiful face on Thursday XX."

Relief swept over her and she realized that Alistair declining to spend the night with her had had her questioning if he just wasn't that into her anymore. And while she logically understood that he had a demanding job that kept him busy at very early hours, she still felt a little insecure that he would turn down the opportunity to spend the night together. His text made her feel better about it. And then it hit Tori like a ton of bricks: she was absolutely, falling-in-love crazy about this man. In Tori's world, this meant that she had now reached the point of no return. The point where every text, every glance, every word and every touch would be analyzed to the point of insanity. She was now navigating through dangerous territory. The territory of totally hurt feelings if things didn't work out. Scratch that, she thought. She wouldn't just be hurt if Alistair decided to break things off with her at this point—she would be devastated.

Sighing, she warmed up some water in the microwave and set about making herself a decaffeinated cup of tea—forgoing her usual late-night caffeine fix in an effort to fall asleep once she was finished writing.

"Frizzy, Flat and Everything in Between: Conair's Newest Range of Hair Care Products Raises the Bar for Beauty," read the title. Satisfied, she began to type. Detailing the evening's event, she touched on the specifics of the styling products including pictures of the tools that had been included in the press packet. She had also snapped a few inconspicuous photos of the stylists at work, showing attendees with half-done hair that demonstrated the effectiveness of Conair's new hair-styling gadgets.

Giving it a once-over, she saved the draft to her *On the List* folder and climbed into bed. Setting her alarm clock to go off a half hour earlier than normal, Tori vowed to wake up early to get the article on the site.

Feeling refreshed after a comatose-like sleep, Tori managed to publish her Conair piece before 7 a.m. Checking out her site analytics she was pleased with what she saw. With every article that she had published, her Internet traffic had grown exponentially. She was now receiving daily hits of nearly 2,500 people, with over 1,800 regular subscribers. People were also commenting more frequently, other sites were linking to her site and Twitter was raving about her reporting. Several comments queried who the anonymous author could be. It was perfect. She was generating buzz, which was exactly what she wanted. The only way to break into the tight-knit industry was to have your work recognized or to know someone. Fortunately, it looked like she was hitting both cylinders. If she managed to play everything just right, she might have a paid writing career sometime in the near future. The thought of that alone was enough to fuel her through eight-hour workdays and five-hour work nights. A little sleep deprivation was nothing compared to setting herself up for a long and successful career.

Pleased with the progress she was making—astonishing, really, given that she had been a fake magazine editor for only two weeks—she sat back and took a few minutes on her couch to enjoy her morning coffee. Tori felt on top of the world. While more responsibility at work was a little poorly timed, she was going to embrace it. She felt like she was killing it on all fronts.

At work that day she felt energized. Far from the yawn-stifling zombie she had been the last two days, she felt perky and full of life. Finding a few minutes to log into her *Fashionist* email account she was taken aback by the hoard of new event invites that she had amassed. Pulling out her phone and writing down the list of events, their dates, times and locations, Tori began to RSVP to one after the other. It was unbelievable. She had gone from the girl who went out at most once every couple of weeks to the woman whose schedule was so jam-packed that personal time was something that she barely had room to pencil in. Still, she wasn't complaining. She definitely understood why so many people were attracted to the industry. It was like being in with the popular kids in high school—not that Tori had ever been a part of the cool crowd during her teenage years. But she was sure that she now knew what it felt like. Being invited to private, sponsored parties felt like being in an exclusive club that everyone wanted to access, but that only a certain set of people actually could.

That night at Chill Ice House, the venue that was hosting the Roots event, Tori ran into several people that she'd met over the past two weeks. She nursed one drink for the entirety of the evening and happily took home her gift bag full of Roots sweatpants, sweatshirts and T-shirts. Back at home she once again fired up her laptop and continued with her near-nightly routine of article writing, publishing the piece this time before going to bed. Stashing her Impotentia papers into her bag for tomorrow morning's meeting, Tori fell into a blissful slumber after texting Alistair and wishing him a good night.

*

"This is great, Tori!" Sierra was impressed with the effort that Tori had put into the Impotentia products campaign. "I'll be honest, I didn't know what to expect of you, but I'm really impressed with your work."

Tori beamed at her. Getting complimented on tangible work and not on her ability to juggle ten coffees at a time was encouraging. It gave Tori a boost of sorely needed confidence.

"Thanks, Sierra! I put a lot of thought and effort into it. I'm just happy that it fits with what you had in mind," she said happily.

Sierra nodded her head in approval as she looked over her work once more.

"The idea of partnering up with a catering and liquor company is a great idea," she said. "In fact, I'm going to see if we can get one of our other clients, Patisserie, to go along as the caterer for the event. It would be good publicity for them and could be done at a very low cost."

"I was also thinking that we could do gift bags?" said Tori uncertainly, thinking about all of the party swag that she had amassed over the past few weeks. "I know that at lots of parties they provide the guests with samples of the product on their way out of the door," she rushed on. "It was just a thought. I don't know if that's something that we want to do, though."

"I think that's a great idea." Sierra looked pleased.

Tori was over the moon—it was her first chance at real work and work-related responsibility and by all indications, she was killing it.

"Keith is going to be very pleased when I meet with him this afternoon. He had his doubts about your dedication to this campaign and I can't wait to tell him that he couldn't have been more wrong."

That unsettled Tori a little bit.

"Doubts?"

"Yes, he said that you didn't seem very happy to be given the opportunity to work on this launch. I told him that you were probably just having a bad day and not to read too much into it."

"Thanks, Sierra," Tori said earnestly. "I just have a lot going on in my personal life right now and it was a little overwhelming at the time. But I'm really happy to be working on this with you. Ever since I started here, I've been waiting for the chance to do some real marketing work."

"How would you like to take a stab at writing the press release for the party?" she asked.

"I would love to!" Tori felt a surge of joy. "I love writing, it's what I've always wanted to do. Thank you so much, Sierra."

Her colleague laughed.

"No worries, Tori. Now, if you can have that copy to me by next Monday, that will give me enough time to look it over."

Tori thought that the copywriting would likely take up most of her weekend—after all, she wanted to turn in her best work—but she wasn't bothered by that. She was going to prove herself and her writing skills valuable to Sierra, Keith and Staten Marketing.

"Done," she said confidently. "I'll have it to you first thing on Monday morning."

And with that, Sierra gathered up the assorted papers and the two of them left the conference room, chatting amicably until they parted ways at Tori's desk.

On an adrenaline rush from the success of her site and the morning meeting, Tori sat back and contemplated everything that she had to do today. Her schedule was jam-packed and she imagined she would be ready for bed by eleven. Hopefully her "I'm doing a great job on everything" high would keep her going until then.

Immediately after work she rushed to Maggie's firm, climbed in the elevator and pressed 18. In the glass-walled lobby of the finance firm the receptionist ushered her through a set of double doors and into a large glass conference room. Five people sat around the table, including Maggie, waiting on Tori to begin the meeting.

Blackstone, Maggie's finance firm, had been generous enough to allow her the use of their office after working hours to conduct her SPCA event planning. A big proponent of charity, they had also agreed to match whatever amount of money Maggie was able to raise.

Her best friend beamed at her as she walked through the doors and settled into her seat.

"Hi, Tori," she said happily. "We're just going over the final plans for the party."

The fundraiser was going to feature a dog fashion show and

an agility competition, and the planning committee had already lined up Purina, Molson and a handful of other sponsors for the event. Maggie had gone all out on the plans. They were selling tickets for $160 per person, which included a gift bag, drinks, snacks and prizes. By the time the meeting had finished—two hours later—Tori had been put in charge of obtaining items for the silent auction. Maggie had also tasked her with doing the advertising for the event. Her plate was more than full at the moment, but Tori was happy to help out her friend.

Throwing her papers into her purse, she hurried home as fast as she could. Her coat and purse lay discarded on her dining room table as she rushed around her apartment getting ready. The Conair styling products she'd received earlier in the week were being put to good use—her flat iron had bitten the big one yesterday morning and she was grateful to have a brand new one on hand. After all, flat irons were expensive, and her budget was stretched so thin at this point that it was threatening to snap. Smoothing down her hair into poker-straight strands, she painted more makeup overtop of what she was currently wearing due to a lack of time.

Sliding on the inky-green dress that she had hemmed and embellished earlier in the week, she stepped into a pair of black sparkly heels and then stood back to observe her appearance. Satisfied with what she saw and with a few minutes to spare, she sat down on the couch for a breather. Ever on time, Alistair dialed her at 7:30 p.m. sharp to let her know that he was downstairs.

"Alistair?" she said, question in her voice.

"Yes, beautiful?"

"What would you think about having dinner at my place instead?" she queried. The last thing she felt like doing was going out for dinner.

"I would love that," he replied.

"Perfect!" she said happily. "I'll buzz you up."

A few short minutes later Alistair appeared on her doorstep, their mouths blossoming into identical smiles as he moved in for a hug. He was dressed up in a sleek, gunmetal-grey suit, sans tie, with the first button of his white dress shirt undone.

"You look as gorgeous as ever." He planted a kiss on her lips as he stepped inside. "What's for dinner?"

Tori thought about that.

"I really don't have much in my fridge and cupboards to work with," she admitted, thinking that she could hardly serve him Mr. Noodles for dinner. "I thought that we could just order in?"

Alistair nodded in approval.

"That sounds great. And it will give me time to work up an appetite." He winked.

Tori laughed.

"What are you in the mood for?"

"Aside from you?" he teased. "I could go for some Thai. Stay in for some Thai, I mean. I have the perfect place." Alistair pulled out his phone, dialed a number and spoke to the customer service rep on the other end. He rattled off a list of items including pad Thai, tofu and vegetables, rice noodles and vegetarian spring rolls before confirming the order and hanging up.

"Delivery at your door in forty-five minutes," he promised. "Now," he said, advancing towards her. "Let's get you out of that dress, pretty lady. I want to make love to you and hear all about your day."

Forty minutes later the two of them lay snuggled up together, naked on the couch. A contented sigh escaped Alistair's lips.

"You know, Tinsley," he said dreamily. "You make me really happy. I love spending time with you. I know it's only been two weeks but I could marry you tomorrow."

Tori's stomach dropped. Marriage?! She wanted nothing more than to be with Alistair forever, but she wanted to do it as Tori. Not as Tinsley.

Alistair caught the look of panic on Tori's face and pulled her closer.

"Come here, you." He kissed her forehead. "You know I'm only teasing. I'm crazy about you but don't worry, I'm not going to get down on one knee tomorrow," he said lightly. "I just feel very comfortable around you. I love how open and honest we are with one another," he continued. "It's exactly the kind of relationship I've been looking for."

Tori sighed at that and leaned her head against his chest. She loved their relationship, too. She just wished that it hadn't started off as a lie. "Open and honest" was maybe not how she would describe their relationship from her side. Maggie was right, she thought reluctantly. The longer she dragged out the lie, the worse the fallout would be. In that moment she felt a sudden surge of confidence and steeled herself to tell him the whole sordid truth.

"Alistair?" She hesitated.

"Yes?" he replied, his fingers playing with her hair.

"I . . . there's . . . there's something that I need to tell you." She felt like there was a lump caught in her throat.

"You can tell me anything," he said. "What is it?"

"Well . . . it's about my job," she said cautiously.

"What about your job?" he asked, curiosity evident in his voice.

"I'm not—" At that moment her phone started to ring and her apartment's buzzer came up on the screen.

"Hello?" she answered.

"Hello, food delivery here for Alistair Chase."

Tori buzzed the guy up, hung up her phone and then headed for her bathrobe. She couldn't very well answer the door wearing nothing.

When she came out of the bathroom Alistair was pulling on his briefs. He grabbed a wad of cash out of his pants pocket and passed it to Tori. Moments later her dining table was teetering with an assortment of Thai cuisine.

Alistair, already feeling at home in her place, rummaged around for a bottle of red wine and two glasses.

"What was it that you were going to tell me about your job before the delivery guy interrupted?" Alistair asked, washing down a forkful of pad Thai with a sip of wine.

"Oh, that." Tori had suddenly lost her nerve. "Um, it was nothing important," she mumbled, poking away at the noodles on her plate.

"You seemed pretty serious?" Alistair pressed her. "Are you sure it's nothing?"

Tori hesitated. Now was her chance, she could tell him right now and absolve herself of her guilt.

"I . . . I've been given a new job," she said. "For Maggie's SPCA fundraiser—I'm in charge of marketing."

God. She'd been given the perfect opportunity to come clean and be honest about who she was, and she'd blown it.

"Oh?" Alistair looked impressed. "Is that going to cut into our time together? Is that why it was so important to tell me?"

All she could do was open and close her mouth, followed by rapidly nodding her head.

A large smile blossomed across his face.

"You're such a good person. I love that you're donating your time to a charitable cause and I am so supportive of that. Don't worry about being busy with your extra work. We'll find a way to spend time together."

Tears welled up in her eyes. Both because of how supportive Alistair was of her, and because of how ashamed she was of herself. She had this amazing man who was crazy about her and she couldn't even bring herself to be honest with him.

They finished their dinner together, but Tori found it difficult to enjoy. Guilt was gnawing away at her. Loading up the dishwasher, she turned to Alistair, who was sipping his wine and watching her intently.

"Would there ever be anything that I could do that would cause you to lose interest in me?" she inquired, seemingly out of the blue.

His eyebrows scrunched down in thought.

"That's a bit of an odd question. Nothing that I can think of," he said. "I like everything that I see so far. Of course we don't know one another that well, so I can't say definitively."

That sealed it for her. She couldn't tell him until they had settled into a more stable relationship. She envisioned Maggie furiously shaking her head in disapproval while Alistair stood up, embraced her and planted a kiss on the top of her head.

"You don't have to worry about anything, Tinsley. I'm not going anywhere."

Tori suddenly felt sick.

Chapter 9: Google Gaffes

The Swarovski and Saks Fifth Avenue parties that Tori had RSVP'd for were being held at the Shangri-La and the Saks Fifth Avenue flagship store, respectively. The Swarovski party was filled with glimmering crystals and an equally glimmering crowd. They stayed for an hour, mingling with the PR representatives and chatting to acquaintances before picking up Tori's press packet and gift bag. She'd spotted Munger across the room at one point, but he seemed reluctant to approach her with Alistair by her side. Maybe she was going to have to bring Alistair to all of her events from now on, she thought. Or maybe Munger had finally gotten the hint? She could only hope. On the way over to Saks she opened up the gift bag from the party and was surprised to find a sparkly Swarovski crystal bracelet. Alistair immediately put it on her wrist. In addition to her favourite Alistair earrings, Tori shone like the sun.

The Saks launch was full of familiar faces—some from the Swarovski party and some from other events that she'd attended in the last few weeks. It seemed to always be the same people that she saw at every party.

The high-end department store was celebrating its collaboration with fashion maven and famed style blogger Bryan Boy on a Saks-exclusive capsule collection. Tori couldn't help but think back to what Marcus had told her the other night—about how a girl named Rachel had been in talks about doing a Saks collaboration until she'd pissed off Corinne. Tori suppressed a shudder.

"Are you cold, Tins?" Alistair put his hand on her shoulder, bringing the wineglass to his lips with the other.

Tori smiled at him and shook her head.

"No," she said. "I just had a sudden chill up my spine."

"Ah." He rubbed her shoulder affectionately.

"I am about ready to get out of here, though." She had no idea what time it was, but she knew that it was likely way past an hour where she would manage a decent amount of sleep. Fortunately, tomorrow was Friday, and all that she had after work was an evening spent together with Alistair to look forward to.

Setting their drinks down, they made their way to the escalator and began navigating the department store maze. At Tori's door they shared a long and steamy kiss before parting ways for the evening. She was dismayed to see that she had stayed out until 12:48 a.m. She was going to have to stay up for at least another hour in order to put together two posts for her site.

Swathed in flannel pajamas with a Diet Coke on her desk, she sat down and started typing. A yawn threatened to escape her lips and she tried to stifle it with her fist. Given she had been at two parties that night she needed two articles for her site. She'd managed to make decent headway with the Swarovski one, but it definitely wasn't publishable. She sighed, saved the draft and headed for bed. Once again, she set her alarm clock for an hour much earlier than she would normally get out of bed. This weekend she was definitely going to sleep in.

*

When the obnoxious beep of her alarm clock went off at

dawn, she blearily reached for her phone. Setting the snooze button to give her fifteen more minutes of much-needed rest, she felt her eyelids droop down again. When the beeping began a second time, fifteen minutes later, she nearly screamed. She had only just managed to fall back to sleep.

Soon after, the smell of coffee drifted through the air as she rubbed her eyes repeatedly to get them to focus. At this rate, she thought, she should be buying coffee in Costco-sized containers. Her eyes finally came into focus and she cringed at her reflection in her hallway mirror. From the looks of it she should be buying anti-aging and de-puffing serum in Costco-sized containers, too.

Setting her coffee on the kitchen table she flipped open her laptop, which sat where she had left it last night, amongst the mess of bags, press releases and gifts that the respective companies had given her the previous evening. Reading over her 1 a.m. draft, Tori tweaked a few paragraphs before adding a title and pressing Publish. She then sent out the requisite tweets to garner more traffic. While her site had been pulling in pretty big numbers lately, Tori was afraid that it may drop. She wanted it to keep expanding, and she figured that the only way to do that was to start getting exclusive scoops on industry insiders to go along with the product and party coverage.

Yawning, she sketched out the bare bones for an article on the Saks collaboration. Unfortunately, she wouldn't have time to finish it before work, so she saved it to the cloud and vowed to finish it during her lunch break.

She just barely made it to work on time—at 8:57 a.m. she had just stepped off of the elevator and into the office. Everyone else was already at their desks, mindlessly working away. Quietly slipping her bag underneath her desk she clicked on her computer monitor. Looking at the list of names she had to call today she let out a sigh. Initially she had figured that it would take her only four or five weeks to get through all of the phone calls. But judging by how her week had gone, she had grossly underestimated the timeline.

Her eyes watering with the strain of holding back another

yawn, Tori realized that it was the first time that she had ever been genuinely excited for her office coffee run. At the moment she needed an espresso almost as much as Munger Carlson needed a lesson in manners. While Alistair's presence had been enough to deter him from hitting on her at the Swarovski party last night, he was still persisting with his late-night dirty text messages. She'd woken up to one this morning and deleted it without even looking to see what it said.

By the end of the morning she had managed to get through the rest of the last names that started with an *A*, but she still had a long way to go. Twenty-five letters' worth of last names to go, to be exact.

During her lunch hour she clicked open another browser and logged into her cloud account. She had never worked on anything personal at the office before, but she figured that as she was doing it off the clock, it wouldn't be an issue.

Wouldn't be an issue unless someone figured out what she was doing, she corrected herself.

Typing like a madwoman she raced to finish the article before her break was over. She had spent some time browsing the Internet in search of other articles that had been posted about the event and so far, she had found five. Not an enormous number, but enough that it would likely dilute traffic to her page.

Five minutes before her lunch break was over Tori hit Publish. Her Saks article focused mainly on the clothes in the capsule collection and included links to participating retailers. From her phone she tweeted out a link to the article along with a series of hashtags from her *On the List* Twitter account. She had amassed a series of followers on the social media site, and while it wasn't numbering into the thousands, it was growing at a steady rate—at the moment she had 943 followers.

With just a few minutes left for lunch, she chowed down on a granola bar that she kept in her desk for emergencies. In her rush to get to work on time she'd forgotten to grab anything for lunch.

"Working on the new product launch over your lunch break?" came Keith's voice behind her. "Good stuff, Tori. I like an employee that is dedicated to their job."

All Tori could do was plaster a fake smile on her face and nod rapidly.

"Keep up the good work," he said, sounding impressed. "I knew that you would give this project your best effort." He turned and headed towards Ryan's office.

Tori felt guilty, but only slightly so. After all, she reasoned, her lunch hour was unpaid, so it didn't matter if she worked on her own stuff. And Keith didn't need to know that the effort that she was putting in was on her own site. And she had been up late at night and early in the morning working on the product launch so it really wasn't a misplaced compliment after all.

Rushing home after work, she checked the analytics on her site and was ecstatic to see that her number of followers and page views had grown. Pleased with the evidence that her sleepless nights and hard work was paying off, she set about tidying her apartment before lying down for a short nap. She and Alistair were going out tonight—he had been evasive about his plans but had finally revealed that he had a surprise planned for her. Remembering his last surprise, the incredibly expensive and unbelievably gorgeous Cartier earrings, Tori was excited but didn't know what to expect.

Her phone suddenly buzzed on her coffee table and she saw a text from Marcus: "Tins! What are you doing tonight?! Private party at the Hazelton Hotel. Come!"

"Can't! Date with Alistair!" she texted back.

Seconds later her phone buzzed and a text from Marcus popped up on her screen again. "Bring him with!" it read. "Scotty Hamilton is in town! It's going to be wild tonight!"

Tori told him that if they ended up in the area that they would pop by, but she had every intention of doing anything but going out. After an exhausting week of work, much of it spent at booze-filled parties, the last thing that she wanted to do was go out and be social. In fact, she was hoping that Alistair's surprise was that they were staying in, having a relaxing dinner and then going straight to bed. To sleep, she clarified.

Nothing doing, Alistair arrived at her place at 6:30 p.m.

She had opted for casual wear tonight—high heels paired with black tights and a black sequined tank top, an effortless look that was the sole result of extreme fatigue. Hair pulled back in a ponytail, she wore minimal makeup and slung a cute triangle purse over her shoulder.

"You look gorgeous as always." Alistair pulled her in for a kiss when she stepped into the lobby.

"Thanks." She smiled tiredly. "You look great as well."

He really did, she thought to herself. His slim-cut navy suit was paired with brown shoes and a white shirt that was unbuttoned at the top. Linking their hands together he led her to the car as they chatted amicably about their day.

"So where are we going?" she asked, buckling herself in.

"I guess you'll have to wait and see," he teased.

Tori smacked him playfully on the arm.

"All right," she conceded, sticking her bottom lip out in an exaggerated pout.

Alistair laughed at her and she smiled back at him as their driver navigated the busy roads to wherever it was that they were heading. Twenty minutes later the car pulled up outside of a dirty-looking brick building. A wooden sign hanging above the door read Rue Morgue Manor.

A morgue? What the hell were they doing at a morgue? she wondered anxiously.

"Um, Alistair," she said meekly. "I know that you said that you wanted this to be a surprise, but what exactly are we doing at a morgue?"

Alistair grinned at her.

"We're taking a taxidermy class," he said proudly.

"Taxidermy!?" she exclaimed, feeling a mixture of revulsion and confusion.

"Yes," he replied. "I Googled you the other day and read the article that you wrote about doing small mammal taxidermy and dressing them up in clothes. You wrote that you couldn't wait to try it out so I thought that I would take you to a class."

Tori's eyes went wide and Alistair suddenly looked unsure of himself. The real Tinsley Tomlinson and her penchant for everything totally fucking bizarre was going to be Tori's downfall. She felt like she might throw up. There was no way that she could participate in a taxidermy class.

"We don't have to go?" he said, looking concerned. "I thought that it might be fun for you is all. Maybe it's not something that you're actually into?"

Tori felt awful. He had set all of this up because he thought that it was something that she would enjoy. But there was no way that she could stomach slitting open a dead animal. God knew what other weird things he had learned about Tinsley during his Google search.

"Alistair," she said gently. "It was so sweet of you to set this up for me, but to be honest it's not something that I'm really into anymore." It was a half-truth considering that she definitely wasn't into it anymore but had also never been into it in the first place. "I don't know if I could stomach it," she continued. "I used to be into some really strange stuff." She made a mental note to do a cursory Google search of Tinsley Tomlinson first thing tomorrow morning. She couldn't believe that she hadn't thought to scope the woman out before deciding to impersonate her.

A look of relief swept across Alistair's face.

"I'm actually glad to hear that," he said with a chuckle. "I thought it was a pretty morbid thing to be into myself, and I don't know if I could stomach it either. I was afraid that I might end up vomiting all over myself during the class. Probably should have just surprised you with a private showing of an Andrei Tarkovsky film . . ." He tapered off.

Andrei Tarkovsky? she thought. Whoever the hell he was she figured that it was something else that Tinsley had written about on the Internet.

"Alistair, I am so sorry," she said sincerely. "I know you went through a lot of trouble to surprise me and I'm sure that you spent a lot of time setting this up."

He waved his hand in an "it was nothing" gesture.

"Maybe next time I'll just ask you what you're into instead of Google stalking and surprising you."

Tori beamed at him gratefully.

"I like that idea," she said. "I've been into a lot of weird things over the years."

"Well"—he grabbed her hand and squeezed it—"what should we do now? I have a bottle of wine in the back and had planned on late-night eats after the class, but it looks like we can go for an early dinner. To tell you the truth," he continued, "I wasn't entirely sure if I would even be able to eat after taking a taxidermy class. I'm a little relieved that you're not into it."

Tori laughed at him.

"I don't think I would have been able to eat anything either. Even the thought of it makes me a little queasy. We could go to a pub?" she suggested. "I know one that has cheap beer and a live band on Friday nights?"

"Done," he said. "What's the address?"

Tori rattled off the address to Grace O'Malley's and their car pulled away from the brick building.

The Irish pub was a run-of-the-mill bar dotted with random knick-knacks and black-and-white photographs hanging on the walls. Christmas lights sprinkled the ceiling and classic rock blasted from the speakers. Sitting on the same side of the booth at a table facing the bar they laughed as Alistair told her about a funny encounter that he'd had with a client earlier that day. Beers in front of them they ordered an array of appetizers, nibbling at them while they talked. Their conversation was easy—they talked about everything from pillow preferences and the merits of Pilates, to favourite ice cream flavours and how to make the fluffiest pancakes.

When the band started up, Tori looked around for the first time. The pub, which had been littered with empty tables when they had first arrived, was now jam-packed. She checked her phone when Alistair went to the washroom, and she saw she had fourteen text messages from Marcus, February, Alexei and a host of other acquaintances who she knew from industry events. All of the messages stated roughly the same thing: "Where are you? You need to be here! This is the greatest party!"

Alistair slid into the booth next to her just as she clicked open the last message.

"Busy?" he asked.

"No, just texts from a bunch of people telling me to go to a party up in Yorkville tonight," she said wearily. "Apparently some guy named Scotty Hamilton is in town."

"We could go if you like?" he offered.

"No. Thank you, though," she said. "I'd prefer a low-key evening. I'm pretty tired out from my week."

"Of course. Do you want to head home for some wine and couch cuddling?" he inquired.

"So much!" she said enthusiastically.

They packaged up the array of leftovers and got into a cab.

"Ugh," Tori said, "I just remembered that we drank my last bottle of wine last night and the liquor stores all closed an hour ago," she lamented, looking at the time.

"I have plenty of wine at my place," he said. "Do you want to spend the night there instead?"

"I'd love to." She smiled.

They wove their way through traffic until they hit the downtown core and pulled into the driveway of a glitzy hotel and residence. She'd known that Alistair lived in an expensive area of the city, but she didn't know he lived in the heart of the financial district. The car pulled up to the curb and Alistair led her to the entrance.

"Good evening, Mr. Chase," a black-uniformed doorman greeted Alistair as he pulled open the door.

"Hello, Vince," Alistair answered back. "How's your evening?"

"Quiet so far, Mr. Chase. But it's a Friday night so I imagine it will be busy before long."

"Not too busy for you, I hope." Alistair shook the doorman's hand. "Have a good night, Vince."

"Same to you, Mr. Chase."

Inside of the lobby, he led her to a small space to the left with tall ceilings. Two banks of black elevators stood there, with the one on the right springing open as soon as he pressed Up.

They kissed in the elevator, which let them off at the twenty-second floor and opened onto a second lobby. A great expanse of marble held a long pond, several velvet-upholstered chairs, a baby grand piano and a concierge desk. Through the floor-to-ceiling windows she could see the night sky lit up by an array of city lights. Another bank of elevators stood to their right. This time, the lift stopped on the thirty-eighth floor. Tori suddenly felt self-conscious about her tiny apartment with her second-hand and discount furnishings.

Unlocking his elaborate white-lacquered door, Alistair ushered Tori inside to one of the nicest condos that she had ever seen. Vaulted ceilings led to hallways on either side of her and an expansive chandelier hung down from the ceiling. Seeing the look of awe on her face, Alistair smiled and offered to give her a tour. Down the hallway to her left was a bedroom that was the size of her kitchen and living room combined. An enormous kitchen in white and black tones overlooked the city and featured a breakfast nook that adjoined a formal dining room. The living room was done up in shades of grey, black and white, and featured a large roaring fireplace that split the living room and dining room into two separate spaces. A forked hallway led off from the living room and into two different rooms. In one room Alistair had set up a den full of books, an old antique desk and a chaise longue. When she stepped into the other room she came upon the biggest bedroom that she had ever seen. She had thought that the first bedroom was the master bedroom due to the sheer size of it, but stepping inside of the second one, she realized how wrong she was. Black velvet curtains ran the length of the room, taking up one entire corner of the condo. A king-size bed sat against the far wall with a television and sitting area in the corner. A dressing table, walk-in closet and ensuite featuring a double sink, a shower that looked big enough to hold a party and claw-foot bathtub adjoined the room.

Tori suddenly felt inadequate.

What was Alistair doing dating her? She could never afford anything close to this. She would probably never make enough money in her lifetime to even rent out a place like this. Alistair should be dating someone like Corinne, she thought.

Apparently she was very wealthy.

"It's a little much for just me," he said after showing her around. "But it's convenient for work, I like the building and I like to have a decent amount of space."

"Decent amount of space?" Tori choked out. "Your ensuite is the size of my entire apartment."

Alistair laughed.

"Yes, and I much prefer your apartment. It's cozier. And it has you in it," he teased. His smile faltered when he saw the look of discomfort on her face. "Is everything okay, Tinsley?"

"Yes," she lied, continuing after a pause. "I just . . . Your place. It's so beautiful. And I could never afford anything like this in a million years . . ." She trailed off, twisting a piece of her hair self-consciously.

"Ah," he said knowingly. "I'm sorry. I didn't mean to make you feel uncomfortable by bringing you here. You should never feel ashamed of where you live and what you can or can't afford. I like you for you, and not for where you live or what you do or what you wear. The same way that you like me for me, and not for the number in my bank account or for what I wear or where I live. Okay?" He looked at her sincerely.

"Okay," she said timidly, starting to feel a little better.

With that Alistair had her rummage up some wine and wineglasses from the kitchen while he set to work in the living room—turning on the fireplace, dimming the lights and putting on some soft jazz. Tori had managed to pick out a pair of glasses from the kitchen but selecting a bottle of wine was another thing entirely. Alistair came to check on her after a while and found her staring at his wall of wine looking completely perplexed.

"Need some help?" he asked.

She nodded rapidly.

"All right, let's see." He skimmed the rack. "Pick a region."

"Um, how about France?" she suggested, picking the first place that came to mind.

"France. Good choice." He moved to a middle section of the wine wall. "How about Châteauneuf-du-Pape?"

"Sure," she agreed. She had no idea what the hell

Châteauneuf-du-Pape tasted like, but she was more than willing to give it a try.

Pulling an old-fashioned-looking bottle out of the wine rack, he set it on the counter and pulled out a corkscrew.

"Would you mind grabbing a couple of plates and napkins and bringing the leftovers?" he asked.

Tori happily obliged and then followed him back into the living room. Snuggled up on the white leather couch with a fuzzy black blanket draped over top of them, they clinked their glasses together and Tori nestled herself under the crook of his arm.

"I wish we could spend every night like this," she sighed happily while taking another sip of wine. "This is perfect."

"Likewise." He smiled down at her. Alistair began to gently stroke her neck and Tori put down her glass, afraid she would nod off and spill her wine.

Several hours later she woke up in the fluffy confines of Alistair's enormous feather-duvet-covered bed.

"Good morning," he whispered over at her, his head resting on the pillow.

"Good morning," she whispered, smiling back.

"You passed out on me last night." He smirked. "Right in the middle of my story. You were snoring like a freight train."

"Nooooo!" Tori was mortified. "Was I really? I was so tired last night. Christ, I'm surprised you could stand sleeping next to me if I was making that much noise."

He laughed.

"I'm only teasing, you weren't snoring. But I did have to carry you to bed. You were like a rag doll. Completely passed out."

"Oh God," she said self-consciously. "I'm sorry! I was so exhausted from the last week."

"No apologies needed." He smiled. "I'm just happy to have you around. Conscious or unconscious," he joked. "I did take off your pants, though, I hope you don't mind. I figured that you wouldn't want to sleep in your pants."

"Definitely not," she said, smiling back at him.

"Good." He nodded approvingly. "Now, do you want to go out for breakfast or should I order in from room service?" he asked.

"Room service?" she questioned. "In your condo?"

He laughed again.

"Yes, since I live in a hotel I have access to room service, maids, maintenance and the concierge." Fumbling through his nightstand he pulled out a leather-bound menu and handed it to her.

Tori propped herself up on the pillows and perused the menu.

"I'll have the French toast," she decided.

"Good choice." He nodded. "That's one of my hangover favourites." Picking up the black cordless phone from his nightstand he pressed zero and requested room service. Adding in an egg-white omelette, bacon and hash browns for himself, he also ordered a bottle of champagne and a jug of orange juice. Clicking off the line, he rolled over to her.

"Breakfast will be served in thirty to forty minutes," he declared.

"Hmm," said Tori. "That gives us just enough time to finish what we never got to start last night." She leaned over and planted a kiss on his cheek.

Alistair placed his hand behind her neck and pressed his lips against hers. The soft kisses turned more passionate and before long both of them were snuggled up together, relaxed, spent and satisfied. She clicked on the television set and they spent a few minutes watching the news before the deep *bing-bong* of the doorbell announced the arrival of their breakfast.

Swathing himself in a fluffy white robe, Alistair threw an identical one at Tori. She picked it up, marveling at the softness of it.

By the time she entered the kitchen, the waiter had pulled their meals out of the warming box and was setting the plates down at the breakfast bar. Cheque signed, Alistair held the door for the waiter while he navigated the wheeled table out of his condo. An uncorked bottle of champagne sat in an ice bucket between their two plates and Alistair poured them each a generous dollop of the sparkling substance before adding a splash of orange juice.

"Cheers." He held up his glass and they toasted.

After breakfast and breakfast mimosas in bed, Tori looked at the time. It was nearly noon and she had so much work to do.

"Damn," she said regretfully. "I need to go. I have a ton of things to work on today."

Alistair planted a kiss on her forehead.

"Damn is right, but I understand," he said. "I love how dedicated you are to your work."

She pulled on last night's clothes while Alistair threw on a pair of jeans and a T-shirt, ordered her an Uber and then accompanied her down to the lobby. He kissed her on the lips and closed the car door behind her, but not before promising to pop by later that evening with takeout.

As the car sped down the street, Tori leaned back on the headrest and closed her eyes. She felt totally recharged, completely relaxed and ready to face the day. It was amazing what twelve hours of sleep, a delicious breakfast and several mimosas could do for a person.

She had almost forgotten that she had an event to attend tonight—Edelman PR was hosting the pre-launch party for one of the city's newest bars and she texted Alistair to see if he wanted to join her. She already knew that the regular gang of fashionistas would be there, but she was always happy if she could spend more time with her boyfriend.

At home, she worked feverishly on her Impotentia event plans and press release. She ran the numbers, sent out inquiries and started making up potential guest lists. Hours later her phone buzzed, shaking her out of her work reverie, and she realized just how late it was. Alistair had texted to her say that he would be over in the next hour. Panicked, she looked at the clock. Good God, she had spent nearly six straight hours working.

By the time Alistair arrived she had managed to get her hair and makeup together but was lounging around in a bathrobe.

He dropped two bags of Chinese food on the table then rummaged through her cupboards in search of plates, napkins and forks.

An hour later they were in a car on their way to Spin—a brand new underground ping-pong bar that played the hottest new music and served up a menu of imaginative drinks. Walking up the red carpet, the clipboard girl ushered them in past a line of waiting people. After all, as the ostensible and now recognizable editor of *Fashionista*, Tori didn't wait in line.

Downstairs the place was packed. Ten ping-pong tables were placed around the room with several arm's lengths between them. She spotted the tall blond hair and sunglasses that signified Marcus's presence and made a beeline for him.

"Tins, darling!" he exclaimed, air-kissing and hugging her. "You missed out on a real rager last night. God, if this hangover ever goes away, I swear on all that is holy, I will never go to another Scotty Hamilton party ever again." He sipped his requisite martini and winced. "Jesus Christ. Hair of the dog isn't even helping." He shook his head in disgust. Then, shrugging his shoulders, he polished off the drink.

Tori looked at him, open mouthed and aghast.

"You know what they say, Tins. Get back on the wagon. I'm not a quitter," he informed her.

Alistair tried to hide his smile as he greeted Marcus, plucking two glasses of wine from a waiter walking by with a tray. Marcus reached across them and also grabbed a glass, replacing the one he took with his empty martini tumbler.

"Lord, I need to get some snacks into me," he moaned as a canape-carrying waitress paused at a group in front of them.

All around the room high-heeled women and men in suits stood around the ping-pong tables. Amusingly, they were at a bar whose entire niche was table tennis but there wasn't a single person playing it.

As the evening wore on, likely owing to several drinks, the crowd began to loosen up. Suddenly there were ping-pong balls flying everywhere. People crowded around to watch the guests play—badly, Tori thought. Not that she was any kind of table tennis star herself. It was funny to watch men and women in designer dresses, sky-high heels and a drink in one hand trying to play table tennis, though. Laughing at the scene she snapped a few photos before a loud ruckus in the far corner drew her and Alistair's attention away. A large crowd had gathered around a table and the two of them wandered over to investigate.

"Oh. My. God," Tori said in disbelief when she saw what was going on. Behind her, Alistair began to laugh uncontrollably. It appeared that Marcus had managed to talk the bartender into bringing him several tumblers full of liquor and he was currently playing a game of beer pong on the ping-pong table. Opposite him was a woman wearing a feather dress who Tori had seen at several events. She appeared to be highly inebriated at this point and her aim was so bad that it looked like she was trying to hit the crowd instead of the cups.

She watched as Marcus threw the ball. It arched up and came down in a picture-perfect parabola, deftly sinking into one of the glasses while the surrounding crowd cheered. Marcus was in his element. Hangover clearly abated, he worked the crowd, urging them to cheer louder with his hands. His opponent picked up the cup that held the ball, pulled it out and began chugging.

It was at that point that Tori noticed for the first time that the cup was full of a clear liquid. She wondered what it could be. Had Marcus finally come to his senses and decided to drink water? She watched the woman in the feather dress wipe her lips and then stumble away. No, Tori thought to herself. Surely he wouldn't? Marcus picked up a glass from his end, apparently thirsty due to his opponent's poor aim, and took a large gulp. She had never seen him drink anything but liquor before, and she suddenly realized that yes, Marcus actually had. He was playing beer pong with vodka.

"Your friend Marcus is a bit of a wild one," Alistair said, still sounding very amused.

"My friend Marcus has a bit of a drinking problem," she replied.

"Now that you mention it, he does seem to be drunk a lot,"

he agreed.

"He's playing beer pong with vodka," she said exasperatedly. "He needs an intervention."

At that point a waiter came by with fresh glasses of liquor and Marcus ordered a bystander to arrange them into a triangle.

"Who's next?" he taunted. "Who else feels like losing!"

A tall, bearded man in a blue-velvet jacket stepped forward and picked up the ball.

"Oh me, oh my!" Marcus fanned himself at the sight of his attractive opponent. "Honey, I wouldn't mind it if you dominated me tonight," Marcus said, clearly referring to a different kind of game he wanted to play.

The man laughed at Marcus and shook his head.

"Tell you what," the man said. "If you win, I'll be your shirtless butler for a day. If you lose, I'm giving my maid the day off."

"You're on!" Marcus looked elated. "You throw first, darling. I'm going to wipe the floor with you so take every advantage that you can get."

The crowd had oohed and aahed throughout the entire exchange, and they were now picking sides to cheer for.

A smirk appeared on the man's face and the crowd went silent as he lined up his shot, tossed the ball and dropped it with perfect precision into the middle glass.

Marcus's jaw dropped open as he stared down at the pong ball now floating in the cup.

"Bottoms up, *darling*," the man laughed, miming drinking with his thumb and his pinkie. The crowd roared with laughter as a flustered-looking Marcus picked up the glass and drank the liquor.

*

They arrived back at Alistair's place just before midnight, collapsing into his king-size bed and quickly drifting off to sleep. Tori had been unfortunate enough to run into Corinne right as they were leaving Spin. The aggressive blonde had shot daggers at Tori and snarkily pushed past her, hitting her shoulder against Tori's as hard as she could. So much for her and Corinne having an amicable conversation, she thought.

Corinne's attitude showed her that no amount of talking was going to turn the tide of her opinion on Tori. Alistair had gone to get their coats at the time, so he didn't see her, and Tori didn't bother mentioning the incident to him. She wanted Corinne as far away from her relationship with Alistair as possible— something that was proving to be difficult given her presence at industry events.

After a quick breakfast she bid Alistair goodbye and headed back to her place to work. For most of the morning she wrote and polished a piece about her night at Spin. Her article included descriptions of the décor, drinks and music, as well as photos of the venue and of people playing table tennis. She'd also written about the vodka pong fiasco, hoping that it would give people a few laughs, which would work to increase her site's traffic.

Marcus had lost the game—badly. He hadn't known it at the time, but his velvet-clad challenger turned out to be an ex-NBA player. Apparently, the difference between sinking basketballs and ping-pong balls was negligible.

With Alistair's help she had put Marcus in a cab with Alexei and made him promise to call her if he needed help managing their inebriated friend. She would have been more concerned about Marcus considering the state that he was in had she not witnessed him drink far more on several occasions.

"Getting Spun at Spin: Ping-Pong and Vodka Pong at Toronto's Newest Sports Bar," she titled the piece. Clicking Publish, Tori pulled out the papers that she had amassed for Maggie's SPCA fundraiser and got to work.

Chapter 10:
Family Matters

The next few weeks passed in a fairly predictable manner: her usual Staten work sandwiched between early-morning and after-work meetings with Sierra, and attending and writing about fashion, beauty and bar events at night while spending as much time as she could with Alistair. She now had a spread of beauty products and clothing that she kept at his place and he had a couple of items of clothing that he kept at hers. She was still dead tired every Friday, but she was enjoying every exhilarating moment of the industry events. And every time she gained new followers, page views and mentions, she got a rush of adrenaline. It was like some sort of drug. She had taken to eavesdropping on people's conversations to glean insider info about people in the industry and, to that end, her site had shot up in popularity. Everyone was wondering who the man or woman behind it was.

She'd made sure to Google "Tinsley Tomlinson" shortly after Alistair's failed surprise and Maggie hadn't been kidding when she said that there was barely anything about the writer online. Aside from a few far away photos of her wearing enormous sunglasses, Tori discovered that she had no social media accounts, there was no information about her on the *Fashionista* website, and there was no indication of where she lived. After reading a few of her articles, all of which touted exceedingly strange trends, Tori came to the conclusion that Tinsley Tomlinson was a new breed of hipster. For Tori's intents and purposes, that suited her just fine. At the moment, everything in her life was going perfectly. She had an amazingly supportive, successful, handsome, fun and down-to-earth boyfriend; she was living out her dream job; her website was racking up the readers; and Sierra and Keith were impressed by the effort she was putting in at the office.

While her guilt at fraudulently gaining entrance to parties had mostly waned (she figured she more than made up for it by the press she was giving the companies through her website), she still felt terrible about lying to Alistair.

*

Alistair kissed her goodbye on Friday morning as he left her apartment. Tori's parents were in town visiting her this weekend so she and Alistair wouldn't get to spend any time together. She was taking a half day off at work to meet her parents, who would be staying at her place.

Work emails dealt with by mid-morning, she clicked open her *Fashionist* account and a flurry of emails filled her inbox. Invites, thank-yous, product offerings, product pitches and correspondences from acquaintances waited to be opened. She scrolled through and clicked on a couple before opening up one from Susan Rich. She knew that Susan was on the board of directors of several charities, and Tori's curiosity was piqued. The subject line read "Fashion Cares Fashion Show Proposal." Intrigued, Tori clicked it open.

Dear Tinsley,

It's been so great getting to know you over the last few weeks.

As you are the fashion editor of Fashionista I would like to personally invite you to walk in the runway show for Fashion Cares on Friday, June 29. With you being one of the foremost authorities on fashion, we would be honoured to have you as one of our special guests for the evening. Fashion Cares raises funds for a host of charitable organizations and over the years we have donated more than $38 million to worthy causes, positively impacting thousands of lives. If you are interested in donating your time to this important event, kindly let me know and we can go from there.

Regards,

Susan

Tori's jaw dropped open. Fashion Cares wanted her to walk in their charity runway show? She couldn't believe it! She scrambled to reply to the email, afraid that if she left it, she might get an email from Susan saying that she had mistakenly sent it to her and that it had been intended for someone else.

Dear Susan,

So great to hear from you! I would be honoured to be a part of the Fashion Cares runway show and I look forward to hearing more about my role.

Cheers,

T.

Beaming with pride, she pressed Send and then sat back in her chair. All of her fifteen-hour days, late-night writing and tired mornings were paying off in spades! Not only had she amassed an online following of just under 10,000, made tons of industry contacts and gotten to go to some amazing events, but she was now being touted as a "foremost authority" on fashion by one of Toronto's most well-known socialites! She immediately texted Alistair, Maggie and Marcus the exciting news. The first two responded immediately with exuberant congratulations. Marcus's reply came in much later, though it was no less enthusiastic. Shortly after that she was out of the office and on her way home. It had been more than six months since she had last seen her parents. They had all been together for Christmas in Sudbury, but since then her mom and dad had been vacationing all over South America.

Rushing upstairs she did a quick inspection of her place. She had been trying to keep it clean all week, but she wanted to make sure that there wasn't any evidence of Alistair left behind. Or of Tinsley. She didn't think that her parents, the beacon of moral superiority, would approve of her lying about who she was in an attempt to jumpstart her career.

Her parents would be sleeping on the pullout couch in the living room. As usual, she would offer them her bed, but she knew that they would decline. Actually, maybe she wouldn't offer them her bed this time, she thought, cringing. She and Alistair had been sleeping in it all week and she hadn't had time to change the sheets.

The cramped quarters of her apartment would be tight for three people, but her mom and dad were only spending two nights in the city and, fortunately, the forecast called for sun. Her phone started buzzing and Tori pressed 9 to let her parents in. Minutes later there was a knock at her door and she was nearly bowled over by her mom as soon as she opened it.

"Mom!" she exclaimed. "Dad!" She was so happy to see

them. They always had a fun time when they were together and she was just sorry that her sister was unable to join them. While they did talk frequently, Zoom and phone dates were not the same as seeing her mom and dad in person. "I've missed you guys! How was the drive down?"

"Tori." Her mom continued to squeeze her tightly. "I've missed you so much." Tori could hear the telltale sign of tears welling up in her mother's eyes. She was a total softie where her daughters were concerned.

"I missed you, too, Mom!" Tori managed to wiggle her way out of her mother's grasp and put her arms around her dad. He stopped struggling with their luggage momentarily to give her a hug back, planting a quick kiss on her cheek.

"Tori, how are you?" he asked.

"I'm great, Dad!" she said enthusiastically. She looked at their luggage and then looked at her dad. Her parents were planning on leaving on Sunday, and yet they appeared to have brought enough clothing with them for a month-long vacation.

"Don't look at me," he said, denying he had anything to do with the obscene number of bags. "That's all your mother's doing. She thinks she's going to do fifty outfit changes per day or something," he chuckled.

Her mom lightly swatted him on the arm.

"Oh, Harold," she said.

Tori reached into the refrigerator and tossed a beer to her dad and a bottle of white wine to her mom.

"Do I get a glass or do I have to drink it straight from the bottle?" she inquired.

Tori, already reaching into the cupboard for a wineglass, snorted.

"If this turns out to be anything like Christmas you may as well drink it straight from the bottle," she laughed as her dad started chuckling. Her mom smirked, pretending to not know what she was talking about. Tori still couldn't stop laughing about finding her mom passed out underneath the spruce tree last Christmas. What had started off as a genial game of charades had ended with her mother lying face down beneath the tinsel-laden boughs.

She grabbed a wineglass out for herself and they all sat in her living room chatting.

"So, how are things going at work?" her dad asked her. He wasn't one for small talk, so conversation with him usually came down to a few things: the weather, work, school (when she had been in university), Maggie and her sister. He was a man of few words who liked to get straight to the point. Her mom, on the other hand, could talk for hours.

"Work is going really well," she said. "My boss has put me on a special project and I'm putting together the launch for a new product," she said proudly.

"Good for you, sweetie!" said her mom.

"Good," her dad said. "Good to hear."

"So, what are we going to do this weekend?" her mom asked. It wasn't often that she was in the big city, but when she was, she had a tendency to want to explore everything. Tori had put together a tentative list of things for them to do during her lunch hour the other day. There were so many things to choose from that she was just going to give the list to her parents and let them pick out what they wanted to do.

It was late in the afternoon by the time that they had settled on a plan for the evening, having spent most of their time catching up and chatting about things on the news and her parents' crazy next-door neighbours. They popped down to Hunter's Landing for some appetizers and drinks where Tori told them all about Maggie's upcoming fundraiser and how Maggie had put her in charge of the marketing.

"It sounds like you're doing really well for yourself, sweetie." Her mom smiled. "You know that we're proud of you. I know that you've always wanted to be a writer, but it really sounds like you're doing well with marketing, and it sounds like you're happy with it," she said, beaming.

Tori smiled, but she felt guilty. She was happy all right. Yes, it was great being given more responsibility at work, but what she was really focused on was her writing career.

After leaving the restaurant, they decided to wander down to the harbourfront to enjoy the sunshine and take in the sights. Strolling around the waterfront they watched boats sail by as they navigated their way through a myriad of cyclists, runners, tourists and citizens all soaking up the sun. Tori was just snapping a photo of her mom and dad in front of the water when she heard someone to her left yell out "Tinsley!" and she was nearly knocked over by Marcus's signature head lock and air kiss combo.

Oh fuck. Tori's stomach dropped to her feet. It was just her luck.

"Tinsley?" Her mom's brow furrowed in confusion at the sunglasses-sporting man who currently had her daughter in a death grip. "Who is—"

Tori quickly cut her off.

"This is Marcus, Mom! Marcus, meet my mom!"

Marcus grabbed her mom around the neck and began gushing about how lovely it was to meet her and how much he loved her daughter. Her mom's eyes went wide as she looked around in confusion.

"Yes, but . . . why are you calling her Tin—" she tried again as Marcus suddenly spotted her dad and grabbed him around the shoulders.

"And Mr. Tomlinson!" Marcus continued, ignoring her mom. "So sorry to hear about your below-the-belt problem. You've got a great daughter there." He winked at Tori's dad.

"I . . . what?" her dad asked, confused. "My below-the-belt problem? What are you talking about?"

"It's okay, Mr. Tomlinson. Your secret is safe with me," Marcus insisted. "And for the record, from my own personal experience, I can assure you that Impotentia is extremely effective, if you know what I mean."

Tori's dad looked aghast.

"Anyway, sorry," Tori interrupted as Marcus opened his mouth, oblivious to the embarrassment that he was causing her. "It's great to see you, Marcus!" She grabbed her parents by their elbows and steered them in the opposite direction. "But we have to go now! We have early dinner reservations! We can't be late!"

"Okay then, Tins," Marcus said, waving goodbye and blowing her an air kiss. "I'll see you on Monday night! Great to meet you, Mom and Dad!" He strolled away, his gigantic man purse in tow.

Ushering her parents along in front of her, Tori's mom looked back at her in confusion.

"What on earth was that about?" she asked. "Why did that man call you Tinsley?"

Isn't that the million-dollar question, Tori thought.

"Uhh . . ." Tori looked around as her dad cut in.

"And why does that man think that I need Impotentia?" he asked indignantly.

"It's a long story," Tori, looking guilty, tried to beg off.

Her mother gave her an appraising look.

"Well, then it's fortunate that we're here for two days."

Tori sighed.

"Okay, let's go and find a quiet booth at the Brewhouse down the street. I'm going to need a few drinks for this one."

They walked along in silence as Tori quietly contemplated how her parents were going to handle it—after all, they'd just told her how proud they were of her. Now they were going to find out that their daughter was a grade-A liar who was leading a phony double life. She felt like crying.

Settling into a corner booth in the unassuming pub, Tori ordered up a double vodka soda and took a hefty drink when the waitress placed it in front of her. Her parents sat in silence, waiting.

"Tori," her mom finally said. "What the hell is going on?"

"I've done something," Tori said. "Something that you're probably going to be ashamed of, and something that I should probably be ashamed of but I'm not. Well, I am very ashamed of one aspect of it, but I have zero regrets about the rest of it."

Her mom and dad had identical looks of puzzlement on their faces as they waited for her to continue.

"The reason Marcus referred to me as Tinsley is because that's who he thinks I am," she began. "This whole fiasco started off over a month ago and it just kind of spiraled out of control. You remember my old fashion and style website, *Fashionist?*" Her parents nodded in unison. "Well," Tori continued, "I received an invite to an industry party—I thought that my work was finally being recognized but it turned out that I was only invited as an accident. There's another website, a huge, internationally known online magazine called *Fashionista*, and one of the editors is named Tinsley Tomlinson." A look of understanding was starting to form on her mother's face. "I only intended to go to the one event, just to see what it was like, but I drank far too much because I was so nervous about being fraudulently invited and not knowing anyone, and I blacked out and passed out all of my business cards, and met loads of people, and took stupid photos and generally made an ass out of myself." She paused and took a deep breath. "And I woke up the next morning with no memory and all of these text messages and emails and event invites, and I was so mortified that I wanted to crawl into a hole and die. And then I talked to Maggie about it and she encouraged me to keep up the charade to kickstart my writing career. And I don't feel guilty about any of it," she said. "I've gotten so many great contacts and been to so many amazing events even if people do think that I am someone else . . ." She trailed off.

Her parents stared at her, open-mouthed and silent.

"Uh," Tori said after a beat. "Are you guys going to say anything?"

Her mom found her voice first.

"That's completely crazy," she said. "But if it's giving you experience and it's not hurting anyone then I don't see the harm in it."

Tori was floored. The last thing that she expected was for her mom to be supportive of her deception.

"But you said that there was one part of it that you're ashamed of. Which part?" her mom asked curiously. "You haven't been skipping out or slacking off at work because of this alter ego, have you?"

"God, no," Tori said firmly. "I know what pays my bills and I would never jeopardize that, not in a million years."

"So, what is it?" her mom prompted her.

"Well," she said guiltily, "I met someone . . . when I was pretending to be Tinsley." Her parents both grimaced. "And I was about to tell him my actual name when Marcus came out of nowhere—he does that, as you saw—and told him that I'm Tinsley and that I'm the editor of this famous magazine," she said desperately. "And I really like him, and everything between us is so perfect, but he thinks that I'm someone I'm not," she said miserably. "I've been lying to him this entire time about my name and my career, and I've been too much of a coward to tell him the truth, and I feel horrible about it. So awful. So, so awful," she concluded. And with that Tori downed the rest of her drink.

"Oh, that's horrible," her mom said, recoiling.

"Tori . . ." Her dad shook his head disapprovingly.

"I know!" she wailed. "I don't know what to do. I tried to tell him the other night and the delivery man interrupted me, and I'm scared that if I do tell him that he'll think I'm some kind of liar and he'll break up with me, and things are so perfect, and he's so perfect, and we're so perfect, and I couldn't take it if he dumped me." The sentences were just spilling out of her now. She had found it difficult to start, but now that she had the floodgates were open and she couldn't hold anything back. "Everything else that he knows and loves about me is true," she said, trying to make her parents understand. "Everything except for my name and my job," she finished.

"Love?" Her mom's eyebrows were currently sitting near her hairline.

"Mom!" Tori said exasperatedly. "Is that seriously the only thing that you took away from everything that I just said?"

"Love is serious, Tori. You've fallen in love with this man? And he's fallen in love with you?"

Her dad sat back and observed. He could handle a lot of things, but the romance department where his daughters were concerned was not one of them.

"Yes," Tori admitted. "I'm completely head over heels in love with him. And I know he feels the same way about me."

"Well, you can't very well carry on a healthy relationship where one partner is dishonest about who they are," her mom cautioned. "I can't imagine how devastating it will be for him when he finds out the truth. But you'd better tell him before someone else does," she continued. "That's a big kind of betrayal, and if you don't tell him first, you'll look even more dishonest."

"You're right," Tori said, sighing. "I know you're right. And Maggie told me the same thing. I just don't know how to tell him." She paused and took a sip of her drink. "Can we talk about something else?" she begged. "Anything? Please?"

There was a pregnant pause before her mom broke the silence.

"You mentioned being mortified the day after the party?" she inquired. "What exactly did you do there?"

"You didn't pass out underneath of any trees?" her dad asked, trying to lighten the mood. "I hear it runs in the family." He smirked at her mother, who gave him a playful smack.

"No passing out underneath of any trees," Tori said. "But I did jump on a waiter's back, deep throat an ice sculpture, make out with a billionaire and do shots on stage with a famous rapper."

Her parents' eyes went wide and her mom uttered the word "Jesus" under her breath.

"Well, you come by it honestly," said her dad resignedly. "Your mother was a wild one back in her day. Luckily for her I came along and tamed her otherwise she'd probably still be swinging from chandeliers."

"Oh, Harold." Her mother smacked him again. Turning to her daughter she gave her a small smile. "Well, honey, while I don't condone what you've done to this poor man and I hope that you muster up enough courage to tell him the truth, I see no harm in you getting out there and making contacts and gaining writing experience," she said definitively. "As long as your marketing work isn't suffering, I say carry on as long as you can."

"Thanks, Mom." Tori felt relieved. She couldn't believe how

good it felt to get everything off of her chest. "Oh," she said, suddenly remembering something else. "And then there's this woman named Corinne who absolutely hates me because I'm dating Alistair," she went on. "That's his name, by the way. And I wouldn't normally care, but she's in the industry and she's really vindictive and super rich, and she ruined the life of the last girl that she decided she didn't like."

"Good God," her mom said. "You're living a real-life soap opera. Is there anything else? Maggie hasn't faked her death or gotten involved in a clandestine love affair with a cabinet minister, has she?"

"No," Tori said earnestly. "That's it. All of it. And a good thing, too. I don't think that I could deal with anything else."

Her conscience felt lighter, if only slightly so. It felt good to be able to talk to her parents about the secret life that she had been leading. Of course, they wholeheartedly did not approve of her continuing to lie to the man that she loved, but aside from voicing their concerns and offering up their advice, there was nothing that they could do.

Noncommittal to her parents' "come clean to him" urgings, she changed the subject and began telling them about all of the exciting events she'd been to and all of the contacts that she'd made.

"And just this morning I received an email from one of the city's most well-known socialites and she wants me to walk in a charity fashion show," she said proudly.

"Wow," her mom said sincerely. "It sounds like you've managed to accomplish quite a lot in a very short amount of time. Good for you, sweetie. Now, tell me more about your man."

The three of them continued on with their conversation that evening, eventually deciding to just eat dinner at the pub. They spent the rest of their night at a cozy fireside lounge where the serious conversation from earlier that day stayed all but forgotten as they reminisced, laughed and made new memories.

*

The next morning Tori woke up to the smell of fresh coffee

and pancakes emanating from her kitchen. Yawning, she dragged herself out of bed only to discover that while she had slept her parents had gone to the grocery store, stocked her cupboards full of food and whipped up breakfast. Her tiny dining table was laden with pancakes, berries, whipped cream and orange juice. *I have such a great family*, she thought as she popped a forkful of pancakes into her mouth.

From Tori's list of things to do her mom had picked out a handful of options. Collectively they settled on spending the morning down at the harbourfront where a vegetarian food festival was taking place. But after a lazy morning spent drinking coffee in their pajamas the sun was midway through the sky by the time that they arrived at the docks. People, with their pets and kids in tow, were everywhere, wandering around to the different vendors, sipping on drinks served in pineapples and coconuts, snacking on festival fare and chatting to each other.

Sunglasses perched on top of her head, Tori checked out the assorted offerings of a chocolate vendor while her mom and dad looked at a table full of bath products next to her. Not finding anything to purchase, she wandered over to her parents and stood back watching the crowd.

Suddenly, out of the corner of her eye she spotted a familiar face. Doing a double take, she quickly realized that it was Alistair. Her eyes darted slightly sideways and she took in the tall, blonde-haired woman wearing a tank top and short shorts who was walking beside him. She watched as the woman gave him a playful shove and Alistair, smiling, put his arm around her shoulder affectionately. Tori felt like someone had punched her in the stomach. Had Alistair been cheating on her all of this time?

Just then he looked in her direction and their eyes locked together. She expected his grin to falter at suddenly being caught in the company of another woman, but instead his smile widened. He said something to the woman, and they began walking towards Tori. Both Alistair and his female companion were beaming.

"Tinsley!" He gave a very hurt and confused-looking Tori a

hug and a kiss on the cheek. "This is my sister, Ashley." He gestured to the blonde woman beside him.

An overwhelming sense of relief swept over Tori. "Ashley, this is Tinsley."

Ashley beamed at Tori before enveloping her in a hug.

"So great to finally meet you!" she gushed. "Alistair has told me so much about you."

Wide-eyed, all Tori could do was stand there with a dumbstruck smile on her face. The sudden appearance of both Alistair and his sister had rendered her speechless. What were the odds of them running into her and her family on a Saturday afternoon in the fourth largest city in North America? At this point she figured that she was being punished by a higher power. Although she admitted that his condo's proximity to the harbourfront and the popularity of the waterfront festivals may have played a part in it, too.

Just then Alistair glanced to her right and noticed her parents, who were standing slightly behind her. His grin widened and Tori's heart sank to her toes. *This is it*, she thought, *it's all over*. She couldn't believe that it was going to go down like this. She wasn't even going to get a chance to confess to Alistair in private. Her mom, her dad, Alistair's sister and half of the waterfront were going to get a front-row ticket to Tori's world crashing down around her.

"Hi," her mom said from behind her, stepping forward to shake Alistair's hand. "I'm Olivia," she said. "Tinsley's mom."

Tori blinked. She could barely believe her ears. Tinsley's mom? Holy hell, her mother was going to go along with it?

"Lovely to meet you." She shook Ashley's hand next and then gestured to her husband. "And this is Tinsley's dad, Harold." She nudged him.

"Uh, hi," her dad said uncertainly, extending his hand to the Chase siblings.

Tori shot a look of desperate gratitude at her mother and received a quick wink in return.

"How are you guys enjoying your stay so far?" Alistair inquired.

"We're having a very lovely time, thanks." Her mom smiled. "Tinsley is a great host. We were actually just on our way to have some lunch if you and Ashley would care to join us?"

Tori's eyes went wide and she stared at Alistair, silently willing him to decline.

"That actually sounds very nice," Alistair said with a grin. "What do you say, Ashley? Are you up for some lunch?"

"Definitely." His sister nodded. "I've really been looking forward to meeting you." She smiled at Tori. "I haven't seen my brother this happy in a very long time."

Despite the warmth of the sun, Tori suddenly felt very cold. Under normal circumstances she would have been happy to have lunch with her boyfriend, his sister and her parents. But given that her circumstances were anything but, a group lunch was the last thing that she wanted. God knew how long lunch would go on for. And God knew how long her parents would be able to keep from slipping up. Her chances of being found out had just skyrocketed. She felt her pulse quicken.

Maybe she could just fake a sudden bout of food poisoning? No, she thought. More lies was the last thing she needed.

"Where should we go for lunch, Tor-insley?" her mom caught herself at the last moment. Tori grimaced. It was already starting.

"I have no idea," Tori said, unable to concentrate on anything but her impending doom. "Alistair? Any lunch suggestions?"

"How do you feel about Italian, Mr. and Mrs. Tomlinson?" Alistair asked. "There's a great place a few blocks away that Ashley and I go to all of the time."

"Italian sounds great!" said her mom. "The Italians make some great wine. And pasta," she added as an afterthought.

Fantastic, thought Tori. It sounded like her mom would be getting into the liquor. Hopefully she would just pass out at the table instead of blowing Tori's cover.

"So, Alistair," her mom chatted as they walked along. "Tinsley says that you're in finance?"

Alistair began telling them about his job and then shifted the subject to them.

"We're both retired," her mom said. "Harold and I spend half of the year vacationing to get away from the snow."

Minutes later they walked in to a quaint little Italian restaurant just north of Lakeshore. It was decorated in a muted palette of soft greys, and enormous circular orbs hung down from ceiling lending a soft glow to the space. An enormous wall of wine sat on display behind the bar and Tori watched as the wait staff scurried around the tables. The restaurant was busy, and the bustling lunchtime crowd nearly drowned out the music coming from the speakers. She half hoped that they would be turned away, but Alistair managed to secure them a spot.

At a large circular table her mom and dad sat to the left of Tori, and Alistair and his sister sat to the right. Their waiter placed long black menus in front of them and whisked off to get them water. Picking up the wine list, Alistair consulted with her parents before selecting two vintages. When the bottles were brought to the table he offered her mom the first taste.

"Great choice of wine, Alistair," she said approvingly as the waiter poured the burgundy liquid into the glasses.

"Thanks." He smiled. "I'm a bit of a wino."

"You and Olivia have that in common," her dad teased as a chuckle of laughter went around the table.

Entrees ordered, they all grabbed a piece of warm focaccia from the basket in the centre of the table. Except for Tori. Her appetite was non-existent. She was too nervous to think of food.

"So, tell me how you two first met," her mom said to Alistair, dabbing at her lips with her napkin.

"Well, Mrs. Tomlinson, the first time that I met your daughter she nearly face-planted into me. And the second time I met her, ten minutes later, she swept me off of my feet." He paused. "Literally. She fell over and dragged me down with her," Alistair finished as her mom, dad and Ashley all started laughing.

By the time that they finally parted ways, it was nearing dinner. To Tori's great shock and surprise, it had all gone fairly smoothly. She still couldn't believe that her parents had covered for her. The topic of her fake job had never been broached, and the only thing that her parents had lied about was her name. She felt guilty about roping her parents into her charade although she reasoned that they had done it of their own volition. Well, at least her mom had done it of her own volition. Her dad had just followed along with it after a warning glance from his wife.

She also felt horrible about meeting Alistair's sister. Ashley was so kind and warm and welcoming, and she genuinely seemed to like Tori. She could only imagine what she would tell her brother once she found out that Tori had been lying to him for the entirety of their relationship.

"I really like Alistair," her mother said approvingly as they walked home.

"I like him, too," her dad agreed. "He's a good guy. And I like his sister, too," he added.

"Yeah," Tori said. "Ashley is fantastic." She paused. "Thank you both for not blowing my cover, but I really wish that you hadn't suggested lunch, Mom."

"Why not?" asked her mom. "I had a really great time at lunch. I thought that we all did?"

"I had a really great time, too," said Tori. "But now I've not only lied to him, but I've lied to his sister, too. She is one hundred percent going to hate me when I finally tell Alistair the truth."

Neither her mom nor her dad had anything to say to that.

"What am I going to do," Tori sighed, phrasing it as more of a statement than a question.

"I don't know what you're going to do, but you'd better do it fast," her mom said. "That man is crazy about you. I can tell just by the way that he looks at you. If you tell him now it will probably hurt him, but he is so clearly in love with you—you, not Tinsley," she clarified, "that I really think that it won't matter to him. In fact, he may even be able to find humour in it. He has great sense of humour," she added.

Tori looked at her, appalled.

"Well, granted, he may not find it humorous straightaway!" her mom backtracked. "But eventually! It will be one of those funny little stories that you share with people for years to come."

Tori felt a renewed sense of hope. She really needed to muster up the courage to have a serious, open and honest conversation with him. She wanted to do it sooner rather than later, but right then and there she made up her mind to wait until after the Fashion Cares fundraiser. After all, it was only a few weeks away, so what would be the harm in a short delay? Now that she had been asked to walk in the show, she really, really, really wanted to do it and on the off chance that things didn't go well with Alistair and he outed her to the industry, she didn't want to put her role in jeopardy.

*

Her parents left late on Sunday night, giving Tori time to finish some last-minute work. She had firmed up the guest list for the Impotentia product launch that she and Sierra were hosting next week and given it a final look over—Sierra had wanted it by Monday as they were going to send out the invitations that week. They had settled on holding the event downtown at Arcadian Lofts. Easily accessible by public transportation, car and foot, it was a popular event space for parties. They would be serving appetizers and drinks (from their client Patisserie, and a beer and wine company that Tori had found), and they would be handing out gift bags with Impotentia's women's products.

Tori had panicked a little when it came to creating the guest list. A lot of the people who should be invited, she realized, were people that she now counted as friends and acquaintances from her industry events. Trying her best to prevent anyone who knew her as Tinsley from attending the Impotentia party, she had intentionally left several names off of her list. There were still fifty-seven people whom she had earmarked for invitations. That seemed like more than enough. Saving the list and sending a copy to Sierra, she sat back feeling satisfied that she had done her job and would avoid being found out.

The next morning, she was right about to dial Charles Ellis's phone number (she was halfway through the E last names on her calling list) when an email from Sierra popped up on her screen. Subject line: "Re: Impotentia Product Launch Invite

List." Placing her phone back in its cradle, she clicked open the email.

"Good work on the list, Tori," it read. "I've added a few more names of people that you missed, but overall, well done. Please send the invites out by tomorrow and have them RSVP by next Tuesday. We'll need a complete head count by next Wednesday."

Seeing Sierra's modified invitees list attached, Tori clicked it open and scrolled through.

Fuck, she thought as she saw the names that her colleague had added. For the most part it consisted of names of individuals that Tori had intentionally left off.

Her heart rate quickened. How she was going to maneuver her way around this situation? she wondered, slumping in her chair. Picking up her phone she texted Maggie.

"Mags!" she typed. "Sierra's just given me the invite list for our launch next week and half of my industry friends/acquaintances are on it!! What am I going to do??!!?"

Her phone buzzed moments later with a reply from Maggie. "Oh, that blows, Tor. I don't know how you're going to get yourself out of this one," Tori read. Well that was helpful, she thought, feeling a little put out. Maggie was usually more supportive than that. She put down her phone.

Maybe she could pretend that she was a brand ambassador for Impotentia? She shook her head at the thought. More lying was not the answer. She would just have to soldier on and hope like hell that she would be able to get through it.

After gaining approval from Sierra about the design of the electronic invitations, she entered in the list of email addresses and pressed Send.

By the day's end a trickle of RSVPs had shown up in her email inbox and she was dismayed to find the names of people that she knew among them.

The rest of her week was spent at after-work industry events where she imbibed, had snacks, mingled with people who, by now, had become friends and amassed gift bags. By Friday nearly all of the RSVPs had come in and the number of confirmed attendees hit ninety-eight. Somehow Marcus had managed to catch wind of the party and had RSVP'd despite having never been invited. February, who was on the invitee list, had also RSVP'd and Tori surmised that she must have passed it along to him.

Damn it, she thought. Marcus already associated her with Impotentia given his pill-popping escapade. She just hoped that she could avoid being with Marcus, Sierra and Keith simultaneously. That would be a recipe for disaster.

Midway through her workday she realized that she had seriously dropped the ball with regards to Maggie's fundraiser. Her work and pretend-work obligations (and Alistair, if she was honest) had completely overtaken her life. She had a lot of work to do for the SPCA benefit, so she begged off of spending Saturday afternoon with her boyfriend in order to get started.

Fortunately, from the number of contacts that she had made, getting products together for the silent auction would be easy. She sent out a mass of emails to different people and companies politely soliciting donations. Thanks to the number of gift bags and free product that she'd received at almost every event she attended, she also had a closet full of high-end hair care products, kitchen gadgets, gift cards, jewelry and electronics that she could throw together for baskets.

In terms of marketing, her strategy was to put in a minimum amount of effort but get the maximum amount of exposure. She didn't know quite where to start, however. She thought about using *On the List* to promote the event but quickly decided against it. All it would take was one person to put two and two together and she would be ousted as the woman behind the website.

Instead, she created a Facebook, Instagram and Twitter account for the fundraiser and made an event invitation for Thursday, June 28 that was open to all. She posted the event to several animal rescue group pages and placed listings on *blogTO* and *NOW Magazine*. Tomorrow she figured that she would print out flyers about the event and then tape them up around the city. Logistically she should have done everything weeks ago and she hoped that she hadn't left it too late. She knew that Maggie was counting on selling out the benefit and she would feel horrible if hardly anyone came out. Effort-wise she realized that she hadn't really put a lot in. She thought back to Maggie's curt text earlier that week and wondered if her seeming flakiness and lack of dedication towards the fundraiser had caused Maggie to be mad at her. Thinking about it, they'd talked very minimally the past few weeks, with most of the communication coming from Maggie asking her where she was at with the silent auction and marketing. Tori had been so busy with work, her website, events and Alistair that the last time she had actually seen her friend face to face it had been the night of the fundraiser meeting at Maggie's office. They hadn't had a chance to sit down girlfriend to girlfriend to catch up on each other's lives in weeks. She sent Maggie a text telling her that she'd just created event pages for her fundraiser and asking her to get together next week after her Impotentia event. Maggie quickly responded with a short thanks, letting Tori know that she was free after work the next Friday for an hour.

One hour? she thought to herself. *Seriously?* Tori felt guilty as she asked her friend to pencil her in. Maggie was definitely pissed at her, she thought. And with good reason, too.

Typing "drinks with Maggie after work Friday" into her phone's to-do list, she then dialed Alistair.

"Hello, beautiful," he answered. "All done with the fundraising duties?"

"Yep!" she said enthusiastically. Although *done* might be stretching it. She'd put in a minimum amount of effort, but she figured that she would really get to it tomorrow with the posters that she planned to put up.

"That was fast," Alistair commented. "Does that mean that you're free to spend the rest of the day with me?"

"That's exactly what that means." Tori smiled.

"Perfect," he said. "Do you want me to come and pick you up? We can make dinner at my place tonight? Or do you want to stay in your neighbourhood?"

"Let's go to your place," she said. "We can pick up groceries and then head over."

Lately they had been spending more time at Alistair's place—this owing to an unfortunate event whereupon a building acquaintance had called out "Tori!" to her from across the lobby. She'd quickly headed for the exit with Alistair in tow and he'd asked, confusedly, if the woman had been calling to her. Tori had feigned ignorance, pretending that she hadn't heard her neighbour, but she'd been a lot more cautious since then.

They spent the evening together in Alistair's kitchen, Tori whipping up a Greek salad to go with grilled veggies and portobello mushroom burgers. She was happy that her schedule didn't include any parties that night. As much fun as they were, and as helpful as they were in boosting her website and sharpening her writing skills, attending several events per week—sometimes two or three in one night—was becoming exhausting.

They polished off a bottle of wine after dinner before heading out for an evening stroll. Alistair had kept to his word of asking Tori what she was into instead of Internet stalking and surprising her with things. It was working out quite nicely although Tori felt bad that she was unable to reciprocate. Her finances, such as they were, were a limiting factor. So, while Alistair continued to show his affection by showering her with costly surprises, she'd taken to making him meals and giving him back massages in return.

They had settled into a very happy weekly routine and were inseparable Monday to Sunday despite all of the events that Tori had to attend and Alistair's crazy work schedule. His sister, Ashley, had tried to get together with her and as much as Tori wanted to, she had used every excuse imaginable to avoid her. It was bad enough that her own boyfriend was unaware of her double life—she didn't want to further deceive his sister. The thought of coming clean to Ashley had popped into her head several times, but each time she talked herself out of it. After all, she reasoned, blood was thicker than water. It didn't matter how much Ashley said that she liked Tori, she knew that if she told her the truth, Ashley would immediately tell Alistair.

After a nightcap at a lounge close to Alistair's condo they headed home hand in hand before snuggling into bed.

Alistair woke her up with coffee and a kiss the next morning. While she had slept, he had popped out to Starbucks and picked up drinks and the *Wall Street Journal.* She had promised herself that she would print out and plaster the city with posters for Maggie's fundraiser that day but while sipping coffee with Alistair an alarm on her phone alerted her that she had a meeting with Susan Rich that afternoon regarding her role in Fashion Cares.

She couldn't believe that she had forgotten about it. Next to her budding website and blossoming relationship it was the thing that she was excited about the most. After downing her coffee, she gave Alistair a kiss, hurried home and threw herself together. The promise that she had made to herself about postering the city was all but forgotten as she raced to the Four Seasons Hotel where she had agreed to meet Susan Rich.

"Tinsley, hi!" Susan greeted her as she walked into the champagne-coloured lounge. Seated on a comfy corner couch in front of a glass coffee table, Susan, wearing a knee-length white dress with large red posies printed on it, stood up and embraced Tori. Air-kissing her twice, she gestured to the seat next to her, inviting Tori to sit down.

"Thank you again for the invitation, Susan," Tori said graciously. "I'm really excited to be a part of the fundraiser."

"I am so happy that you agreed to do it." Susan smiled. "Tea?" she asked, her eyebrows raised in question.

"Please." Tori nodded as Susan lifted up the silver pot, pouring steaming-hot liquid into a bone-coloured cup.

"As I mentioned in the email," Susan continued, placing the silver pot back onto the table, "we will need you to be at the venue two hours beforehand for a quick run-through and hair and makeup prep. We're utilizing local designers for the show and you'll be wearing a Lucian Luce gown. He will be in contact with you to set up a fitting appointment. Our emcee for the evening is Peter Wilders from Wilders Entertainment, and you'll be joining Suzanne Roberts, Arlene Dickinson, Joella Lim and a host of other models for the evening."

It was late afternoon by the time Tori bid Susan goodbye and headed home. Two of Susan's friends—fellow society women whom Tori recognized from events—had shown up and joined them for tea. Kara Morris was a sixty-ish-year-old housewife who spent most of her days shopping 'til she dropped and engaging in philanthropic endeavours. The other woman, Mimi Earle, was in her late forties and had built her fortune in the fitness industry. Tori had expected to be given a bit of a cold shoulder, but the women could not have been kinder. They had welcomed her into their group and embraced her like an old friend. She'd actually exchanged numbers with Mimi, who had asked her if she wanted to go for drinks one night. Not contributing much to the conversation, Tori had listened to their gossip and squirreled away information for later. She had wanted to start posting insider info on *On the List*, but she didn't want to put any opportunities or new friendships in peril.

On a high, she called Alistair as soon as she stepped into a cab.

"Hi, honey," he answered warmly.

"Hi, handsome," she answered back.

"How did your meeting go, Ms. Supermodel?" he teased.

"It was really great!" Tori said excitedly. "I'm really looking forward to the event."

"I'm happy for you," he said sincerely, a smile evident in his voice. "I'm really looking forward to it, too. I can't wait to see you all dolled up and strutting your stuff down the runway," he laughed.

"'Dolled up' and 'strutting'?" she giggled. "It sounds like someone has been spending too much time with Marcus."

"Well, if I am it's entirely your fault," he shot back in mock indignation before softening his tone. "What are you doing tonight, pretty lady?"

"Well," she teased back, "I was planning on doing you."

"Hold that thought," he said. "I'll be over in ten."

She had laughed, told him she would see him soon and then

hung up the phone. Given she was just nearing the downtown core, there was a good chance that he would arrive before her. As it was, Alistair had pulled in less than thirty seconds after she did, and they took the elevator up together.

Minutes later they were both stripped down naked and running their hands over each other's bodies, sharing passionate kisses in the process. By the time that they tired each other out and Alistair lay fast asleep beside her, Tori had completely forgotten all about the vow that she had made yesterday morning to finish the marketing work for Maggie's fundraiser.

Chapter 11: Blending In

At work that week, Tori spent most of her time taking care of last-minute details for Thursday's Impotentia party. While still apprehensive over her two lives colliding for one night, she was also a little excited. It was her first real marketing project and she wanted it to go well.

On the day of the event, she spent the entire morning stuffing gift bags. In all, she'd stuffed 120 bags full of Impotentia's new products along with the press release that she had (proudly) written up, and a USB stick full of digital images. They had received ninety-eight RSVPs but knowing people's propensity for showing up with a plus one in tow, she figured that too many gift bags would be much better than not enough. The event was slated to start at 6:30 p.m., so she headed over to the venue around noon to ensure that the set-up was running smoothly. Sierra had given her the go-ahead to take charge but to let her know if she had any issues. She and Keith were going to show up half an hour before the event was to begin.

Fortunately, the event space was only a few blocks away

from her office. Gift bags in tow, she'd taken the elevator up to the fourth floor, walked past the carpeted lobby and through the glossy black double doors that opened into the loft.

Bunches of glittery pink, blue and silver helium-filled balloons dotted the room and a banner reading "IMPOTENTIA" hung up near the back wall. A table up against a far wall held a black-clothed bar, as did the wall opposite it. Patisserie, the catering company (and Staten marketing client) that they were using to keep the guests fed, had been kind enough to provide them with barware and their servers were currently setting up the liquor stations. A local winery had agreed to sponsor their event, as had a small, newly launched craft brewing company. She watched as their delivery companies carted in boxes full of booze and dropped them beside the drink stations. On the other side of the room chefs outfitted in aprons, black pants and hats carried their tools of the trade to the back room to set up for the snacks that they would be serving.

It was exhilarating watching it all come together and Tori was excited that after all of her hard work, in a few hours she was going to finally see the fruits of her labour. Of course, that excitement was twinged with an equally strong feeling of dread. She was hoping that if she just avoided being in the same place as Keith or Sierra and any of her friends at the same time, that she might just be able to keep her charade going. Her heartbeat began to quicken, and she took a few deep breaths in and out to calm her nerves. The stress of everything had been getting to her lately. Between her nine-to-five job, working on this product launch, going to industry events, writing for her website and spending time with her boyfriend she felt like she was constantly on the verge of a meltdown. She just hoped that she could keep it together long enough to make it through tonight as, in several short hours, she would have one less thing on her to-do list.

By the time 6 p.m. rolled around, Tori was on pins and needles. University marketing majors had been taken on as interns to act as the "list" and gift bag girls for the evening. That ensured that Tori's industry friends wouldn't come face to face with their friend Tinsley checking people's names off of the guest list. Wearing a plain sleek black jersey dress (the last thing she wanted was to draw attention to herself) that she had brought with her to work, Tori kept her hair down and her makeup to a minimum.

"This looks great," Sierra gushed as she took in the room. Everything had come together just the way that she had envisioned. Even Keith was impressed.

"Great work, Tori. And Sierra," he added as an afterthought.

And shortly after that, the press started to trickle in in ones and twos. Keeping a wary eye out for anyone that she might know, Tori stayed far away from her boss and colleague. Only fifteen minutes had passed since the event had started before Tori recognized someone. Out of the corner of her eye, she'd spotted an editor for *Elite Magazine* come through the doors and scan the crowd.

Standing by the bar, Tori grabbed her wine and turned the other way. While she wasn't on a first-name basis with the woman, she still wanted to avoid her. For the next ten minutes she stood talking to the gift bag girls while trying her best to avoid eye contact with Sierra or Keith. The two of them were both busy chatting up the guests and showing them the products laid out on a back-wall table. The photographer (a student who they had hired for a reasonable price) walked around the room asking people to pose for photographs. She tried to discreetly turn away anytime the camera was aimed in her general direction.

Trying to avoid Sierra and Keith as they moved around the room turned into a choreographed dance routine. When Keith moved forwards, Tori moved backwards. When Sierra moved left, Tori moved right. She had talked to a couple of individuals that she knew from the industry—Kellyanne from the *Globe and Mail* and Veronica from *Toronto Life*. They tittered about the products and then exchanged gossip. Veronica was going to the Thomas Sabo jewellery party at Soho House in half an hour, which Tori was planning on attending, too. Although Tori would have to stay at the Impotentia party until the bitter end.

They had planned to wrap everything up by 8:30 p.m., which gave attendees a two-hour time frame in which to drink, snack, talk and snag a gift bag. From previous events that she had attended, though, she knew that there were always one or two stragglers who would stay until they were ushered out.

She had been keeping an eye out for Marcus to prevent his usual over-the-top enthusiastic greeting, and while talking to a sexual wellness columnist, she spotted his perfectly coiffed mop of blond hair. Excusing herself from the conversation she edged towards the back of the room to try to approach Marcus from behind.

"Marcus!" she exclaimed in a voice that was barely above a whisper. He whipped around, sunglasses firmly planted on his face and oversized Louis dangling from his arm, and smiled.

"Tins!" he said enthusiastically, throwing his arm around her shoulder. She managed to drag him off to the side by pointing out the nearest bar.

"I'll have a white wine," Marcus said cheerfully as the bartender dutifully poured out a glass and handed it to him.

"Cheers, Tins." He clinked his glass against hers before taking a large sip. "How long have you been at this party for?" His eyes roamed around the room in search of friends, acquaintances and potential bedmates.

"Oh, a while," Tori said vaguely. "I've just been mingling and having wine." *And avoiding my actual work colleagues*, she thought to herself.

"Well, once around the room and then I'm heading over to Soho House," Marcus declared. "Join me?"

"Ah, I might," she said, not wanting to commit when she knew she couldn't. "But I'll probably just meet you there."

"Suit yourself." He smiled. "Now, let's go check out their products." Marcus gestured to the product-laden table on the other end of the room. Tori grimaced. Sierra was standing right next to it with a welcoming smile on her face.

"Uh, you go on ahead, Marcus," she said. "I've already heard the sales pitch. I'm going to run to the washroom. I'll catch up with you in a few."

Downing his wine and ordering up another glass, Marcus whipped his hair around and strutted towards Sierra. Tori headed through the double doors and into the women's washroom. Leaning against the sink, she took a few calming breaths before wetting a paper towel and blotting cold water on her neck. The combination of nerves, alcohol and the summer weather had her sweating like crazy. Oil-blotting sheets took care of the sheen on her face and a quick under-eye powder dealt with the mascara marks. Steeling herself, she left the safety of the washroom and walked back into the party.

Marcus was still chatting with Sierra, who was now gesturing in the direction of Keith. Around her, people were mingling, having drinks and snacking on appetizers. Every so often one or two people would start in with the goodbye air kisses and head towards the door, the students doling out gift bags as they left.

Having managed to maintain her relative anonymity up until this point, Tori was mildly horrified when the sound of Marcus's voice caught her attention and she turned to see him standing right behind her, deep in conversation with her boss, Keith.

"Great new products," she heard Marcus say. "I've used the male enhancement pill myself," he admitted. "Of course, I didn't know that's what it was initially! I popped it after finding it in my friend Tinsley's purse." He paused for a moment. "She's actually around here somewhere." He craned his neck to see over the crowd. "Not the party favour that I was necessarily looking for," he continued. "But it was a good time had by all." Tori could see Keith's eyes bulging. She ducked behind a waiter and made her way to the bar in order to avoid detection.

"Beer? Wine?" the bartender inquired.

Tori waved her hand.

"No, thank you. Just water, please," she said wearily. She didn't want to drink too much at her own event. But at the Thomas Sabo event later tonight? She was going to pull a Marcus.

She definitely hadn't meant to or anticipated getting her two lives tangled up, but she had to admit that right now it was working. The product launch was looking to be a massive success, and she knew that there would be a ton of coverage tomorrow, including her own.

The number of gift bags was dwindling down and so was the crowd when Marcus finally separated from Keith and sought her out.

"There you are!" He had February—who had just shown up five minutes ago—in tow as he made his way over to the bar.

"One more for the road, I think." He nodded politely at the bartender, who deposited a glass of white wine in front of him.

"Tinsley." February hugged and air-kissed her. "Are you coming to Soho House with us?" she asked.

"No," Tori replied. "I'll have to catch up with you later. I have a quick commitment that I need to take care of."

"That's cool," February replied, tossing back her locks. "Should we grab our gift bags and get out of here, Marcus?" she asked.

Tori was a little taken aback. February hadn't even looked at the products that they were celebrating the launch of tonight. She hadn't talked to Keith or Sierra, and she didn't seem interested in the items in the slightest. It took a fair amount of effort on her part to keep her facial features in check. She just hoped that February, as an editor for *Elle Magazine*, would at least read the press release and give the Impotentia products a write-up. She was beginning to understand why she was garnering so many invites—her *On the List* email account had been receiving an astronomical number of invitations to everything from video game launch parties to the opening of craft beer breweries. She guessed that her articles garnered a decent amount of publicity for the companies and their products.

The duo gave Tori their goodbyes and left for Soho House while Tori, relieved that everyone whom she knew on a friend and acquaintance basis had gone, began to relax.

"Great work on putting this launch together, Tori," Keith said from beside her. "From the attendance alone, it looks to be a success, and we couldn't have done it without you." He beamed proudly.

"Thanks," she replied, jubilant that not only had she managed to avoid being found out but that her first real work opportunity had gone so well. "I put a lot of effort into it so I'm glad that you're happy with it." She smiled, unable to keep the happiness out of her voice.

After the last of the stragglers had been ushered out the door, Tori, Sierra and Keith grabbed a glass of wine and toasted to a successful evening. The caterers were cleaning up and the waiters went around picking up dirty plates and cups. Sierra handed Tori one of the leftover gift bags, of which there were only two, and then the three of them got to work with packaging up the presentation table full of products and the banner. The marketing students were thanked and sent home with three hours of marketing-related work experience to put on their resumé.

She texted Alistair minutes after the room had been cleared out to see his whereabouts. They had agreed to meet around 10 p.m. to head to Soho House.

"Just left the party," Tori texted. "Where are you?"

Moments later her phone buzzed as a reply popped up on her screen. "Hi, gorgeous. Just left my place, want to meet at Soho House?"

"Sure," she texted back. "I'll be there in 10."

Tori figured that she would walk over. It wouldn't be an expensive taxi ride, but she was trying to save every penny that she could. The last two months of constantly being social had seen her using her credit card like a trust-fund kid. She was terrified to see her statement at the end of the month.

She was still basking in a high from her launch's success on the way over to the party. Okay, so it wasn't exactly "her" launch. It was Sierra's launch, too. But Tori had put so much effort into it that she felt like she was the main player. A slight breeze blew through her hair as she crossed the street, walking across the pavement carefully in her high heels. The city's streets were bustling at this hour—downtown Toronto on a Thursday night felt more like a Friday, with bumper-to-bumper traffic and hordes of people drinking and dining on outside patios and navigating their way to different venues.

Soho House was situated just outside of the Shangri-La Hotel, and she hurried across the six-lane University Avenue as quickly as she could, ignoring the flashing hand signal as it urged her to slow down.

Regaining her composure on the other side of the street, she headed for the Soho House entrance on the corner. Pulling open the large wooden door, she found herself face to face with none other than Munger Carlson.

Fuck, she thought to herself. *Just my luck.*

"Tinsley." A smile spread across Munger's face as he moved in for an on-the-lips kiss. Tori recoiled and tried to move backwards but there was a small group of people standing directly behind her.

"Munger!" She managed to turn her face sideways at the last minute causing Munger to plant his lips on her cheek. Undeterred, he pulled her forwards, wrapping his arm around her waist.

"You've been avoiding me, Tinsley," he said into her ear as she tried to extricate herself from his grasp.

"Yes, I have," she said matter-of-factly. "I'm here with my boyfriend tonight."

"Boyfriend?" Munger said, raising his eyebrows and peering around. "I don't see a boyfriend anywhere. Join me for a drink, Tinsley."

"No, thank you," she said firmly, having wiggled away from his arm. She stepped back as far as the people behind her would allow for, but it wasn't nearly far enough. She had had it with the billionaire's constant harassment. "And in addition to that, please stop texting me, and please stop talking to me," she said, a culmination of stress, lack of sleep and two glasses of wine causing her to blurt out. "I don't want to see you and I don't want to talk to you. I don't like you, Munger."

His eyes narrowed at her.

"Well, aren't you a real bitch," Munger shot back at her nastily. "No one turns me down, and no one speaks to me that way," he said menacingly.

Tori breathed a deep sigh.

"Whatever you say, Munger," she said wearily. "I'm past the point of caring. Now please let me by so that I can see my boyfriend," she said. Tori's "give a fuck" had clearly worn out.

Munger's mouth dropped open in outrage. Tori supposed that no one had ever stood up to him before. She squished herself up against the wall and slid past him to the receptionist waiting at the door.

"Tinsley Tomlinson," she said to the woman in a confident, no-nonsense tone. "*Fashionista Magazine*. Here for the Thomas Sabo party."

"Certainly, Ms. Tomlinson," the woman said, typing something into her computer. "I'll just need to see some ID."

Tori sputtered.

"Sorry, what did you say?"

"I just need to see your ID," the woman repeated.

Tori grabbed her purse and fished around for a bit.

"Sorry," Tori said, hoping her expression looked genuinely apologetic and not panicked, which was how she felt. "I seem to have misplaced my ID."

The woman looked uncomfortable.

"Oh, well I'm sorry, Ms. Tomlinson," she said. "But I can't let you upstairs."

Tori was completely taken aback.

"Ahem," a snarky-sounding voice came from behind her. Tori turned around to see a big blonde-haired, designer handbag-toting woman with expertly applied makeup who had it out for her. It was Corinne. She sneered at Tori.

"If you wouldn't mind moving out of the way so that *actual* members could get in, that would be great."

Tori immediately flushed and moved backwards until she came up against a brick wall. She watched in embarrassment as the receptionist scanned Corinne's card and she waltzed by, turning to give Tori a nasty smirk as she made her way upstairs.

Her cheeks stained red, Tori shrank against the wall. It was mortifying being refused entry to the private club. It was even more mortifying to have your enemy watch the whole thing go down. She pulled out her phone to text Alistair when she heard someone call out "Tinsley!" Her head snapped to the left and she saw Susan Rich approaching her from the entrance.

"Susan!" Tori said with a touch of relief.

Susan smiled. "Are you having trouble getting in?" she asked sympathetically.

"Yes," said Tori. "It's just, I seem to have forgotten my ID."

"Ah," said Susan. "Well then why don't you just come in as one of my guests. You don't need identification for that."

"Thank you, Susan. Really. I really appreciate it," Tori said with sincere gratitude.

The receptionist smiled at the duo as she scanned Susan's card. "Perfect," the receptionist said. "The Thomas Sabo party is on the rooftop."

On their way up the stairs the two of them talked about the upcoming Fashion Cares fundraiser, which was now only two weeks away. When they reached the roof they were greeted by another woman—this time it was a short, curly-haired lady holding a clipboard. She crossed their names off of her list as soon as she saw who they were, and they walked past her and into the sizeable crowd. Glass walls allowed for unobstructed views of the city and lights, strung across the open-air roof in a zig-zag pattern, lit the area in a warm glow. While Susan excused herself to go and talk to a friend, Tori craned her neck for any glimpse of her boyfriend.

With no sign of Alistair in sight Tori made her way to the bar, figuring that at least if she went there that she could find Marcus. She had just made it to the counter when she spotted Alistair. Standing in a far-off corner wearing a slim-cut navy suit, he was sipping a cocktail and talking to Corinne.

Frowning, she debated on what to do. After a few seconds she squeezed her way through the crowd in Alistair and Corinne's direction. She had just popped out of the other side when she saw a laughing Corinne place her hand on Alistair's upper arm. Still embarrassed by the blonde witnessing her being denied entrance downstairs, Tori walked over to them, her face flushed with annoyance.

"Hi," she said tersely, looking at Alistair.

"Hi, honey." A smile lit up his face as he saw Tori. He leaned over her, grabbed her around the waist and planted a kiss on her cheek. Corinne looked positively apocalyptic.

"How was your event?"

"It was good," she said, pasting on a small, disingenuous smile.

"Glad to see that you managed to make it in." Corinne gave Tori an equally disingenuous smile. Tori stared back at her.

"Right," she said. "Well, Alistair, why don't we go and check out the jewellery?" she suggested.

"Sounds like a plan." His hand found hers and squeezed it lightly. "Excuse us, Corinne." And with that they turned away from the blonde dragon lady and made their way through the throngs of people.

"Are you really that keen to check out the jewellery?" asked Alistair.

"No," Tori replied. "I just wanted to get away from Corinne." She quickly told him what had transpired downstairs.

Alistair shook his head. "I'm so sorry, Tinsley. I had no idea. I knew that Corinne could be nasty but that's really out of line."

"What were you doing talking to her?" Tori asked, trying to keep the frustration out of her voice. Alistair kept saying that he disliked Corinne but if that was the case, then why did she keep turning up between them?

"Nothing," he replied, a hint of annoyance in his voice. "She came over and started talking to me about a new project that she's working on. What am I going to say? 'Sorry, Corinne, but I don't want anything to do with you'?"

Tori scrunched up her mouth before letting out a sigh.

"I suppose you're right," she said. "I'm sorry. I just feel like every time I turn around, she's either coming up in conversation or in person. And I know you don't like her, but I can't help but think that she's trying to steal you away."

Alistair laughed at that.

"I have absolutely zero interest in that woman. If I did, I would still be dating her." He ruffled Tori's hair affectionately and then planted a kiss on her shoulder. "Now you on the other hand. No one can hold a candle to you, Ms. Supermodel."

Tori felt a little calmer.

"Thank you," she said a little sheepishly. "I suppose I'm just stressed out," she said, trying to rationalize her paranoia.

Later, after grabbing a drink and looking at Thomas Sabo's latest collection, Tori excused herself to go to the washroom. Upon exiting the stall, she came face to face with Corinne, who was reapplying her lipstick in the mirror.

Tori set her purse on the counter while she washed her hands. Turning off the taps she reached over to grab some paper towel before bracing herself for a confrontation. She was fed up with the socialite's constant attitude and snark towards her and was going to try to put an end to it.

"Look, Corinne," Tori said, turning to her, trying to keep her voice level and void of venom. "I don't know why you seem to hate me so much, but if it's because I'm dating Alistair, then that has more to do with you than it does with me." She paused for a moment watching Corinne's eyes narrow. "I mean it's not my fault that Alistair isn't interested in you. I wouldn't take it personally," she said. "There are loads of guys who haven't wanted to go out with me—" She swung her arm wide to emphasize her point and knocked over unzipped her purse in the process, the contents scattering across the tile floor, bouncing, clanging, fluttering and rolling. She let out a whispered curse and then crouched down to pick up her things.

She gathered up business cards, lip gloss, keys, mints, loose change, credit cards and ID that lay scattered on the ground. Reaching for a rogue dollar Tori turned her head slightly to see Corinne bending back upwards before shooting Tori an innocent look.

She was immediately suspicious. Had Corinne swiped something of hers from off of the floor? Surely the woman wouldn't stoop to stealing?

"You know, you're right, Tinsley," Corinne said sweetly.

"I'm sorry that we got off on the wrong foot. Let me help you get your things together." And with that Corinne helped pick Tori's purse contents up off of the floor.

Tori's jaw dropped open and she sat rooted to the tiles. Was trying to reason with her really all it had taken to turn Corinne from Ice Queen to Nice Queen?

Corinne passed Tori all of the things that she'd scooped up from the floor and Tori sincerely thanked her, hoping that the truce would last. Corinne waved her hand in an "it was nothing" gesture before exiting the room. Standing up, Tori did a quick inventory of her purse contents before fixing her hair in the mirror and going back out to join her boyfriend.

"Should we get out of here?" he asked, handing her back her drink.

"Let's," Tori replied. She had planned on a wild and crazy blowout but now that she was here the first thing that she wanted was a good night's rest and the last thing that she wanted was a hangover.

Saying a quick goodbye to assorted friends and acquaintances, they made their way downstairs and into a car. Tori didn't think that her feet could take the six-block walk in her heels. She'd been standing for the better part of seven hours and her feet felt puffy and tender to the touch. They crawled into bed and snuggled up together—Alistair kissing her neck while Tori busied herself with him down below.

Chapter 12:
The Mix-Up

"Congratulations again on the launch, Tori," Sierra said to her the next morning. "I know that it was a team effort, but you really were an integral part of it. We received a ton of media attention and the Impotentia executives are very happy."

"That's great!" Tori beamed. "Thank you again for giving me the opportunity. I really appreciate it and I feel like I gained some really valuable experience. I couldn't believe how many people showed up."

And it was true. She was still amazed at the number of people who had shown up to a party that she had planned. She thought back to high school when she had told everyone that she was throwing a party at her house on a Saturday night and only four people had shown up. *If only they could see me now*, she thought.

"You're more than welcome." Sierra smiled. "Oh, and by the way," she added. "I found pictures from our event on Twitter." An odd look crossed Sierra's face. "It's a little strange, though. You're in a few of them but people have you tagged as

'Tinsley'."

Tori tried to keep the panic that she suddenly felt off of her face.

"Tinsley?" she managed to choke out in a strangled voice. "That's weird." She cleared her throat before continuing on. "Maybe they mistook me for someone else," she said, avoiding her colleague's gaze. She'd thought that she had managed to avoid the camera all night, but the photographer must have taken some candid photos when she wasn't looking.

"Yeah, that must be it," Sierra said thoughtfully. "Strange." She shook her head. "Anyway, great job again, Tori."

"Thanks." Tori smiled back. She was happy that the campaign was finished as it was one less thing she had to worry about. What she had to worry about next, though, was Maggie. She was meeting her after work for the one hour that her best friend was giving her, and she had a feeling that it wasn't going to go well.

They'd agreed to meet at Hunter's Landing, their usual drink and catch-up place, around 5:30 p.m. Settling into the squishy leather booth, Tori ordered a martini and waited. Ten minutes later Maggie sat down across from her with the smallest ghost of a smile. This was definitely not going to be like old times, thought Tori.

"Maggie!" Tori said enthusiastically, trying to prevent the conversation from turning sour. "I'm so glad that you were able to pencil me in for today."

Maggie looked at her, unsmiling.

"Yeah. Thanks for coming, Tori," she said. "I haven't heard much from you about where you're at with the advertising and silent auction for my fundraiser."

Tori felt instantly guilty. She'd really flaked out on her responsibilities for Maggie's fundraiser. She hadn't even gotten around to creating the posters that she'd intended to post around the city.

"I know, and I'm so sorry," Tori said. "I'm putting up posters around the city this weekend."

Maggie took a deep breath.

"It's one week until the event, Tori. And you haven't really done anything." She paused. "You know, I don't know who you've turned into lately. The Tori that I know would have put in all of her effort to make this a success. You've offered to help out, but it feels like you're barely committed. If you didn't want to do it, you should have just said so in the first place instead of telling me that you would do something and then flaking."

Tori felt awful.

"You're right, Maggie," she admitted, feeling disgusted with herself. "I've been a shitty friend lately. I've been neglecting my responsibilities and I'm so, so sorry for that. You know I care about you and you know that I wouldn't intentionally screw you over. I'm sorry if I've been coming across as uncaring and flaky."

"Thanks, Tor," said Maggie, her face void of emotion. "Apology accepted. Anyway"—Maggie grabbed up her purse, threw down ten dollars and started to stand up—"I have to go."

Tori grabbed the ten dollars and stuffed it back into Maggie's purse.

"I'll take care of the bill," said Tori. "You didn't even order anything."

Maggie sighed, pulled the ten dollars back out of her purse and dropped it on the table.

"It's okay, Tor. We both know how thin you're stretched most of the time." Maggie put on her jacket. "And don't bother putting up posters this weekend," she said. "I have someone else taking care of it." And with that Maggie walked out.

Apology unaccepted, it seemed.

Tori felt terrible. She quickly finished her martini and headed home. It didn't matter if Maggie had assigned someone else the job of putting up posters around the city for her SPCA fundraiser. Tori was going to make up some flyers and put them up herself. She felt awful for letting her friend down, especially because she knew how important it was to Maggie.

Changing into her comfy clothes as soon as she arrived home, Tori cracked open a Diet Coke and spent the next hour designing a poster. After going back and forth on the font size and placement, she finally decided that it was done. The black-and-white poster featured a picture of two rescue dogs along with details of the event and Maggie's phone number and email address for anyone who wanted to get involved. She was just about to hit Print when a notification popped up on her SPCA Fundraiser Facebook page. She'd only had one comment before that, inquiring as to whether or not people could bring their dogs to the benefit.

Clicking the red notification square, she saw that someone had left a comment on the event's wall. "I thought that this was taking place on June 29?" someone named Emil Stanway had written.

She had a moment of panic.

June 29? That's the same night as Fashion Cares! No, she thought. *It can't be.* There was no way that she'd mixed up the date. Was there?

Abruptly getting up from her chair, she headed to her bedroom. The file folder containing all of the SPCA event details sat on her desk. She picked it up and leafed through the documents. Her eyes stopped on one of the pages that read "Confirmed Schedule" along the top in bold letters.

Fuck.

She'd gotten the dates mixed up. While they had originally chosen Thursday, June 28 for the event, they had changed it to Friday, June 29 at their last meeting! And Tori had completely forgotten about it. What was she going to do now? she thought. Not only had she royally neglected her volunteer duties but now she wouldn't even be able to attend! She'd promised Maggie that she would be there to run the silent auction table, but it was during the same time as Fashion Cares, which was something that she'd agreed to thinking her night was free! And she couldn't very well back out of it now—she was an integral part of the show. Not to mention the fact that she was counting on it to boost her industry cred.

Oh God, she thought. Maggie would never forgive her.

Tossing the folder onto her desk she hurried to her computer and changed the date on the Facebook event. Then she replied to Emil Stanway that he was correct, the benefit was on the twenty-ninth and that she hoped to see him there. Next, she changed the date on the poster that she had created before printing off 150 copies. Tomorrow morning she was getting up bright and early to poster the entire downtown core.

Minutes later her phone buzzed and a message from Maggie appeared on her screen. "I'm sorry for being so short with you this afternoon," it read. "I'm just stressed out, and I'm afraid that my event is going to be a failure :(."

She couldn't believe that after she, Tori, had neglected her responsibilities and been such a terrible friend, that Maggie was apologizing to her. She felt horrible.

"It's okay, Mags," she wrote back. "I fully get it. I totally dropped the ball on the marketing but I'm going to do everything I can to ensure that your event is a success." She hit Send and sat back feeling miserable.

Seconds later, her phone buzzed again. "Thanks Tor," the text said. "I appreciate it. You're a good friend."

Good friend? she thought. She was the worst friend. Burying her face in her hands, she picked up the stack of posters and put them in her bag before texting her boyfriend.

"Remember how I said that I have a lot of work to do for Maggie's fundraiser?" she texted. "I'm going to spend tomorrow postering the city and thought that it may be more fun with two people."

Her phone buzzed less than a minute later.

"I would love to help," Alistair replied. "I'll be over at 7 with coffee and croissants."

Tori smiled at that before putting down her phone and turning back to her computer. She needed to have a postering strategy. She didn't want to just tape flyers onto every telephone pole in sight. She needed to hit up pet stores and other local businesses that would be supportive of Maggie's cause.

Tens of Google searches later and she had several maps printed out and stores marked off as potential poster locations. As the sun went down, she spent the remainder of her evening sending out emails to media outlets, radio stations and local celebrities, asking them to please use their Twitter, Facebook and Instagram accounts to get the word out about the benefit.

Clicking her computer off just before midnight, she threw on her pajamas and curled up in bed. It was the first night that she'd had to herself in weeks but it was far from the relaxing evening that she craved. After the Impotentia launch she'd thought that she would feel less stressed. How wrong she had turned out to be.

*

Alistair arrived bright and early the next morning with coffee and croissants in hand. Between the two of them they had 150 posters, five area maps, ten rolls of tape, a box of pushpins and two water bottles to keep themselves hydrated. They also had mini flyers to give to people that they passed in the street, which Tori had printed out last night after being unable to fall asleep.

She was glad that Alistair had agreed to help her. With the sun shining and a slight warm breeze it seemed more like they were out for a leisurely stroll than working. Initially she'd been wary about approaching businesses to advertise for Maggie's event but nearly every shop—coffee, pet, liquor, grocery—was more than happy to put a poster on display. After all, who didn't love pets?

By the time that they were out of flyers they were exhausted—it had taken them nearly the entire day to poster the city. Tori checked the pedometer tracker on her phone and was astonished to see that during the course of the day they had logged over 30,000 steps.

"No wonder my feet are so sore," she groaned, showing Alistair the screen.

"Poor girl," he said sympathetically. "Tell you what, how do you feel about a massage followed by wine in the Jacuzzi?" he asked.

"Oh God," she said, leaning up against him. "Please don't tease me. Throw in some sushi and jazz music and I'm in."

"Done." He squeezed her shoulders. "I'll email my concierge to set it up."

They'd trekked around the city hitting up everywhere from

the Distillery District to Dovercourt, and the harbourfront to Hazelton Avenue. The sweaty and disheveled pair finally finished up near the Royal Ontario Museum.

Hopping in a cab they pulled up to Alistair's condo and immediately jumped in the shower when they made it to his floor. The warm water felt heavenly after an entire day spent walking in the sun.

Half an hour later they were lying on massage tables in a candlelit room, listening to the calming sounds of nature emanating from a speaker. Exhausted, Tori fell asleep a few minutes into her massage and only woke up when Alistair whispered in her ear.

"Wake up, Sleeping Beauty," he teased.

She'd groggily lifted her head up and rubbed at her eyes.

"I'll meet you in the Jacuzzi," he said, giving her a quick kiss on the cheek.

Between the wine, the warm water and the pulsing jets, Tori didn't last long. She dozed off again, this time in the hot tub, and Alistair decided that they should call it a night. Back at Alistair's condo they opted to forego sushi and jazz, collapsing into bed instead and quickly falling asleep.

Tori felt refreshed the next morning. Looking at the clock she was shocked to see that she'd slept for ten hours. Incredibly, Alistair was still sleeping.

Make that snoring. She winced as he let out a particular loud snort.

Quietly getting out of bed she headed for the kitchen to brew a pot of coffee. Just as she'd hit the start button a thought popped into her mind. She was friendly with a large number of media personalities in the city. What if Tinsley contacted them and asked them for a favour? She tiptoed back into Alistair's bedroom and grabbed her phone.

"Marcus," she texted. "I need you to do me a favour. If I send you something would you send out a Twitter blast about a fundraiser this Friday?" She hit Send and then put down her phone. She didn't expect to hear back from Marcus right away knowing his proclivity for liquor and late nights.

After a relaxing brunch with Alistair she headed home and set to work emailing her industry friends. From her *Fashionist* account, of course. The emails requested that the recipients send out tweets and Facebook and Instagram posts promoting the SPCA event. Happily, she received a handful of "No problem!", "Sure" and "Done!" replies back by late afternoon.

Confident that her contacts would reach a wide audience she next emailed Lucian Luce, the designer whose gown she would be wearing, regarding her fitting appointment the next day. After work she was going to head over to his studio to try on the dress that he had created for her. Susan Rich had had Tori send Lucian her measurements and a headshot before he designed her gown. Tomorrow's fitting would be the first time that she was seeing it and she couldn't wait.

Later that evening Alistair came by and Tori made dinner. They snuggled together on the couch sharing a bottle of wine while she racked her brain about what to do about the silent auction table on Friday. She couldn't leave Maggie high and dry. She would have to find a replacement. Then an idea popped into her mind: she could call up the same university that they'd used for the Impotentia launch to see if any marketing students would be willing to work as interns for the night.

That bit of stress relieved, Tori could finally relax. The only thing that she had to worry about now was telling Maggie that she couldn't come to her fundraiser. That and falling down on the runway. Which was crazy. She was so comfortable with Alistair and everything was going so well that she'd almost forgotten that she'd been living a lie. She'd transitioned so smoothly into the role of being Tinsley that being found out didn't even register on her "things to stress about" radar anymore. She'd almost forgotten that she'd been lying to her boyfriend for the entirety of their two-month relationship.

Extricating himself from Tori's embrace, Alistair kissed her goodbye before heading home for the night. He had a big meeting in the office first thing in the morning and was going to be up and out of bed at a very early hour.

Like the night before, Tori fell asleep almost immediately.

Unlike the night before, however, her dreams were full of terrifying imagery that jolted her awake, leaving her heart racing and her mind poorly rested.

Chapter 13: Unfriendly Terms

She felt haggard the next morning as she trudged into work; nightmares had kept her up for most of the night.

"Have you read *On the List*, yet, Tori?" Sierra asked as she passed by her desk.

Tori's eyes went wide.

"Um, no," she lied. "I haven't. What's that?" she asked, feigning ignorance.

"It's only the hottest fashion, lifestyle and gossip site on the web!" her colleague raved. "You should check it out. I know that you've always wanted to write for a magazine. You could pick up some pointers from the author. She's a really great writer and she has her finger on the pulse on all of the hottest scenes in the city."

"Thanks!" Tori said enthusiastically. "Um, for the suggestion!" she stumbled. "I'll have to check it out!" A small jolt of pride shot through her. Sierra was complimenting her work? Sure, Sierra wasn't the editor of *Vogue* or anything, but an objective compliment was something that Tori treasured. While she appreciated it when her friends and family told her that she was a great writer, she didn't necessarily believe them. After all, they were supposed to be your biggest supporters, but their opinion was seriously biased.

Compliments from unsuspecting coworkers aside, Sierra was right—her blog was one of the hottest sites on the net. Google Analytics revealed that *On the List* was one of the most-visited websites for Toronto, Montreal and the surrounding regions. Incredibly, her subscriber count had just breached the 60,000 mark the other day.

Turning to her phone list with a smile on her face she dialed R. Franklin's number and waited for him to pick up. Fingers tapping on her desk she did a quick run-through of her to-do list for the next four days as the phone continued to ring. Tonight, she had her gown fitting and then dinner with Alistair; tomorrow she had two product launches; Wednesday there was a pre-opening store preview; and Thursday—thanks to her mixing up the date of Maggie's fundraiser—she was completely free. *Well, maybe not*, she thought. She'd see if Maggie needed help with any last-minute things that evening. And if not, she was going to spend the night with her boyfriend.

While she was still racked with guilt at having to tell Maggie that she was bailing on her event, at some point during the night she'd come up with a quasi-solution to her double booking. She really didn't want to bail on her best friend, but she really didn't want to bail on Fashion Cares either—they were both very important to her in very different ways. And so, instead of completely forgoing her best friend's event she figured that after the fashion show she would hurry over to Maggie's fundraiser. Sure, her best friend might be pissed at her but at least she would appreciate that Tori had made the effort.

She hoped, anyway.

"Tori?" came a voice from behind her.

She hung up the phone.

"Mmm?" Tori turned around and saw Keith standing behind her. Why did he always do that? Who did he think he was, Houdini?

"I'd like to meet with you in my office on Friday morning,"

he said to her, straightening his tie. "Ten a.m. sharp."

"Great!" she responded cheerily. "I'll see you then!"

Her heart started beating faster. This was it! She was getting a raise! Hadn't Keith said as much when he presented the Impotentia launch to her? What had he said? If it all went well, she would be getting a raise!

Unable to concentrate on her phone task she took office coffee orders before bounding out the door. Bubbling with excitement as she made her way to the local Starbucks, she realized that there was really no one she could call. Alistair was out, so was Marcus and the rest of her industry friends. She knew Maggie would be excited for her, but she didn't want to take attention away from her fundraiser. She could call her parents?

"Hello?" her mom answered on the first ring.

"Mom!" she said enthusiastically.

"Hi, honey," her mom replied. "Is everything all right?"

"Everything is great!" Tori responded. "Hold on a sec." She rattled off the drink order to the blue-haired cashier. "Sorry about that." She turned her attention back to her mother and handed the cashier two bills. "I think I'm getting a raise!" Tori said excitedly.

"A raise? Oh, that's great, sweetie! Why do you think that?" she asked.

"Because Keith said that if I did well with the product launch that he would give me a raise, and he just told me that he wants to meet with me on Friday!"

"Well, I hope that's what the meeting is about," her mom said. "You've been working really hard lately, honey. And I know how stressed out you've been." She paused. "But just in case the meeting isn't about you getting a raise, I don't want you to get your hopes up."

The high that Tori had been riding on suddenly decreased in altitude.

"Yeah," she said to her mom, trying not to sound too put out. "I guess you're right. The 'chickens before they hatch' thing, I guess."

"Tori!" the barista called out her name.

"Anyway," she continued. "Sorry, Mom, I have to go."

"Okay, sweetie," her mom said. "I'm rooting for you. I just don't want you to be disappointed if the meeting doesn't turn out to be what you think it is."

"Yeah," Tori said unhappily. "I know. Thanks. Bye, Mom." She hung up the phone.

Well, she thought to herself. That phone call had certainly put a damper on things. But she knew that her mom was right. Keith had given no indication that their Friday morning meeting was about a raise. For all she knew he could be foisting another product launch onto her.

She grimaced at the thought.

It wasn't that she hadn't enjoyed the challenge of putting together the event for Impotentia—it was always good to learn new things and to prove yourself at work—but she knew that marketing was not what she wanted to do with her life. Because of that she didn't want to dedicate valuable time outside of regular working hours to her marketing job when she could be using them to work on her future career.

Walking down Queen Street after work she double-checked the address of an old brick building on Portland before opening the door and ascending the creaky old stairs. Lucian's studio was on the third floor, and Tori was huffing and puffing by the time she made it to the top.

To the left of the landing stood an oak door with a frosted glass window that said LUCIAN LUCE in bold black letters. Turning the brass knob, she gave the heavy door a bit of a shove and it swung inwards.

"Tinsley!" came Lucian's voice from across the room. He stood up from his desk where he had been drafting a pattern.

"Lucian!" she replied back. "I hope I'm not interrupting you?"

He waved his hand in dismissal.

"Not at all." He smiled, putting his pencil behind his ear. "Give me one second and I'll grab the dress." With that he disappeared into a back room.

Tori looked around. It was a spacious, high-ceilinged room with enormous glass windows on the far wall. Mannequins dressed in Lucian's designs dotted the entrance to her left, and to her right sat a reception desk with LUCIAN LUCE in big bold letters adorning the front. Enormous pattern drafting desks, sewing machines and sergers stood around the room, and there was fabric and drafting paper scattered everywhere. On one wall, tens of Lucian's hand-drawn designs were pinned to a large corkboard. On another, a large mirror amplified the size of the space. Behind the desk stood racks of clothing and she walked over and started looking at the gowns. He was known for his elegant and dramatic gown designs, and was known to employ the use of feathers, silks, French lace, dramatic necklines and sexy silhouettes.

She was just fingering a black-feathered cape when she heard Lucian emerge from the back room and turned to see him holding a white garment bag in his hand.

"Come and see!" he said excitedly as he hung the bag up on an empty clothing rack.

A big smile crossed her face as she hurried over beside him.

"I can't wait to see it!" Tori said as he started unzipping the bag. "I love your designs, Lucian. I was so happy when Susan told me that I would be wearing one of your pieces."

"Just you wait." He winked. "This dress is going to look incredible on you."

And with that, he pulled the gown out of the bag and held it up for Tori to see. The dress was so gorgeous that she nearly gasped. It was a floor-length, curve-hugging design made out of deep red velvet with a plunging neckline and short off-the-shoulder sleeves.

"Lucian, this is one of the most beautiful gowns I've ever seen," she said sincerely. "I can't believe that I get to wear it!"

"I'm glad you like it," he said, smiling. "Now try it on!" He pressed the dress into her hands. "From the looks of you I don't think that I'll need to make many adjustments, but we'll see. The dressing room is behind that clothing rack." He motioned to a white door just visible behind the mountains of clothing.

She dropped her bag on the reception desk before heading for the fitting room. The smooth fabric slid up her body and she noticed the contrast between her porcelain skin and the red dress. The combination was dynamite. Pulling her hair around to one shoulder she grasped the zipper and pulled it up to the top. Lucian was right, she thought—the dress fit her like a glove.

"There are some pumps in there, too," Lucian called from the other side of the door. "I don't know if they're your size but put them on so that we can get the full effect."

Tori looked around and spotted two pairs of nude high heels in the corner behind her.

"Okay," she called back, reaching for the shoes.

A few seconds later she pushed open the door, excited to see her reflection in the mirror.

Lucian let out a shriek when he saw her.

"Tinsley! That dress is to die for on you! Oh my God. It's like it was made for you!"

She took a few steps forward before moving over to the mirror. Lucian wasn't kidding, she thought—she looked incredible. She could hardly believe that she would be wearing this gown for all to see on Friday. He motioned for her to twirl and then came over, making her turn this way and that, adjusting the straps and smoothing down the bunched-up train before declaring that he didn't need to do any work on it.

After Tori changed back into her work clothes Lucian gave her the garment bag and she was on her way. Carefully hoisting the bag in the air, she hailed a cab and made for home. She still couldn't believe her luck! When she'd promised Lucian that she would return the dress to him the day after the fundraiser, he'd declined.

"Nonsense," he insisted. "You keep it. You look so good wearing it that it's an amazing advertising opportunity for me."

Tori had been stunned.

"Are you serious, Lucian?" she'd asked. "I can really keep it?"

He'd laughed before telling her that yes, he was serious, and that yes, he wanted her to have it.

"You're not going to believe what I'm wearing on Friday," she texted Alistair after getting into the back seat of a cab.

"????" he responded seconds later. Tori smiled and texted him back a fire emoji. She couldn't wait for Friday.

Her phone buzzed again. "Maybe you can give me a preview tonight?" she read with a grin.

"Not a chance," she wrote back and pressed Send.

Another message from Alistair quickly popped up on her screen—this time it was a sad-face emoji quickly followed by him telling her that he was wrapping things up at the office and would be over in an hour.

The next day at work Tori agonized over how and when she was going to tell Maggie about being unable to attend and run the silent auction table at her fundraiser. She'd heard back from the university and two students had volunteered to run the silent auction table on Friday. She had been exchanging emails with them all morning, trying to get everything coordinated.

She would much prefer to tell Maggie over the phone, but Tori knew that it was something that she had to do in person. It was something that she was dreading, especially after the "I'm sorry, you're a good friend" text that Maggie had sent her last Friday. Tori decided that she wasn't going to tell her best friend that she was going to head to her fundraiser right after the fashion show. She figured that it would be better if she surprised her. That was one of the things that she had learned at her job, at least—under promise and over deliver. Still, she knew that she would have some serious making up to do to Maggie after Friday night.

Mustering up her courage Tori grabbed her phone and typed out a quick text to Maggie. "Hey, Mags," she wrote. "Meet for coffee tonight? I have to talk to you about something." She sat there staring at her phone, several seconds passing before she took a deep breath and hit Send. Putting her phone down and picking up the consumer list, she grabbed her office phone and dialed the number for M. Fund.

Several phone calls later Tori had forgotten about the text that she'd sent to Maggie. When her phone finally buzzed, however, the dread came flooding back to her.

"Sure," Maggie's reply said. "Unless you want to bring coffee to my office after work? I'll probably be here until around 9 tonight."

"Okay, great," Tori texted her back. "I'll bring the coffee."

Sitting back in her chair, Tori tried to craft a speech in her head. Eventually she decided that it didn't matter what she said because it all boiled down to "I'm a bad friend."

She'd cobbled together several themed gift baskets to be used for the silent auction, and a few of her contacts had also given her generous donations. Colby, who owned a Niagara Falls vineyard, had given her a two-night stay at his chateau complete with wine tours, a romantic dinner for two and two cases of wine. Another contact, James, owned a high-end jewellery shop up in Yorkville and he had donated a yellow diamond necklace valued at over $12,000.

She was hoping that the auction items that she'd amassed would go a long way towards easing Maggie's inevitable anger towards her. Not that she could blame her best friend. Bailing on her was a very, very shitty thing to do.

By the end of the day Tori was on pins and needles. Usually her workday dragged by, but today it seemed that no sooner had she taken her lunch than everyone was packing up to go home.

Sighing, she turned off her computer, grabbed her purse and headed out the door. Maggie's favourite coffee shop, Aroma, was out of the way, but Tori was going to do everything that she could to soften the blow. She popped into the sparsely populated café and ordered a vanilla-bean latte with extra foam and a box of calorific but oh-so-delicious maple-dipped donuts and honey crullers.

Sunglasses perched on her face she entered Maggie's office building with her heart in her stomach. Nothing doing, she thought as she climbed into an elevator and began her ascent. The lift pinged as the car came to a halt and the doors slid smoothly open. Smiling at the receptionist she headed through the glass doors and into the offices of Blackstone. She spotted Maggie working feverishly behind a bank of computers on the far side of the room. Walking up behind her she dropped the donuts and drinks on the desk beside her.

"Hi!" Maggie turned around and gave Tori a sheepish smile.

"Hi." Tori smiled back. "Busy?"

Maggie rolled her eyes.

"Incredibly. My boss wants a huge report on his desk first thing tomorrow morning and there's a whole section that I haven't even started on yet."

"Well," said Tori. "Maybe this will cheer you up?" She held up the drink tray, removed the vanilla-bean latte and handed it to Maggie.

"You went to Aroma!" Maggie said happily. "Thanks, Tor!" She took the proffered drink and then looked down at the desk and noticed the donuts. "Oh my God," she practically drooled. "You didn't!"

Tori nodded.

"Maple-dipped and honey crullers?" she asked excitedly.

Tori laughed.

"Yep! Half a dozen, to be exact. I figured that since you were going to be at the office all evening maybe a few donuts would perk you up."

Her best friend put down her latte and reached for the box, her eyes lighting up as she grabbed a maple-dipped donut and gleefully took a bite.

"Ughhhh," she moaned. "This is exactly what I needed," she declared.

Tori pulled up a seat next to Maggie and removed her own latte from the cardboard holder. The trek from the coffee shop to Maggie's office had rendered the liquid cool enough to drink and she took a sip, savoring the smell and taste of cinnamon.

"Talk to me," said Maggie. "What's new and exciting in your neck of the woods?"

Tori took another sip of her drink.

"First off, you'll be happy to know that I spent nearly nine hours posting up and giving out flyers for the fundraiser on Friday."

Maggie looked pleased at that.

"Awesome! That's great," she said as she bit off another piece of the pastry.

"And I also had several of my industry contacts promote the event on their social media accounts," Tori rushed on. "And I've amassed some really great items for the silent auction."

"Such as?" her best friend inquired.

"A MAC makeup basket, a spa package worth over $5,000, a sports memorabilia basket, a yellow diamond necklace that's worth over $12,000, a trip to a winery, dinner for eight at Morton's and a whole lot more."

Maggie's eyes went wide.

"Holy Christ, Tor!" Maggie looked impressed. "That's amazing! I can't believe that you got all of that!"

"Yeah," said Tori. "I was happy that so many of my contacts came through for me. I hope that it brings in a lot of money for the SPCA."

Maggie popped the rest of the donut in her mouth and began to chew. "Me, too!" she said through a mouthful of pastry. "So, what did you need to talk to me about?"

Tori took a deep breath. In for a penny, in for a pound, she thought.

"Well," she started, unsure where exactly to begin. "Remember a few weeks ago when I told you that Susan Rich had asked me to be in the fashion show for the charity fundraiser Fashion Cares?"

"Of course," she responded, licking donut glaze off of one of her fingers. "What about it?"

"Well . . ." Tori paused, pursing her lips together. "It seems that I had a slight mix-up with my dates."

Maggie's eyebrows furrowed.

"Dates?" She looked confused. "You're taking multiple dates? You're not just going with Alistair?" she asked.

"Uh . . ." Tori was apprehensive. "No. I mean, yes. I am just going with Alistair. I meant calendar dates. Like days of the week," she clarified.

Maggie's eyes narrowed in suspicion and she sat there in silence, waiting for Tori to continue.

"I mixed up the date of your SPCA fundraiser," Tori said finally.

Her best friend's eyes narrowed even further.

"So what are you saying?" she asked, a hint of aggression in her voice.

Tori looked at the ground. She wanted to be anywhere but here at that moment.

"I'm saying that I agreed to do the Fashion Cares fashion show this Friday because I thought that your SPCA fundraiser was on Thursday. And that I can't back out of the fashion show."

Maggie looked like she was about to explode.

"Are you fucking serious!" she exclaimed. "You're flaking on my fundraiser? The one that you agreed to help out with over two months ago?" She looked incredulous. "I cannot believe that you're going to some stupid fashion charity event instead of supporting me! You know, the person who is supposedly your best friend! The one who is always there for you, who always encourages you and who always has your back!"

Tori's face was frozen in a grimace.

"I'm sorry, Maggie!" Tori genuinely felt awful. "I really am! I feel completely horrible about this! But I'm a part of the show. And the designer custom-made my gown—I can't back out!"

"You're unbelievable." Maggie looked at her former best friend in disgust. "First the advertising and now this? Remind me to never ask you for anything. Ever. Again," she emphasized.

"Maggie!" Tori pleaded with her. "Listen to me! It's not intentional! I only realized that I had mixed the dates up on Sunday," she said. "And I already have two replacements for the silent auction table! I never would have agreed to Fashion Cares if I thought that your fundraiser was on the same day!"

Maggie ignored her, angrily typing away on her keyboard.

"Yeah," she finally sneered. "Right."

"Please believe me, Maggie," Tori urged. "Do you honestly think that I would ditch your fundraiser because I thought that something better came along?"

The aggressive clacking of the keyboard continued, and Tori stood up from her chair, turning to go.

"I don't know what you'd do anymore," Maggie said without looking at her friend, her voice quivering in anger. "I don't know who you are anymore, and I don't want to know."

Tori felt like she'd been punched in the stomach. She knew that she hadn't been the greatest friend to Maggie lately, but her best friend didn't even want to know her anymore?

"I'm sorry, Maggie. I really am." Tori walked out of the office and into the elevator lobby. Tears welled up in her eyes as she waited for a lift to stop on her floor.

Maybe she should have told Maggie that she was going to come by as soon as the runway show ended? She knew that it was shitty of her to bail on the duties that she'd volunteered for, but it was probably less shitty if Maggie knew that she wasn't intending to bail on the event altogether.

When she finally made it home her eyes were red rimmed and puffy. Sunglasses had hidden them for most of her walk home, but they couldn't mask the tear streaks down her cheeks. She knew that she had to get ready—she had two separate launch parties that she had to hit up tonight—but going out and being social was the last thing that she wanted to do. Mindful of why she was doing all of the going out in the first place she wiped off the mascara smudges underneath her eyes and threw on some lipstick. She didn't even change her outfit before heading back out the door and to the parties.

The next two days flew by for Tori. On Thursday at work she texted Maggie, hoping she'd had a little time to cool down.

"Hey," she'd written, "I'm going to have the auction items delivered to the venue tomorrow at 4. The university volunteers will be there by 5 to set up. I know that you don't want to talk to me right now but please let me know if you need any help setting up tonight. I'll do whatever you need." She'd hit Send with a nervous feeling in her stomach as she waited for a response.

Three hours later, when she still hadn't received a reply, it hit Tori—her friend didn't want anything to do with her anymore. Maggie wouldn't even acknowledge her existence. She felt sick over the whole situation. When Alistair had commented on her somber disposition, she'd told him the whole story.

"Whoa," he'd said, looking at her with a grimace. "That's . . . that's pretty rough, Tins."

She buried her head in her hands.

"I know!" she'd wailed. "It's entirely my fault, but I never would have agreed to it if I'd had the correct date!" She looked at him pleadingly. "You believe me, don't you?"

"Of course." He smiled. "You're a good person, Tinsley. And a good friend. Maggie knows that, too, and I'm sure she'll come around. But you can probably understand that she's really angry right now."

That made her feel a little better.

"I should have just told her that I was going to come there after the fashion show instead of showing up as a surprise," she said glumly.

"Hey," he said, rubbing her back. "I know that your heart was in the right place, you just misjudged how this one would play out."

Her heart swelled; she was so lucky to have a boyfriend like him. Then another pang of guilt shot through her. God, he still didn't know who she was. She hoped that he would be this understanding when she finally revealed that she'd been lying to him. She had promised herself that she would do it after the Fashion Cares event and she meant it. Not that same night, necessarily, but on the weekend. She had decided that she was going to sit him down and tell him everything. It had been gnawing at her, and so had her mom. Tori didn't think that her life had ever felt so tumultuous as it had in the past two months. She was terrified that he would hate her after he found out, but she knew that she couldn't just keep lying to him forever.

By the end of the workday she had come to terms with the fact that she wasn't going to hear from Maggie. She was still going to show up at her fundraiser tomorrow night after the fashion show, even though it would probably just look like she was only doing it to try to get on her good side now.

With the evening free she and Alistair spent the night down by the waterfront enjoying the warm weather before stopping in at a restaurant on the lake for dinner. After dinner they walked back to Alistair's condo where he drew a relaxing bubble bath for two. Snuggled up in their robes after toweling off, the duo spent the rest of the night cuddled up in bed watching Netflix.

Chapter 14:
Revelations

At work the next day, Tori felt an odd mixture of sorrow and excitement. She'd left Alistair's early that morning to drop off the silent auction items with her concierge. Alistair had arranged for a courier to ferry everything to the venue for her. With the rollercoaster of emotions that she'd experienced in the past four days she'd almost forgotten about her meeting with Keith that morning. Her phone had alerted her fifteen minutes before she was supposed to meet him in his office.

What was she going to do for fifteen minutes? She couldn't concentrate on anything. Not only was she amped up about the fashion show tonight, but she had no idea what Keith wanted to meet with her about. While she knew that her mom might be right and that maybe the meeting had nothing to do with her getting a raise, she still held out hope. And so did her bank account.

At five minutes to 10 a.m. she got up from her desk and walked over to Keith's office. She could see him typing away at his computer and tentatively knocked on the door.

Keith immediately looked up and made a "come in" motion before clicking something on his screen and gathering up a bunch of papers that were scattered across his desk.

"Tori!" he said genially. "Have a seat, thanks for coming."

She sat down and put her hands in her lap.

"No problem," she said. "What did you want to meet with me about?"

"Well," he said, scratching the side of his face. "First off, I wanted to congratulate you again on putting together the Impotentia launch. I'll admit that I initially had my doubts, but you proved me wrong."

Tori smiled.

"And because of that, I'd like to offer you a promotion," he said, waiting for her reaction. "To junior marketing associate."

A jolt of happiness shot through her.

"Are you serious!" she asked as Keith nodded back at her. "Thank you so much! Do I get my own office?" she asked. "Do I get a raise?"

Keith chuckled.

"You're very welcome," he said. "You've earned it. And to answer your question, no, you don't get your own office, but you'll get a new cubicle, and yes, you get a raise."

Tori felt like she could kiss Keith. A promotion—and the raise that went with it—could not have come at a better time. She was barely making ends meet as it was, and a raise would go a long way towards paying off her credit card and making sure that she didn't have to subsist on Mr. Noodles every month.

"Of course," Keith continued, "you know that with the promotion there also comes more responsibilities."

Her heart sank a little at that, but she understood. You didn't make your way up the company ladder by slacking off. She just hoped that she would be able to continue to juggle her two jobs—one fictitious and one that actually financed her.

"Understood." She nodded.

"Great," said Keith. "In that case, I'll have papers drawn up for you to sign on Monday. I'll let you know when they're ready."

"Thank you so much again, Keith!" she said sincerely. "I really, really, truly appreciate it!"

And with that Keith dismissed her.

Bounding over to her desk, she gleefully picked up her phone and texted her mom to tell her about her promotion.

"Congratulations, Tori!" her mom wrote back. "Your dad and I are both really proud of you, honey. Good on you."

Feud with Maggie aside, Tori didn't think that her day could possibly get any better.

She left the office early that afternoon as she had to be at the Fashion Cares venue by 5 p.m. There, the "models" were having their hair and makeup done followed by a quick dress rehearsal.

Garment bag in hand she arrived at the Ritz Carlton fifteen minutes early. As she walked across the open-air lobby full of men and women in business attire, she thought about just how far she had come in two months. It was crazy. She had gone from being a naïve and nervous nobody to being asked to walk in a charity fashion show for the city's wealthiest and well-known people. Not that Tori would ever dream of comparing herself to a model. She definitely didn't possess abs of steel or a perfectly rounded rump, which is what made this all the more spectacular. She was being recognized as a fashion expert. Scratch that. Tinsley was being recognized as a fashion expert.

Taking the elevator up to the third floor, she walked out onto a carpeted entrance bustling with activity. Event staff were carrying boxes and setting up tables. Everyone was dressed in black. Tori, bewildered by all of the people running around, made eye contact with one short-haired man wearing black who was walking around with a headset and clipboard, who pointed her in the direction of the ballroom.

"Around the corner, down the hall and through the doors to your right," he said flippantly. "Go to the back of the runway and behind the curtains you'll find a door. Sophia should be there and she'll point you in the right direction."

Tori thanked him and wove her way around the staffers until

she reached the ballroom. It was massive. Glittering chandeliers hung down from high ceilings and tall tables and chairs stood sparsely around the room. In the middle of the area, jutting out from the far wall, stood the runway. Spotlights were attached to a rectangular metal contraption that hung above the elevated white platform. The lights on it flickered to different colours as she watched—the lighting technician on the opposite side of the room was obviously still trying to figure out the right combination.

Black-outfitted people flitted about inside, but there were far fewer of them inside of the ballroom. Or maybe it just looked that way to her given the expansive space.

Heading across the red, tan and gold hued carpet she made her way to the runway and went back behind the curtains.

"You're a part of the fashion show?" a woman with pink lips and black-rimmed glasses who was wearing a headset overtop of her short, spiky blonde hair asked her.

"I am," Tori replied. "Are you Sophia?"

The woman smiled.

"I am! And you're?"

"Tinsley." Tori extended her hand.

"Ah, yes. I remember reading your name on our model list." She picked up the clipboard that was resting on top of a speaker beside her and glanced down at the sheet. "Follow me," she said. "I'll get you situated for hair and makeup."

Still lugging her garment bag, Tori followed Sophia through a set of white metal doors and into a jam-packed room that was whirling with activity. Garment racks lay positioned around the room and hair and makeup stations surrounded by bright white lights were currently being set up by the stylists.

"Your garment rack is right here." Sophia pointed to a metal rack that read "Tinsley Tomlinson" on one side and "Mercedes McCormack" on the other. From the looks of the black dress hanging on the one side, Mercedes was already there. Tori hung the bag on her side as Sophia continued.

"Daniel here is going to be doing your hair and makeup today." She gestured to a lanky man with pin-straight blonde locks. The tattooed man smiled at her and held out his hand. He was wearing a black T-shirt paired with black skinny jeans and a black tool belt around his waist.

"Great to meet you, Tinsley," he said in a bubbly manner. "Love *Fashionista*!"

Tori smiled back at him.

"Great to meet you, too."

"I'll be back to check on you in a bit," said Sophia before she turned on her heel and headed towards a woman holding a garment bag who had just walked into the room.

Daniel implored her to take a seat before he pulled a barber's cape out from a bag behind him and draped it around her, fastening it tightly at her neck. He asked to see a picture of her gown so she showed him one that she had taken when she had tried the dress on at home on Monday. And with that, Tori sat back and let him take the reins. He was, after all, a hair and makeup expert.

Forty-five minutes later, after Daniel had spritzed and blow-dried, and combed and flat-ironed her hair, she had a loose but elegant chignon resting at the nape of her neck.

"What do you think?" he asked, setting down his styling tools and standing back appraisingly.

"It's perfect!" Tori smiled earnestly. "It's going to look amazing with my dress! Thank you, Daniel"

Nodding his head in approval, Daniel spun her around in the chair and picked up his makeup kit. Rummaging around for a minute he pulled out two different bottles of foundation and held them up to her face.

"You just wait, Tinsley," he said merrily. "You haven't seen anything yet." And with that he set to work applying foundation, mascara, eyeshadow, eyeliner and a myriad of other makeup items that Tori was clueless about. He worked like an artist, Tori thought as she felt the soft brush strokes on her face.

A long while later, Daniel instructed her to press her lips together before applying a quick swipe of lip moisturizer. Since Tori had sat down in the chair the room around her had erupted into an organized chaos. Every styling station was occupied with women in various stages of being made up. Finally, Daniel stood up from his hunched-over position, looking pleased. He grabbed the back of the chair and turned it with one hand.

"Voila!" he announced as Tori caught sight of her reflection for the first time.

She could barely believe it. She looked like an entirely different person. Daniel had filled in her eyebrows, given her winged eyeliner and contoured and highlighted the hell out of her face. The finishing touch was a red lipstick that would match up with the colour of her dress. Tori's face erupted into an ear-to-ear smile.

"Daniel," she said, oozing gratitude. "Thank you so much! I don't think I've ever looked so beautiful in my life!"

The stylist beamed at her and she stood up and gave him a hug.

"You're going to look jaw-dropping up there on the runway," he promised.

At that moment a long-haired brunette lady with high cheekbones and a beaked nose came by, her arms laden with boxes.

"I have a bunch of shoes for you," she said, bending over and placing several boxes on the floor. "Holt Renfrew has lent them to us and the bottoms of them are all taped up, so choose whichever ones you want to wear. Size seven, right?"

"Right," said Tori. "Thanks! I'll put everything beside my garment bag."

Fifteen minutes later all of the women were ushered—still in the clothes that they came in—to doors leading to the runway. They were given a quick rundown of what to expect, and who they would be following before the music started and they filed out onto the runway one after another. The short dress rehearsal was enough to ramp up Tori's adrenaline. She could hardly believe that in a short amount of time she would be up there with all eyes on her.

Sophia had instructed everyone to get into their gowns at this point even though they had at least an hour before the runway show started. Guests for Fashion Cares were only just being let into the venue now.

After zipping up her dress she grabbed a couple of shoe boxes and made for a mirror. After discarding the first pair—a cute pair of Sophia Webster butterfly heels—she slid on a pair of gold satin Manolo Blahniks and stood back to evaluate their effect.

"WOW," she heard someone say to her left. "You look positively stunning."

Tori turned and saw Alistair, who had obviously talked his way backstage, with two glasses of champagne in his hand. "I've never seen you look more beautiful," he said sincerely.

Tori grinned.

"I'd kiss you right now, but I wouldn't want to get lipstick on you." Her eyes sparkled.

Alistair walked up and placed a champagne glass in her hand.

"Then I'll kiss you," he said, looking at her hungrily before bending his head and planting kisses all up her shoulders and onto her neck. "What I wouldn't give for five minutes alone with you right now," he growled.

She let out a low moan.

"You can have five hours alone with me later tonight," she said mischievously. "Cheers." She clinked her glass against his before delicately bringing it to her lips and taking a sip. "How is it out there?" she asked. The thought of walking down a runway with hundreds of people staring and judging had started to make her nervous.

"It's really crowded," Alistair said. "Tons of people. Great music, lots of snacks."

The apprehension she felt must have shown on her face because the next thing she knew Alistair started rubbing her back.

"Hey," he said. "You're going to do great." He paused. "And you know how I know that? Because you're great. And even if you go out there and fall flat on your face and make a complete ass out of yourself, I'll still love you."

Tori was dumbstruck. *Love? He just said that he loves me!* At that moment, red lipstick be damned, Tori leaned up and kissed him fervently.

Eventually the cue came for the models to start lining up and Tori found her place. Standing between a local TV news anchor and the heiress to the Weston fortune, Tori was positioned somewhere near the middle of all of the other models. After giving her a final good-luck kiss, Alistair slipped back into the party.

"Excuse me! Everyone! Hey, everyone!" The room quieted down as Sophia called for everyone's attention. "There's been a slight change to the itinerary tonight," she said. "Peter Wilders, who was supposed to emcee the fashion show tonight, has come down with a cold that's rendered him incapable of talking. Fortunately, his daughter volunteered to take his place. I'm sure you all know her—she's very involved in the industry." Sophia opened one of the metal doors and motioned for someone to come in. "Everyone, I'd like you to give a warm welcome to Corinne Wilders," Sophia announced as Corinne, dressed in a silvery silk dress and strappy high heels, her mane a tousled mess of sexy curls, strutted into the room.

The lineup of ladies, as well as the stylists and staff members, all put their hands together and clapped politely. Corinne flashed a winning smile before addressing the room.

"Thank you, everyone," she said. "I know that you'll all do fantastic. You all look like gorgeous models so there's no need to feel like you're an imposter up there tonight," she said, her eyes darting around until she met Tori's—giving her a sweet smile.

That was strange, Tori thought. Had Corinne used the word *imposter* intentionally? Did she know Tori's secret? Or was it just a coincidence that she used that word? There was no way that she could know, Tori calmed herself, thinking rationally. If she did know, she probably would have told on her before the show and Tori would have been asked not to participate.

With a wave and "Best of luck," Corinne left and the metal doors banged shut with a clang. Minutes later she heard the muffled sounds of someone talking into a microphone. And with that that music started. Sophia opened the door and ushered the first model—a tall, shapely woman wearing a black pleated ballgown—to the runway. Seconds later Tori heard the crowd burst into applause as the woman made her entrance to an upbeat dance song without any words. As each successive woman was sent out, each woman came back—most of them with a flushed face and an enormous smile. Tori felt her stomach tighten as she got closer and closer to the door. Finally, Sophia signaled that it was her turn. With a knot in her throat she pulled the hem of her dress up and walked up the two stairs leading to the runway. From behind the curtain she saw Mindy, the TV personality in a glittering pink cocktail dress, turn at the end of the runway and make her way back. Waiting until Mindy was halfway to Tori, Sophia prodded her back and whispered "GO!"

Taking a deep breath, Tori stepped out onto the runway and stood there, momentarily frozen to the spot. A burst of applause erupted in the room along with several cheers and catcalls. Her face blossomed into an enormous smile as she took her first steps down the brightly lit catwalk. Passing Mindy, Tori scanned the crowd as she neared the end of the runway, eventually finding Alistair's eyes—his smile was a mirror image of her own. She was about to turn around and walk back when suddenly Corinne's voice came through the speakers.

"Excuse me! Mr. DJ!" she said loudly. "If you could cut the music, please!" And with that the music abruptly turned off.

Tori was just as confused as the crowd, who started tittering amongst themselves. What was Corinne doing? Her smile faltered.

"I'm sorry, everyone," Corinne said, her voice sounding anything but. "I just couldn't let this charade go on for any longer."

A wave of nausea overtook Tori as her heart started beating out of her chest. No, she thought. It couldn't be. Was Corinne about to out her? Right here? Right now? In front of everyone?

Corinne started walking down the runway, her silk gown flowing around her. "Would you like to tell everyone who you really are?" she said, smiling nastily at Tori, her voice amplifying through the room due to the microphone in her hand.

Tori was speechless, her feet frozen to the floor. She couldn't believe that Corinne was doing this to her.

"What's the matter, Tori?" she said meanly. "Has being found out left you speechless?" Tori looked out into the sea of confused faces, her heart somewhere in her stomach. "Why don't you tell everyone how you're not Tinsley Tomlinson of *Fashionista Magazine*," Corinne pressed on. "Why don't you tell them how you're really Tori Tomlinson, an entry-level marketing assistant with a super lame, zero-reader lifestyle blog who tricked her way in here and tricked her way into the industry? Why don't you tell them how you pretended to be Tinsley Tomlinson for the last two months, and why don't you tell them how you lied to them all," she ended triumphantly.

Gasps punctuated the crowd, as the confused chatter turned into a higher, more confused buzzing, with people yelling out "No way!" and "What is she talking about?!" and one "How high are you right now, Corinne?"

Tori felt like she was going to cry. She stood rooted to the spot, unable to speak.

"Tell them!" demanded Corinne, shaking the microphone at her.

"I . . . I . . ." Tori stammered, unable to form a sentence. She looked around at the crowd, her eyes welling up with tears.

"Look," Corinne implored the crowd. "She can't even defend herself. She's a total fraud."

Tears began streaming down Tori's face. She looked towards the crowd and locked eyes with Alistair, who looked completely dumbfounded. Tori, trying to hold back sobs at this point, emphatically mouthed "I'm sorry" to him. Slowly, he shook his head, the stunned look morphing into one of disappointment and disgust. Still shaking his head, Alistair turned and made his way through the crowd towards the exit.

She felt her world come crashing down as the shock of her deception being revealed so publicly and embarrassingly washed over her. Pushing her way around Corinne, she turned and fled to the backstage area, pausing to snatch up her purse before pushing her way through a fire exit.

Which, of course, set off the fire alarm.

Head down, she walked quickly across the street towards the park. Tears streaming down her face, she picked up the hem of her dress as her purse buzzed continuously on her arm—phone calls and texts, no doubt, from those who had once counted her—as Tinsley—amongst their friends. She slumped down once she found a park bench, the Ritz entrance just visible through the brush. She looked up as she heard Corinne's voice from the entrance to the hotel.

"Alistair, wait!" Corinne called.

Tori sat up straight, sobbing as she strained to see what was going on. She saw Alistair, about to duck into the back seat of a black town car, pause upon hearing Corinne's voice as the faint wail of sirens went off in the distance. Tori watched as the blonde slunk over to him and exchanged a few brief words before Alistair got into the back seat of the car with Corinne following close behind.

That was it for Tori. The embarrassment and fallout from being revealed as a fraud was a devastating blow. She knew that in addition to losing friends and contacts, she had likely killed any and all career opportunities in the writing industry. At least, she thought, she still had a paying job. At Staten. But the loss of Alistair was something that she didn't think she could ever get over. She'd deceived him so badly that he'd turned to a woman who was the polar opposite of Tori in every way possible. Well, she thought, maybe not every way. At least Corinne was honest about who she was—mean, snobby and vindictive—from the beginning.

As she watched the car drive away, she felt her heart break in two and she bent forwards on the bench, dry heaving between sobs.

Chapter 15:
The Fallout

She spent the next two days in bed. With her phone and computer turned off she divided her time between watching Netflix and staring off into space. On Friday, she'd cried herself to the point of exhaustion on the park bench while sirens and red lights flashed all around her—all thanks to her hasty escape through the fire exit. She'd watched as people flooded out of the hotel, all dressed in formal attire, and waited for the firemen to clear the building. She'd stayed glued to the park bench, completely listless, her brain and heart in shatters. Eventually, when the air began to send a shiver up her spine, she heaved herself up from the bench and hailed a taxi to take her home.

It served her right, Tori thought to herself, agonizing over everything for the thousandth time that weekend. While she hadn't started out intending to lie to everyone, she had kept up the charade long enough to cause serious damage. She'd fucked up her relationship with her best friend (having obviously not gone to Maggie's SPCA benefit after the fashion show as she had intended). She'd fucked up her relationship with her boyfriend—the man whom she loved and thought that she was going to marry. She'd fucked up any chance she had of making it as a magazine editor. It was all too much for her to bear.

She was dreading Monday morning. She'd thought about calling in sick and then realized that it wouldn't look very good to no-show at work right after receiving a promotion. Lying in bed on Sunday morning she finally worked up the courage to turn on her phone. She grimaced as a flurry of notifications for texts, emails and voice mails flooded the screen. Pressing Ignore she scrolled through her contacts list and pressed Mom and Dad. Two rings later, her mother answered.

"Mom," Tori wailed. "My life is over. I've completely ruined my career, my reputation, my friendships, my relationship."

"Tori, thank God!" her mom said, sounding relieved. "I've been trying to get a hold of you for the past two days! I wanted to see how your event went on Friday, but I couldn't get a hold of you. And then Marcus called last night—no idea how he got our number—and told us what had happened. He said that he had been trying to reach you but that you had turned off your phone and you weren't answering any emails." Her mom took a deep breath. "Sweetie, I am so, so sorry for what happened to you on Friday," she said soothingly. "What that girl did to you is completely appalling."

Tori snuggled deeper into her comforter and shifted the phone against her ear.

"That's not even the worst part," Tori said, her voice quavering as she explained about Alistair and her flaking on Maggie.

"Oh, Tori, you didn't," her mom said, sounding disappointed in her daughter. "Maggie has been your best friend since childhood. I can't believe that you would bail on something that's so important to her. Honey, what were you thinking?"

"I know," Tori sobbed into the phone. "I'm a horrible person." She sniffled. "Maggie hates me, Alistair hates me, the entire industry hates me. And now you're disappointed in me.

My life is over," she cried.

"Honey, I know that right now it seems like you'll always feel this way, but I promise you, you won't. Five years from now, none of this will matter," she tried to console her. "You really let Maggie down and have a lot to atone for, but if you put in enough effort and you seriously want to save your friendship, then I know that Maggie will forgive you."

Tori sniffled.

"I don't know," she cried. "How can she forgive me? I was such a bad friend. I've been a bad friend to everyone," she wailed, thinking of how she had lied to not only Maggie and Alistair, but to all of her industry friends and contacts as well.

"Well," her mom said. "You've got to find some way to make up for what you did, Tori. Plain and simple. And as for your other so-called friends—if they are really your friends, then they will stick with you. If they were only friends with you because of who they thought that you were, then you don't need them in your life anyway." She paused. "And as for Alistair, honey, I'm so sorry," she empathized. "Give him some time, and if he doesn't come around, then he's not right for you anyway. If he really loves you, then he'll understand and he'll be willing to try and work things out with you."

"I don't know," Tori said, feeling uncertain. "I don't know if he'll even talk to me. If he even *wants* to talk to me. I don't even know if I can face him."

"Tori," her mom said heavily. "There are some things in life that you can't control. You can only control your own actions, you can't control others. And as painful as it might be, if he decides that he doesn't want a relationship with you anymore, then you're going to have to accept it. But if you don't even try to make amends, I think you will regret it for a very, very long time. Maybe send him an email," her mom suggested. "Maggie, too. It will give them time to think about things."

Tori began to sniffle.

"Do you want me to come down for a few days?" her mom asked. "Maybe you can take some time off of work. I know that they appreciate all of the hard work and after-hours effort that you've been putting in lately."

Tori tried to compose herself enough.

"Thanks, Mom," she said, her voice shaking. "I'll write them both an email. And you and Maggie were both right. I know that I should have told him. And I shouldn't have flaked on Maggie and my responsibilities. That's not me. I feel like I don't even know who I am anymore." She sniffled. "I suppose my magazine writing career is over as well."

"Not necessarily," her mom said. "You've gained a sizeable online following. You have tens of thousands of supporters, and you're a really great writer. To be honest, I still don't think that it was terrible of you to sneak into those parties—you did give them coverage, after all, and now you have something to put on your resumé. Who knows, maybe some of those people will now start inviting you, Tori Tomlinson, to the events," she said practically.

Tori thought that that was very unlikely, but she didn't voice that to her mother.

"Thanks for listening, Mom," Tori replied with a sigh. "I think I'm going to go to bed now. Well, sleep. I've barely left my bed since Friday night."

"Of course, sweetie," her mom replied. "You know that I'm always here for you, for whatever you need. Why don't you take a hot bubble bath, put on some relaxing music and take some NeoCitran," she suggested. "That way you'll get a good sleep."

"That's a good idea," Tori said, grateful for the suggestion. And after saying their goodbyes, Tori did exactly that and fell into a lemon-flavoured deep sleep less than fifty minutes later.

She felt like a zombie at work the next morning. While normally she had to haul ass to make it there by 9 a.m., this morning she'd shown up at 7 a.m., hoping to avoid seeing anyone on her walk to work. She was counting on keeping her mind away from the catastrophe that was Friday night by focusing on her marketing duties. Unfortunately for her, it turned out that word had spread about Staten's former entry-level marketing assistant and now junior marketing associate's runway debut on Friday. Sierra, wearing a dark grey dress, had stopped by her cubicle.

"So," she'd said harshly before seeing how distraught Tori looked and softening her tone. "Sorry." Sierra looked genuinely apologetic. "I just can't believe that you were doing that for two months and nobody knew."

Tori looked at her pleadingly, hoping Sierra would get the message and go away.

"I mean . . . wow," Sierra finished lamely. "I can't even imagine how humiliating it must have been for you up there with everyone watching. If that happened to me, I'd probably move across the country."

"You're not helping, Sierra," Tori sighed. "Anyway, I don't want to talk about it. I just want to be alone, thanks." Tori turned back to her work.

"Suit yourself," Sierra said, sounding miffed as she walked away.

Tori had spent the rest of Sunday evening, after she'd woken up from her NeoCitran coma, going through the text messages, voice mails and emails that had been left on her phone. The messages ranged from "Tinsley? Tori? What the hell was that all about?????" and "You lying bitch" to "It's not that big of a deal! Kind of artsy, really! A real-live performance piece!" and "Please text/call/email me back! I'm worried about you!!" She hadn't replied to any of them.

Noticeably absent from the nearly one hundred messages that she'd received was anything from Maggie or Alistair. That, of course, had further convinced her that she had lost two of the people in her life who were the most important to her. She'd vowed that after work on Monday, she was going to spend the rest of her day crafting emails for her former (?) best friend and former (?) boyfriend.

"Tori," the voice of Ryan, the senior marketing manager, came from behind her.

Jesus, thought Tori. Was she going to have to relive Friday night every twenty minutes today?

"Yes?" she said defeatedly, turning around.

"There's someone at the front desk who wants to see you."

Her heart leapt for a minute—maybe it was Maggie or Alistair?

"Thanks, Ryan." She tried to stay calm as she jumped out of her chair and headed for the front desk. She turned the corner and, while it wasn't Maggie or Alistair, Tori was glad to see who it was.

"Marcus," she said, sounding deflated.

"Tins—Tori!" he corrected himself before lifting up his sunglasses and waltzing over and enveloping her in a dramatic bear hug. It seemed that his air kisses were momentarily forgotten. "Can you step outside for a minute? Maybe grab a coffee?" he asked.

"Uh," Tori said. "Let me ask."

"No problem, Tori," came Keith's voice from behind her. Tori turned around. She hated the look of pure pity that he was giving her right now. "And take all of the time you need," he said. "I'd like to see you in my office afterwards."

With that, Tori grabbed her purse from her desk and followed Marcus out into the lobby. They rode the elevator down in silence; Marcus finally spoke when they made it outside.

"So," he started as they followed the sidewalk to the nearest Starbucks.

"So," Tori said back.

"The Impotentia that I took from your purse?" Marcus asked, one eyebrow raised in question.

Tori cast her eyes downwards.

"Yeah," she admitted. "It was in my purse because, as you just saw, I work for the company that does their marketing."

Marcus looked thoughtful at that.

"And the Impotentia product launch?" he asked. "How you kept running away from me?"

She nodded her head rapidly.

"Yeah," she said, feeling defeated. "I didn't want anyone to find out that that's who I actually work for." Tori scrunched up her face.

"Well, Tins—ori," he caught himself. "I hope you know that none of that matters to me," he said firmly. "I don't care who you do or don't work for, because either way, you're fabulous. And if you need anything at all, I'm here for you. I know that most of our friendship has consisted of us drinking together at industry events, but I count you as one of my good friends."

Tori was touched.

"Grab that bench," Marcus said as they approached the coffee shop. "I'll go get us drinks." He sauntered through the door leaving Tori alone on the bench. Minutes later he returned, his oversized Louis swinging off of his arm, his other arm holding a tray with two drinks. He sat down and placed his bag in between them, passing Tori her cup—a caramel macchiato from the smell of it—and taking his own.

"Everyone is suuuuuper pissed at Corinne right now," Marcus said, adjusting the sleeve on his cup. "Some people are still processing your little charade, but most people seemed really willing to forgive you once they heard the whole story." He paused and took a sip of his drink. "Corinne on the other hand has been raked over the coals for causing such an uproar at a charity event. Susan Rich and a whole host of other socialites and board members have basically blackballed her, and barred her from future events," Marcus snickered. "God, the irony." He started laughing. "While trying to destroy your life she inadvertently killed her own career."

Tori felt a little better at that. The mean girl hadn't triumphed like she had intended.

"How did Corinne find out the truth about me anyway?" she asked.

"It seems that she somehow got a hold of your old university student ID card and did a bit of sleuthing," said Marcus. "That's what I heard from Alexei, at least."

"But how . . ." Tori racked her brain for a moment before it hit her. "The night of the Thomas Sabo party at Soho House!" she said. "I knocked my purse over in the washroom and she helped me pick everything up. She must have swiped my ID there," Tori said unhappily. No wonder she hadn't noticed her student ID card was missing, she thought. It wasn't something that she normally carried around with her, but it must have gotten jumbled up in her mess of cards.

"I wouldn't put it past her," Marcus said. "But honestly," he continued, "the gall of that woman. Trying to use a charity fundraiser for her own little nefarious purposes. What a bitch." He wrinkled his nose up at the thought.

"Well," said Tori, "it's not exactly how I would have chosen people to find out about it, but I suppose it is better now that it's all out in the open." She paused. "I mean, don't get me wrong, it's been brutal dealing with the fallout, but at least no one thinks that I'm someone I'm not anymore. And I'm glad that everyone sees Corinne for who she really is."

Marcus smiled at her. "That's what I love about you, Tori," he said. "You're such an upbeat, positive person. Whether or not you're the editor of an international magazine is completely beside the point."

"Thanks, Marcus," Tori said sincerely. "Can I tell you another secret?" she asked hesitantly.

"Of course," Marcus said, scrunching up his brow.

Tori took a deep breath.

"You know the city's hottest fashion, lifestyle and gossip website, *On the List*?" she asked.

Marcus nodded his head affirmatively.

"Well," Tori continued, "it's mine. It's my website. I'm the author."

Marcus looked like someone had hit him over the head with his Louis.

"Are you serious, Tori?" he asked, looking excited. "Do you know how perfect this is? You already have a huge following and the publicity that you'll get from this will be enormous!" he declared. "You can definitely use this to your advantage."

"Do you really think so?" she asked uncertainly.

"I know so," he replied. "I'm sure it probably seems like your life is in a bit of a free fall now, but I guarantee you that by the end of the week, you'll reckon that impersonating Tinsley was one of the smartest moves that you could have made. The industry rewards ballsy people," Marcus said confidently. "Why do you think I get invited to so many events?" he asked. "I spend most of my time drinking away their liquor budgets but give them a decent amount of press in return with my antics."

They spent the next thirty minutes discussing Tori's site. Marcus finally convinced her that she should let her readers know who she was in her next post.

A little while later they made their way back to her office. Marcus gave her another big bear hug and a kiss on the cheek and told her to call him tomorrow. She'd gone straight to Keith's office after that where her boss had told her that, due to a few phone calls—one of which came from a very well-known, very wealthy and very influential family (three guesses as to who that was, she thought)—she was being placed on an indefinite (but paid, she thanked God) suspension.

She spent the remainder of her day at home, crafting together two separate emails—one for her former (?) best friend and one for her former (?) boyfriend. To Maggie, she told her how sorry she was for being such a shitty friend. How she knew that she had let her down and how she had actually intended to show up to the SPCA fundraiser after the fashion show but there was an incident that made it impossible (and that she could ask Alistair if she didn't believe her). She also wrote that she wanted to do whatever she could to make it up to her friend because she didn't want to lose her, but she understood if Maggie didn't feel the same.

To Alistair, she started off by explaining the whole situation that had led to him believing that she was someone that she wasn't. She told him how it had eaten her up to know that she was lying to him every day and how she had gotten up the courage one week after they started dating but she had been interrupted by the delivery man and had lost the nerve after a conversation they'd had shortly after. She told him how she had intended to tell him that weekend, that she'd been afraid to tell him before the fashion show in case he outed her to the industry. She told him how much she regretted not being honest with him now, and how she really hoped that he could find it in his heart to forgive her because she loved him. Very, very, very deeply.

She went to sleep that night with the aid of another NeoCitran packet, and she woke up the next morning with her conscience feeling a bit lighter. She checked her email but there were no responses from either Maggie or Alistair. She wasn't surprised as she figured that they both needed time to process things, but it was still disappointing all the same.

Sticking to Marcus's plan she spent most of that day writing a new piece for her website. In the early afternoon she hit Publish, and sat back waiting for the onslaught of comments and emails that she was sure would come. "How I Got on the List," the title of the piece read. In it she explained who she was and how she had come to create the site, although a good number of people from the comment section had seemed to guess already. Given that she hadn't written a piece on Friday night's Fashion Cares event and that word had gotten out that a woman who had been outed on the runway, several people suspected that it was her. One or two of them had also managed to track down the name of her employer. *Scary how easily people can stalk you on the Internet*, she thought.

Marcus's intuitions had been right and from the time she hit Publish until the time she went to bed, she fielded emails, phone calls and text messages from people who couldn't believe that she was the creator of the website.

The next morning Tori awoke to find several surprising emails in her inbox. It seemed that the publicity that she'd gained from her gaffe on Friday night and from the revelation that she was the brains behind *On the List* had made her a hot commodity. She had nearly fallen over when she opened one from *InStyle* asking her if they could arrange a Zoom meeting about her potentially becoming one of their contributing editors. There were also emails asking her for interviews, and emails praising her for her creativity concerning how she had marketed herself. She could hardly believe it. Over the next few days she realized that Marcus had been right! Apparently the industry did reward the bold.

In addition to the tentative job offer from *InStyle*, she also had several other companies vying to have her join their publishing corporation to write her story. Two other magazines had also reached out to her expressing interest in hiring her for an associate editor position and a contributing editor position. She'd also had emails from several high-profile companies who wished to advertise on her site, all hoping to capitalize on the buzz that *On the List* was generating.

It was bittersweet for Tori, who, less than one week ago, had been convinced that her future in the writing industry was all but over. She kept hoping that she would hear from Maggie or Alistair and opened her inbox each morning full of hope.

She had almost given up hope, in fact, when she checked her email on Friday morning and saw an email sitting there from Maggie. Her stomach knotted and she brewed up a cup of strong coffee before sitting down at her computer and opening up the message.

"Tori," the email started. "First off, no matter what we're fighting about or whether or not we are on talking terms, I am so, so, so, so, so sorry for what happened to you on Friday night. I'll admit that at first, I didn't believe your email when you said that you had planned to come to my fundraiser on Friday after your show. However, I met Alistair last night at a finance function. One of his colleagues started telling me this wild story about what had happened to him at a charity event last Friday. He told me that his colleague, Alistair, had been dating the woman that was exposed and I asked him to point Alistair out to me. I went over and introduced myself and we had a long conversation. You're right that you haven't been the best of friend to me lately, but I also think that I need to cut you some slack. It's not your fault that you were saddled with extra responsibilities at work, and I was the one who encouraged you to pretend to be Tinsley to further your writing career. I think that I was a little short-tempered with you when I shouldn't have been. Without you, I never would have been able to bring in such great items for the silent auction table, and I never would have raised as much money as I did. And while you did initially neglect your marketing job for the fundraiser, you really came through for me in the end. We sold out all of the tickets and I couldn't be happier. I would have been glad to see you on Friday night and I'm sorry that you were humiliated so publicly. I think that we've both been pretty stressed out lately and so I apologize for being snarky towards you. I definitely don't want our friendship to end over this and I wholeheartedly accept your apology. Love, Mags. PS Call me when you have a chance. We need to talk. About Alistair."

Tori let out a breath of air that she had been holding and burst into tears. She was so relieved that Maggie had forgiven her. She had been struggling the past few days to accept the fact that her best friend no longer wanted to talk to her.

And Maggie had talked to Alistair, Tori thought to herself. And she wanted Tori to call her to talk about it. Tori didn't know whether that was good news or bad news. But as her inbox sat filled with emails that were, seemingly, from everyone *but* Alistair, Tori was betting on it being the latter.

After spending the morning replying to emails (Tori was astonished by how many event invites she was amassing, although they all came to her *On the List* account instead of her *Fashionist* one), she picked up the phone around noon and dialed Maggie.

"Tori!" came her friend's voice from the other end of the phone. "Oh my God. I am so sorry," she empathized. "How are you?"

A lump caught in Tori's throat.

"I'm . . . doing okay, thanks. All things considered," she replied. "I read your email and I'm so relieved that you've accepted my apology."

"Oh, Christ, Tor," said Maggie. "I think what happened to you on Friday night is punishment enough for anything and everything that you've ever done wrong in your life. I mean, what a complete bitch," she ended.

"Yeah," Tori sighed. "She's really not a nice person."

"Alistair, on the other hand," Maggie said. "He is a very, very nice person. I'm sorry that I wasn't introduced to him sooner."

"How is he?" Tori asked, trying to sound nonchalant.

"He's . . . well," Maggie said. "He's still trying to process things."

Tori went silent.

"But I know he still cares a lot about you," Maggie continued. "He filled me in on what happened on Friday, and I filled him in on how I encouraged you to keep the charade going. He seemed very put out," she ended.

"I wrote him an email, too," Tori said woefully. "He hasn't responded to me. I'm afraid that he won't respond to me."

"I think that you still have a chance," Maggie said, choosing her words carefully. "But I think that you need to go and see him in person," she said.

"What if he refuses to see me?" Tori asked.

"Well, at least then you know that you tried," her friend said. "I would fight tooth and nail for that one.

Chapter 16: All Apologies

The next morning Tori woke up bright and early. She had no idea how Alistair was going to react to her showing up on his doorstep but given the storm that she'd weathered in the past week, she was feeling optimistic.

She'd kept it simple, opting for a quick swipe of mascara and some nude gloss and a white breezy dress with short sleeves. Throwing her phone in her purse she got into cab at 8 a.m. She didn't want to risk him leaving for the day without seeing her.

A million thoughts raced through her head as the vehicle navigated its way to Alistair's building. Both Maggie and her mom had sent her good luck messages this morning. Both of them were rooting for her, and both of them had let her know that if he didn't go for it, that it had more to do with him than it did with her.

The car finally pulled up to the curb of Alistair's building—the streets were virtually empty, it being the early morning on a weekend. Getting out of the car she gently closed the door and walked towards the entrance. Vince, Alistair's regular doorman, was there.

"Vince," she said pleadingly. "I have a massive favour to ask you."

Minutes later she was on her way up to Alistair's condo. She was grateful that Vince had agreed to help her otherwise she would have never gotten up. The security in his building was like a penitentiary. After taking the second elevator up to Alistair's floor she stood rooted to the tiled landing for a moment, working up the courage before she finally knocked, gently, on the door.

Thirty seconds later she knocked again, this time with more force.

"Coming," said a confused-sounding voice through the door. And seconds later the door swung inwards to reveal Alistair, clad in grey sweatpants and a black T-shirt. A look of momentary surprise swept his features.

"Hi," Tori said timidly.

Alistair paused for a beat.

"Hi," he replied back.

"Can I come in for a minute?" Tori asked, her heart in her throat.

He let go of the door and walked wordlessly towards his living room where he took a seat on his couch.

"Thank you," Tori said, following him and sitting in the chair opposite him.

He was still silent.

"I know that you talked to Maggie on Thursday, but I want you to hear this from me," she said. She took a deep breath and let it out before she started.

"As you already know, my name's not Tinsley. It's Tori. And I'm not an editor. I'm an junior assistant at a marketing firm," she said miserably. "Or at least I was before this whole debacle. I've always wanted to be a writer, and when I received an invite to a vodka launch, I thought they'd just gotten my name wrong. And then I realized that they had, and I drank five Mango Mungers to calm my nerves, and then I woke up the next morning with no memory and with tens of text messages and emails addressed to Tinsley. I never wanted to lie to you," she continued, tears welling up in her eyes. "But Marcus introduced me before I had a chance to tell you the truth, and then it just got completely out of control," she said, her voice wavering. "And then you told me all of that stuff about your dad lying to your mom and I knew I couldn't ever tell you the truth because you would never forgive me. I tried a couple of times to tell you, but I was too much of a coward to go through with it. I've been killing myself over it ever since I met you because I love you. I love you with all of my heart and now I've fucked it all up." She started sobbing.

Alistair's face was inscrutable.

"I was going to tell you the day after the fashion show," she cried. "I didn't know how you would react, and I was afraid that you might out me to everyone beforehand if you took it badly. I want so badly for you to forgive me." She wiped at her tears. "And I understand that it's my own fault. I just wish it didn't hurt so much. I wish I'd never lied to you. I love you, and I'll never forgive myself for deceiving you for as long as I live. I just wanted you to know how sorry I am, from the bottom of my heart," she said. "And I wanted you to hear the truth, from me. In person."

Alistair sat there, still stone-faced.

After a few beats she stood up and wiped away the tears that were streaming down her face. Hiccupping, she reached for her purse and walked to the door, fighting the urge to turn back and plead with Alistair one last time. She managed to snap the door shut behind her before she completely broke down. It didn't matter that he could, in all likelihood, hear her crying. She made it down the elevator, into the lobby and outside of the building before she collapsed, overcome by defeat, exhaustion and emotion. With her back against the building and her knees drawn up, she sobbed as she reflected on the mess that she had made. Sure, she had made up with Maggie, and sure she had managed to snag several offers for full-time, well-paying writing gigs, but she had lost the man that she loved. And the realization of that was enough to forever dull her shine.

Sobbing with abandon, her head wedged between her knees, Tori suddenly felt someone sit down next to her. She raised her head and glanced to her right. Through puffy, tear-filled eyes she saw Alistair sitting next to her, his knees drawn up in the same position as hers.

"What . . . what . . ." she sobbed, barely able to form a sentence. "What . . . are you . . . doing . . . here?" she asked between sobs.

Alistair let her sit in confusion for a moment and let out a long sigh before answering. "Tinsley. I mean Tori. Tori," he said again firmly.

"Look. I know what I said about my dad lying and not being able to forgive him for it. And I don't condone your lying on any level, much as it seems to have worked out for you career-wise. But I fell in love with you. Whether your name is Tinsley or Tori or Theresa, I love you. And whether you're a fashion editor for *Fashionista* or a junior marketing assistant for an erectile dysfunction pill, I love you. What you do doesn't make a difference to me, Tin—" He caught himself. "Tori. I love who you are as a person. The private parties and the alcohol-soaked friends and snobby social climbers—that stuff isn't for me. In a way, I have to admit that I'm a little relieved that that's not what your life is really like." He leaned over and wiped the tears from her cheeks. "Although I suppose it's something that I'd better get used to, now that you'll be doing it full-time."

Tori was confused.

"But? . . . You'll get? . . . Used to it?" she hiccupped, sounding like a miserable Valley girl.

A shadow of a smile appeared on Alistair's face.

"Yes. I'll get used to it." He grabbed her hand and squeezed it tightly. "Assuming, of course, you haven't changed your mind about being in love with me in the ten minutes since you left my place?"

Tori started sobbing again as Alistair gathered her into his arms and planted a kiss on top of her head.

Acknowledgements

Carlin Koster—for providing endless inspiration, entertainment and encouragement, an ear to listen and a friendship that I cherish. Maggie—for being the best sister and eagerly reading through several drafts of this novel and providing helpful feedback. Duanne Jahns—for reading my manuscript and providing me with encouraging words and advice, and for our virtual friendship that always makes me smile. Mom and Dad—for always picking me up when I'm feeling down and believing in me even when I have a hard time believing in myself. Grandma and Grandpa—for always raving about my writing and constantly encouraging me to write a book.

About The Author

Jacqueline Parrish is an Indigenous writer from Treaty 8 territory who lives in Toronto, Canada. Her work has appeared in international print and online magazines, and academic journals. She enjoys writing chick-lit, rom-coms, and satire, and often draws inspiration from friends, family and bizarre situations she frequently finds herself entangled in.